THESE THINGS I'VE DONE

THESE
THINGS
I'VE
DONE

Rebecca Phillips

An Imprint of HarperCollinsPublishers

HarperTeen is an imprint of HarperCollins Publishers.

These Things I've Done
Copyright © 2017 by Rebecca Phillips
All rights reserved. Printed in the United States of America.
No part of this book may be used or reproduced in any manner
whatsoever without written permission except in the case of brief
quotations embodied in critical articles and reviews. For information
address HarperCollins Children's Books, a division of HarperCollins
Publishers, 195 Broadway, New York, NY 10007.
www.epicreads.com

ISBN 978-0-06-257090-1 (trade bdg.)

Typography by Torborg Davern
17 18 19 20 21   PC/LSCH   10 9 8 7 6 5 4 3 2 1
❖
First Edition

For Jason, who never had any doubts

THESE THINGS I'VE DONE

one   # Senior Year

I AM A STATUE.

"Dara." My mother touches my arm. Gently, of course, the same way she's been doing pretty much everything since I got back last week. "Mr. Lind asked you a question."

I shift my gaze to Mr. Lind, Hadfield High's principal and yet another addition to the long line of concerned adults in my life. "Sorry," I say, not wanting to add that I was too busy focusing on being a statue to hear what he said. Striving to be motionless isn't something healthy, coping girls are supposed to do.

Mr. Lind smiles with his lips closed and tries again. "I see from the transcripts Somerset Prep sent us that you did especially well in World History last year. Is that something you'd like to pursue in college?"

"Not really." The only reason I liked history so much was because I got to submerge myself in the distant past, where people faced things like war and death and famine and somehow, miraculously, moved on.

"Actually, Dara wants to be a police officer," my mother pipes up.

The principal nods at me, impressed, and leans back in his leather desk chair. "Is that so?"

"Mom," I say.

She fidgets. "Well, you do. Did."

Did. Exactly. And now I don't want to be anything, except maybe a statue. I've developed quite the talent for keeping still.

The office grows quiet. Outside the closed door, I can make out voices, laughter. Teachers and staff gathering to prepare for tomorrow, the first day of the new school year. Mr. Lind, well aware of my unique circumstance—along with everyone else in this town—called last week to suggest this meeting, a preemptive strike for what's to come. Now, if I have a mental breakdown in the middle of math class, he can say he did his part. He'd given me this special attention and tried to ease my way back into the general population of Hadfield High, where everyone knows me and knows what happened and what part I played in it all.

My hand twitches, and I press it firm against my thigh. Steady.

"Mrs. Shepard."

Mr. Lind is speaking again and I focus on his mustache. Who has a mustache anymore? He looks like he's straight out of an old detective show, wide and bald and sweating in his ill-fitting suit.

"I know Dara's reentry won't be easy, but I think with the support of the staff and her counselor, it'll be a positive step for her. For everyone."

Dara's reentry. Like I've been in prison for the past thirteen months instead of eight hundred miles west at my aunt and uncle's house. Like I have to be integrated back into society. Like I'm a dangerous criminal at risk for reoffending.

Maybe that's how everyone will think of me now. I'm guessing my presence offends a lot of people around here. Including, I think, Mr. Lind. We've been sitting in his office for twenty minutes, and he still hasn't looked me in the eye.

My mother opens her mouth to say something and is interrupted by a light knock on the door. Lind, grateful for the interruption, bellows, "Come in!" without bothering to stand up from his desk. A woman I've never seen before pops her head in and says something about a meeting that's about to start.

"Ah." Lind huffs to his feet. "Duty calls. Mrs. Shepard, Dara, thank you for coming in today. If there are any problems, anything at all, don't hesitate to contact me. Okay?"

Mom and I stand too, and Lind smiles at Mom before throwing me a cursory glance. He fulfilled his duty and now he wants us gone.

"Thank you so much," my mother says as she shakes his hand. "I appreciate you calling us in here today. Dara's been . . . well, it's not easy."

"Of course not." He walks us to the door and shows us out. The office is bustling with people and noise, and the air smells like burned coffee. "We'll see you tomorrow morning, Dara. You have your schedule?"

I nod. It's in my back pocket but I haven't even looked at it. I picked my courses during late registration two days after I arrived home, and I know even if the classes I chose were already full, they would make an exception for me. That's what happens sometimes when people know you've been through something horrible—they bend rules to accommodate your fragile mental state.

"It's okay, baby," my mother says as we step out into the early September sunshine. "If it doesn't work out, you can always go back to Somerset. Jared and Lydia said the offer is always open."

I glance at her and notice, for the first time, that her pale blond hair—the same shade as mine—is shot through with silver. Even though I was gone all year, the strain of dealing with me has taken a physical toll.

"I know," I say, though I'm positive I'll never go back. Aunt Lydia and Uncle Jared's offer to take me in last year was a generous one, but I'm determined to do my senior year in Hyde Creek. It's my home. It's the setting for all my memories, both the good ones and the really, really bad. And after more than a year away, I'm back to face all of them.

The drive home is short, and I feel my mother's eyes on me at every stop sign. I'm not surprised when she detours down a side street, avoiding Fulham Road altogether. I wonder if she always avoids driving there, or if she only does it when I'm in the car.

"I'm going to pick up your brother," Mom says as she pulls into our driveway and kills the engine. "I'll be right back, okay?"

She searches my face as she says this, as if trying to determine if she can leave me unsupervised for longer than thirty seconds. I haven't been alone in days. Mom took the entire week off work and has been sticking to my side like a burr. She doesn't even take a shower unless Dad is home.

I go inside while Mom heads down the street to collect my brother from his friend Brock's house. Taking advantage of the quiet, I wander around the main floor, letting the memories flow through me uninterrupted. Each room holds a small reminder of Aubrey—the kitchen, where we baked countless cookies and cupcakes. The main floor bathroom, where we spilled nail polish on the counter and left a red stain that has never fully faded. The living room, where we sprawled on the couch to watch movies. My room, where we did homework and sang along with Taylor Swift.

My aunt and uncle's condo didn't trigger any memories. There, I didn't have traces of my dead best friend everywhere I looked.

But now I'm back, and so is she.

"Dara?"

My mother's voice is overly casual, but I hear the worry underneath. "In here," I say from the kitchen, where I'm leaning against the counter and examining my schedule.

Mom enters the room, the furrow between her eyes relaxing at the sight of me. My brother, Tobias, is behind her, his freckled face smudged with dirt. He smiles when he sees me, but it's a shy smile, unsure, and it disappears quickly.

"Hey," I greet him, stuffing my schedule back in my pocket.

"Hi." He walks past me to the fridge and extracts a carton of chocolate milk. I watch him, my chest aching. I wish I could call him "Tobes" and ruffle his shaggy brown hair and ask him if he's excited about starting fourth grade tomorrow. I wish I could pick him up and swing him around and then chase him through the house when he wiggles free and runs. But I'm not that person anymore, and we both know it.

I manage to hide out in my room until Dad gets home from work, then the four of us sit around the dining room table and eat dinner together. Like a family, the way we've been doing all week. Mom doesn't mention our meeting today with Mr. Lind, but my dad knows about it. He doesn't discuss it with me, though, or ask how I feel about starting school tomorrow. He hasn't had much to say to me since I got home. Instead he's been weird and distant, like he's not sure how to relate to me anymore.

I manage to get down half a plate of my mom's homemade mac and cheese before escaping to my room again. The food is an iron ball in my stomach, and I have the urge to shut my door, crawl into bed, stick in my earbuds, and block out everything. I don't want to sit in here, pretending to read a novel but not absorbing anything. I don't want to look at my schedule or plan my first-day-of-school outfit or wonder if I'll be able to sleep tonight.

I especially don't want to think about tomorrow, when I'll have to walk into school and face the kids I've known for years, people who remember Aubrey and what happened between us on Fulham Road on that warm, sunny, almost-summer morning.

And even worse than that, I'll have to face Ethan.

Ethan, who I haven't seen since that day at the graveyard almost fifteen months ago, when a box containing his sister—and my best friend—was lowered into the cool, damp earth. He knew I was there, but didn't look at me once. That suited me fine because I didn't want him to have to look at me.

But now that I'm back, I no longer have any choice in the matter. And neither does he.

The iron ball in my stomach shifts and I sprint across the hall to the bathroom, shutting the door behind me. Then I lean over the toilet bowl and retch.

My first order of business the next morning is to check in with Mrs. Dover, my guidance counselor. More reentry cushioning.

I get to school early but not early enough, as there are several people hanging out in the lobby, talking and laughing and taking selfies with their phones. I slip by and head into the main office, where I tell the receptionist that Mrs. Dover is expecting me. She waves me through.

Mrs. Dover's door is open and I stand silently at the threshold, waiting for her to glance up and notice me. When she does, she smiles. Unlike Mr. Lind, her dark eyes don't flick away from mine. Mrs. Dover and I already know each other; she used to teach freshman English and I was in her class. But even if I hadn't been, I'd still know her. Everyone does. It's hard to miss someone who looks like a taller version of Halle Berry. Boys trip over themselves when Mrs. Dover passes by. Or at least they used to, back in freshman and sophomore year. I have no idea what changed around here while I was away.

"Dara." She stands up from her desk and comes over to clasp my hand. "Welcome back."

I mumble my thanks. I notice that my foot is tapping

against the carpeted floor, so I shift my weight onto it, forcing it still.

"Nervous?" Mrs. Dover moves back behind her desk and motions me to the chair across from her.

I slip off my backpack and sit down. "Yeah."

"That's understandable," she says, her eyes on me again. The warmth and directness in them makes me feel both uneasy and comforted. She knows what happened, has probably read the newspaper articles and heard all the gory details like everyone else, but I can sense she's not going to judge me. I wonder why. Maybe she still remembers the girl I was, the plucky little ninth-grader who laughed openly and lived fearlessly and got into mischief with her best friend.

But that was then. Both those girls are gone now.

"It'll take some getting used to," Mrs. Dover goes on. "Being here without Aubrey."

I swallow. My eyes, dry and swollen from lack of sleep, itch like crazy but I don't rub them. Applying pressure might release the tears that have been hovering on the brink for days.

Mrs. Dover lowers her gaze to some papers on her desk, giving me a moment to collect myself. When she looks at me again, I'm steady. In control.

"It's a very brave thing you're doing, Dara," she says in her soft, even voice. "Coming back here. Facing everyone. This has to be scary for you."

I nod, unable to speak. My mother said the same thing

when I told her I wanted to come home and do my senior year at Hadfield. That I'm brave. What I didn't tell her then, and what I don't tell Mrs. Dover now, is my decision has nothing to do with bravery. In therapy I learned about forgiveness, and that forgiving yourself means living in the present and letting go of blame. It means self-acceptance. A nice thought, but one that's a lot easier in theory. I'm not ready to let go yet.

Mrs. Dover watches me quietly for another moment before adding, "If you ever need to talk, my door's always open."

The first bell rings, a warning that classes start in five minutes. I grab my backpack and meet Mrs. Dover's eyes. "Thank you."

She nods and stands up, squeezing my shoulder as she walks with me out to the reception area. "Have a good first day, Dara," she says, and just like that, I'm on my own.

My first class is English, on the second floor. I join the mass of bodies heading toward the stairs, tucking in my elbows so I don't accidentally jostle someone. No one even looks at me. Everyone is caught up in the first-day-of-school frenzy, comparing schedules and summers and tans. I float by unnoticed, my body tense as I wait for someone to recognize the tall girl with hair the color of butter who disappeared the summer before junior year and didn't come back. Until today.

But no one does, and I'm just starting to wonder if I'm invisible when I turn a corner and almost collide with Paige Monteiro and Travis Rausch, who are walking hand in hand in the opposite direction. Their eyes pop at the sight of me. Travis hasn't changed much—he might have gotten a bit taller. Paige isn't as skinny as she was at the end of sophomore year, and her hair is shorter, but otherwise she's the same too.

"Dara?"

She says my name like I'm an unwelcome surprise, here to ruin her day. My mind scrambles for something to say to them, but Travis takes Paige's hand and leads her away from me before I can even open my mouth.

Cheeks burning, I glance around the crowded hallway. A couple of people are watching me curiously, like they're trying to place me. Others whisper back and forth, eyes wide as they wait to see what I'll do next. They know exactly who I am.

I start walking again, head down and long hair draped over my face, protective. My neck is sweating, and I feel like puking up the granola bar my mother made me eat on the way to school, but that's okay. This is part of the reason I came back here, why I wanted to face all these people who know who I am and who Aubrey was and what happened to her.

Because they'll never let me forget that my best friend fell into the path of an oncoming pickup truck and was crushed to death right in front of me.

And they definitely won't let me forget that I'm the one who pushed her.

two

Sophomore Year

"DO YOU SEE HIM ANYWHERE?"

Aubrey stood on her tiptoes, adding a few inches of height to her tiny frame, and peered across the crowded cafeteria. Her features shifted into a familiar concerned expression—eyebrows bunched, front teeth clamped over bottom lip. I called it her mother-hen face.

"Aubrey." I hooked my fingers into the strap of her backpack and dragged her toward the food line. "He's fourteen now. A freshman. He can take care of himself."

We took our place in line and she glanced around again, brown eyes scanning the room for a moment before returning to rest on me. She shrugged. "You know what he's like."

I nodded. Yes, I knew what her brother was like—shy, sensitive, a lamb in a den of lions. But I also knew what Aubrey was like. She was fiercely protective, even though Ethan had grown about a foot over the summer and no longer needed his big sister to look out for him.

We shifted forward in line.

"Maybe I should text him," Aubrey said, twisting her long dark hair into a side braid.

"Maybe you should leave him alone and let him make friends during his first week of high school."

She unwound her braid and raised one dark eyebrow. We both knew Ethan had trouble making friends. That was why he'd been sitting with us for the past two days. "Maybe my best friend should stop acting like such a beeyotch."

I stood perfectly straight and glared down at her, pretending to try to intimidate her with my stature; judging from the way Aubrey smirked at me, it wasn't working. I was already five-eight at fifteen; my six-five father liked to tease me that I'd be taller than him one day. My mother, almost as short as Aubrey, said I was "tall like a supermodel," which always made me laugh. Supermodels were also super skinny and super beautiful, two qualities I super lacked.

Aubrey paused in her search long enough for us to buy slices of pizza and squeeze into a table near the cafeteria entrance. Then she continued to keep watch, her leg jiggling against the table as she absently nibbled her crust. Unlike me,

Aubrey only fidgeted when she was worried. I was never still, not even when I slept.

"Is there still hazing for freshmen?" Aubrey asked, pizza slice sagging in her hand. "Is that a real thing or just something that happens on TV?"

Okay, she was being ridiculous. Ethan was only one grade below us. My brother, Tobias, was seven and I didn't fuss over him nearly as much. Then again, Tobias and I had the type of parents who worried and cared and hugged. Aubrey and Ethan had the kind who chose work over fun and only paid attention when someone screwed up. Growing up with detached parents had forced Aubrey into the nurturer role, and Ethan into someone who needed nurturing.

But we all had to grow up sometime.

"Would you relax?" I glanced over my shoulder and caught a glimpse of buzzed dark hair and one pale, bony arm. Seconds later, the rest of Ethan followed, his gangly body emerging through a cluster of seniors. "See?" I said to Aubrey, jerking my chin toward him. "He hasn't been stuffed into a Dumpster after all."

Aubrey's eyes zeroed in on her brother's face, which looked unusually red, even from here. As he drew closer and saw us watching him, the shade deepened to *overripe tomato*.

"Where have you been?" Aubrey demanded as Ethan sat down across from her. "Are you okay? Do you need your inhaler?"

"I'm fine." His eyes—wide and dark brown like his sister's—flicked toward me for a moment. His skin was slowly returning to its usual paleness, but his behavior still seemed off. "And so is my breathing."

Aubrey's mother-hen face relaxed somewhat and she pushed the slice of pizza she'd bought him across the table. Ethan rolled his right shoulder as if working out a kink as he took a large bite.

"What's wrong with your shoulder?" I asked him.

Aubrey glanced up quickly, concern flooding her features again.

"Nothing," he muttered through a mouthful of cheese.

We stared at him, suspicious, until the tomato-red flush returned to his cheeks.

"I hurt it," he said, swallowing. "In gym."

Aubrey's eyes narrowed into slits. "You didn't *have* gym this morning."

He shrugged, the movement causing him to wince. "I'm fine," he repeated, finishing off his lunch.

Liar. I tilted around in my chair and looked at him. "Who was it?"

Anger flashed in his eyes, and I knew I was on the right track. I noticed what went on in the halls of Hadfield High. Juniors were the most likely culprits, probably because sophomores were still low on the food chain and seniors had better things to do than torture freshmen. But even though the

15

school year had barely begun, a few obnoxious juniors had already made cruelty into a sport. Mostly they were all talk, lobbing insults as you walked by, but sometimes—if they were extra bored or if one of them felt like showing off—they took things further. And Ethan—skinny, quiet Ethan—was perfect fodder for idiots like them.

"Who was what?" Aubrey asked, her gaze bouncing between us.

Ethan sighed and craned his neck toward the table by the window, where the junior jerks in question shoved food into their mouths like they'd never learned table manners. "The one in the red shirt who looks like he should've graduated five years ago."

I knew exactly who he meant. Wyatt Greer, king of obnoxious assholes. Last year, he'd tripped some kid in the auditorium, causing him to fall and break his nose.

"He hurt you?" Aubrey's coloring rose to rival Ethan's. "What did he do?"

Ethan turned back around, his left hand reaching up to massage his shoulder. "Punted me into a locker. By *accident*, of course. He even said he was sorry."

"Accident, my foot."

"Someone should slam Wyatt Greer into a locker," I said, glaring over there as I sipped my cranberry juice. "See how he likes it."

"He's like two hundred pounds," Ethan pointed out. "He wouldn't budge."

"True." My gaze lowered to my orange plastic cafeteria tray. "It would probably work better if something slammed into *him*."

"Like a truck?" Aubrey said, huffing out a breath.

"We're not that lucky." I removed the paper plate containing my leftover pizza crust and picked up the tray, testing its flexibility. It was pretty solid. Not easily breakable.

Ethan caught on to what I was pondering, and his mouth curled into a tiny smile. "Dare ya."

Those were my magic words. And also my nickname. The name *Dara* means "compassion," but I preferred to believe it translated to *daring*. My mom claimed I was born fearless. I was the little kid who'd climbed to the highest branch in the tree, jumped off the diving board first, retrieved the lost baseballs from the scary old man's yard when no one else was brave enough. I loved the thrill, the admiration in people's eyes when I faced down something scary and won.

I was Dare-ya Shepard, the girl who never backed away from a challenge.

"Dara?" Aubrey called as I started in the direction of the junior jerks' table, tray clutched in my hands. Intent on my goal, I ignored her.

As luck would have it, the guys stood up as I approached,

leaving their lunch mess on the table as they set off toward the exit. I positioned my tray in front of my stomach and held it tight, angling past groups of people until I was directly in Wyatt Greer's path. He didn't see me coming; he was snickering to the guy next to him, probably bragging about the skinny kid he'd pushed into a locker right before lunch. This fueled my anger even more, and I rammed my tray into Wyatt's abdomen as hard as I could without injuring my own organs in the process. He grunted and doubled over.

"Oops," I said, slapping a hand to my chest. "I'm so *sorry*. Total accident."

He scowled at me, wheezing like Ethan did during a particularly bad asthma attack. "Watch where you're going, stupid," he growled. Such a charmer.

One of Wyatt's friends watched me curiously, a half smile on his lips. I'd seen him around last year. Justin Gates. Also a junior, and a really cute one too. Tall, blond hair, magnetic smile. Too bad he had such awful taste in friends.

"Sorry again," I said to Wyatt. "So clumsy of me."

Before Wyatt or any of his fellow cavemen could react, I turned and bolted back to the table, plastic tray still in hand. When I got there, Aubrey was shaking her head in disapproval and Ethan was laughing so hard, his eyes shimmered with tears.

"That," he said between spasms, "was awesome."

I grinned and sat down next to my best friend, flinging an arm over her shoulder. Her tiny body buckled under my exuberance. "Ethan dared me," I said by way of an excuse.

She shot me a dark look, then another at her brother, and ducked out from under my arm. "You're impossible."

"That's why you love me."

Ethan smiled timidly at me and was just about to say something when tall, blond Justin materialized beside our table. All three of us shut up and stared at him.

"Hey," he said, meeting my eyes. "Did my friend do something to offend you back there or what?"

For a moment all I could do was gape at him, amazed that someone as hot as him was talking to me. "Yes," I finally said. He seemed more curious than angry, so I figured it was okay to be honest.

Justin smiled, showing off straight, white teeth, and I felt the impact of it all the way to my knees.

"In that case, good job. Very impressive aim."

I smiled back, praying I didn't have pizza gunk between my teeth. "I was shooting for lower, actually."

His laugh, full and pleasant sounding, was even better than his smile. "That bad, huh? Well, I apologize on his behalf. Wyatt can be kind of a douche."

"Kind of?" Aubrey said, and Justin turned to her, his smile growing. Aubrey's cheeks went pink, making her pretty face look even more appealing.

"Okay," he said slowly, his eyes glued to hers. "He can be a *complete* douche."

"Much better."

They laughed, and Justin shifted a few inches closer to her. Suddenly it was like I didn't exist. The two slices of pizza I'd eaten burned in my stomach, and I cursed myself for actually thinking for one second a boy would be interested in *me* when my best friend was smart and talented and pixielike and I was . . . well, the exact opposite of all that.

Ethan watched his sister with a vaguely confused expression. He'd probably never seen her flirt; in Aubrey's life, school came first, violin practice came second, and boys fell way down to the bottom of the list.

"Aubrey McCrae." Justin leaned over, hands spread on the table, and grinned. "I've seen you around. You're like some sort of violin prodigy, aren't you?"

Aubrey flushed even harder and gathered her hair over her shoulder, unconsciously sectioning it off for a braid. She did that when she was nervous. "I just practice a lot."

"She's a prodigy," I said, poking her arm.

Justin glanced at me like he'd forgotten I was there and immediately returned his gaze to Aubrey. "Well, prodigy, I guess I'll see you around," he said, gifting her with another luminescent smile as he backed away.

Aubrey gave him a tiny wave and loosened her hair, arranging it over her blazing face. Ethan and I exchanged raised-eyebrow looks.

"Thanks for introducing us," he said, reaching for his backpack.

She smiled in a dazed sort of way, like someone who'd just been given fantastic news but hadn't had time to process it yet. "Sorry. I was kind of . . . stunned."

Clearly, or else she might have realized that Justin had noticed me first. But it was hard to stay bitter when she looked so damn giddy. I nudged her with my elbow and leaned in to whisper, "He's cute."

"I know," she whispered back, then caught Ethan's eye as he stood up to leave. "Try to avoid the hallway where the juniors hang out, okay, Eth?" she said to him in her normal big-sister voice.

"Yes, Mother."

He slung his backpack over his good shoulder and left without another word. Aubrey watched him go, mother-hen face back in position.

"See?" I said. "He's old enough to take care of his own problems now."

"Says the girl who assaulted Wyatt Greer with a cafeteria tray."

"I had no choice, remember?" I grabbed the tray in question and piled all the lunch trash on it. "Ethan dared me."

three   **Senior Year**

MY PARENTS WORK WAY MORE THAN THEY USED to. My mother is an accounts payable clerk for a car rental company and does extra accounting jobs on the side. My father is a roofer and does extra construction jobs on the side. These side jobs started shortly after I landed in therapy for anxiety and post-traumatic stress disorder. The matching dark circles they're both sporting these days are for me, because they're doing what's necessary to make sure I'm okay.

Mom took an extra day off yesterday, but she's back to working at the office this morning. It's raining, hard, so Dad offers to drop Tobias and me off at school on his way to one of his leaky roof repair jobs.

"When are you going to get your license?" my father asks me once we're on the road.

I shrug. I could've learned to drive last year while I was staying with Aunt Lydia and Uncle Jared—they even offered to enroll me in driver's ed—but every time I pictured it, me controlling a vehicle while people crossed in front of me and strolled down the sidewalk beside me, my heart would start galloping. What if I hit one of them? What if I *killed* one of them?

It's not worth the risk.

"Soon," I say.

Dad nods and focuses on the rain-slicked road. I study him for a moment, take in the increasing thinness of his wavy brown hair and the new lines around his mouth. Has he lost weight? Mom has. So have I.

Tobias says something in the backseat, but his words are drowned out by the sudden roaring in my ears as Dad turns the truck onto Fulham Road.

I close my eyes as the memories flood in, vivid and strong:

The sickly-sweet smell of garbage baking in the sun.
The small pink foot with the blue-painted nails that looked so
out of place against the filthy curb.
The bright red blood, seeping across the hot asphalt.
So much blood.

"Dara, honey. I don't know what I was thinking. I'm sorry."

I open my eyes and see my father's ashen face. We're parked on the side of the road, windshield wipers working overtime against the downpour. The spot where Aubrey took her last breath is several yards behind us. I can't see it anymore. I can't smell it anymore. All that's in my nose is the scent of the coconut air freshener hanging off the mirror and my father's aftershave.

"I'm okay," I say, and I'm surprised my voice still sounds like my voice. I glance back at Tobias. He's pale as the white fabric of his T-shirt. "I'm okay," I tell him.

"You couldn't breathe," he says in a small voice. "We got scared."

My father's hand trembles as he shifts the truck into drive and merges back into traffic. "I can take you back home, if you want," he says.

"No." I run my hand over my face and it comes back damp. Sweat or tears or both, I have no idea. "I need to go to school. I'll be fine."

He looks at me, uncertain. I take a deep breath to prove my lungs work, and force my body to remain still. Dad sighs and drives me the rest of the way in silence.

"Check your phone at lunch," he says as I get out of the truck. "I'm sure your mother will be texting you."

I consider asking him not to tell her what happened, but

I know even if he doesn't tell, Tobias will. So I just nod and shut the door.

As soon as I get inside, I head directly to the bathroom and lock myself in a stall.

Clearly I'm not ready to face Fulham Road. It's been fifteen months since Aubrey was killed, but being there made me feel like it just happened yesterday. Am I ever going to be able to drive or walk there again without crying and hyperventilating? *Baby steps, Dara,* my therapist liked to remind me during every session. *Be patient with yourself. Grief is a process.*

What about guilt? I wanted to ask. *Is that a process too?* But the words never came. Next Monday after school, I'm starting back up with my old therapist, the guy I saw before going to stay with my aunt and uncle last year. Continuing with my weekly therapy was the one condition my parents had when they found out I wanted to come home. Maybe I'll ask Dr. Lemke about guilt.

I flush the toilet for no reason at all and exit the stall. Chloe Stockton stands at a sink, brushing her hair. We've never been close friends, but we were assignment partners a couple of times in sophomore biology and got along well. She's one of the nicest girls in our grade.

"Hi," I say, turning on the tap. Our eyes meet in the mirror, and I see the expression of dawning horror some people get when they look at me now. *Oh my God, it's her.* This look was all over the place yesterday, on students, teachers . . . even the damn janitor side-eyed me as he passed by with his mop. By lunchtime, the entire school knew I was back.

Or so I assume. I still haven't seen Ethan. Maybe his parents ordered him to stay away from me. That wouldn't surprise me; I'm pretty sure they still hate my guts. Or maybe he's avoiding me all on his own because he hates me just as much. Last week, my parents sat me down and told me it would probably be best if I gave the McCraes some space for now. Seeing me again after all this time might bring everything back to the surface, Mom said, and they'll need time to process it.

"Um, hi," Chloe mumbles, quickly stuffing her brush in her purse. She turns and leaves before I can say anything else.

I take deep breaths as I dry my hands. *It's fine*, I tell myself. I knew what I was getting myself into when I decided to come back. Of course people aren't going to act delighted to see me. Of course they're going to stare and whisper and avoid me when they don't know what to say. I expected this.

I don't want to be treated like nothing happened. I don't want to forget.

First-bell rings as I'm leaving the bathroom. I glance around to see if Chloe is nearby, whispering to friends about how she'd just run into that freak Dara Shepard in the bathroom, but all I see are strangers. Young kids, mostly. This year's new freshmen, hanging out near their lockers. No one notices me as I walk down the hall toward the stairs. My locker and my first class are both on the second floor.

My brain is still foggy from the flashback in Dad's truck, so it takes me a few moments to realize I'm approaching the music room. I wait for the heart-pounding, head-roaring, can't-breathe feeling I get whenever I'm confronted with an Aubrey memory, but all I feel is a slight tingling in my stomach. Maybe because the music room is a *good* memory.

By the time I met Aubrey, in sixth grade, she'd already been playing violin for seven years. It was a no-brainer that she'd play in our middle school orchestra. Even back then she was all business, with ramrod straight posture and a serious face that rarely curved into a smile. I knew we'd be friends about a week into the school year, when I accidentally poked Gavin Kilroy in the back of the head with my cello bow and Aubrey burst into uncharacteristic giggles. From then on, I made it my personal mission to bring some laughter into her life. Even if her talent *did* intimidate me at times.

Our orchestra teacher, Ms. Valdez, lit up like a sparkler the first time she heard Aubrey perform. I was much less impressive on the cello, but that was okay because we had Aubrey. Then, a year later, we had Ethan, who also played the violin ridiculously well. By the time they both got to high school, they were known as the orchestra's two majorly talented stars.

I wasn't a star. I gave up the cello at the end of freshman year and joined the volleyball team instead. Aubrey was disappointed.

The music room door is locked, but when I peer really close through the small window, I can make out a few music stands and chairs. Aubrey sits in one of them, back perfectly straight as her bow juts through the air. Long, curly hair shields her face, but I know her eyes are closed, her face calm and dreamy.

I can see it so clearly.

"Is it true?"

The voice jerks me back, and the vision of Aubrey flickers out like a lightbulb going from bright to broken. I breathe through the ache in my chest and try to pull myself together before turning around. There's a trio of girls standing a couple of feet away from me, huddled together and staring. Ninth-graders, going by their size and still-childish features. One is blond and the other two are dark-haired. I've never seen any of them before in my life.

"What?" I say, confused.

"You're Dara, right?" asks one of the dark-haired girls. When I nod, she asks again, "Is it true?"

"Is what true?"

She exchanges a quick look with her friends before turning back to me. "That you killed your best friend over some guy."

My body goes cold, but I resist the urge to shrink away and force myself to meet her eyes instead. "Where did you hear that?" I ask over the rising noise-level around us. The hallway is filling up fast, people retrieving belongings from lockers and heading off to class. The bell's going to ring any minute, and I still haven't made it upstairs.

"It was all over school yesterday." Dark-Haired Girl #1 looks at me steadily while her sidekicks divide their gazes between my face and the floor. Her air of confidence reminds me of mine at that age. She's clearly the brave one, the one who steps up when no one else will. "So?" she prompts when I don't respond. "Did you really, like, off your best friend?"

I clench my hands to stop them from trembling. Who would say something so nasty about me? "No, I didn't *off* her. It was an accident."

"That's not what *we* heard," she says, nudging the blonde with her elbow. "Someone said you—"

"Back off."

The girl frowns at me for a second, as if I were the one who said this, but the words didn't come from me. The voice is deep, authoritative, and located a few feet to the left of us. I turn my head, expecting a teacher, and meet a pair of familiar brown eyes. Aubrey's eyes. Ethan's eyes. But obviously it's not Aubrey, and this tall boy with the angular face and broad shoulders and grown-up-man voice can't be Ethan. Can it? The same gawky, baby-faced Ethan I saw at the graveyard fifteen months ago?

"We were just curious," the girl says in a snotty tone. Her friends nod quickly, eyes round as they look up at Ethan. "We wanted to know if the rumors were true, that's all."

"I *said* back off." He steps forward, and I realize *I* have to look up to see his face too. Ethan has never been bigger than me. He must be six feet tall now. And he's let his buzzed hair grow out so it curls over his ears and forehead. And he's wearing an Iron Maiden T-shirt.

Iron Maiden? *Ethan?*

"Sure, whatever," the girl says, turning away. She shrugs at her friends and they stroll off down the hall like they don't have a care in the world.

The bell rings, signaling the start of first period, but I'm still standing here, dumbstruck. I look up at Ethan, expecting a disgusted glare or some nasty words or *something* to let me know he's offended by my presence. But all he does is brush past me and disappear just as fast as he arrived.

At lunch, I head for the cafeteria.

Yesterday, Mom took me out for lunch—a sort of reward for making it through the first half of the day, I guess—so this is the first time I've been inside the cafeteria since sophomore year. Everything looks basically the same. A new vending machine near the entrance is the only noticeable difference. Well, and the fact that Aubrey isn't going to walk in any minute and join me in line for pizza.

I move forward in line and scan the room. I don't see Ethan, or Travis and Paige, but there are plenty of other familiar faces. A few of them are turned my way, watching me with big eyes. Everyone else seems to be ignoring my existence. It feels surreal, like the person I was the last time I stood here is just as dead as Aubrey. Like I'm a ghost.

I buy pizza and a water and carry both to a mostly vacant table near the wall. As I bite into my slice, my gaze lands on the two girls at the other end of the table. I know them. Katherine and Saskia. We were on the volleyball team together sophomore year and became pretty good friends.

They notice me a few seconds later. I stop chewing, wondering if this will be a repeat of earlier today, when Chloe practically ran out of the bathroom to get away from me. But Katherine and Saskia don't run. Instead they wave at me casually, as if my presence in the caf were a totally normal thing. Like I've been on vacation for the past year and now I'm back— no big deal.

"Hey, Dara," Saskia calls down the table. "You joining the team again this year?"

I swallow the bite in my mouth and think about my year on the team. The coach assigned me the middle blocker position, because of my height and because I was confident and quick on my feet. Fearless. But the only one of those qualities I still possess is my height, and it's not nearly enough.

"I don't think so," I say. Saskia and Katherine glance at each other and shrug, then go back to whatever conversation they were having before I sat down. They don't look at me again for the rest of lunch.

✳   ✳   ✳

It's after eleven and I'm lying in bed, contemplating the new mature-looking Ethan and the way he came to my rescue today, when I hear my parents arguing downstairs. I get out of bed and slink over to my open door.

"What were you *thinking*?" I hear my mother say. The anger in her voice makes me feel uneasy. My parents rarely spoke to each other this way before last year.

"I told you, I *wasn't* thinking," Dad replies. His voice is calmer than hers. Mostly, he just sounds tired. Sad. "I didn't even realize where I was driving until she . . . God, she looked so wrecked."

"We need to take it slow with her, Neil. Just being there, close to where it happened, destroys her. She goes through it all over again. That's why I avoid that road when she's in the car. You never should've—"

"I know. I shouldn't have gone down there. She's obviously not ready for it yet."

"She just needs time. Before she went to stay with Jared and Lydia, Dr. Lemke said—"

"I know what Dr. Lemke said. We have to be patient. Follow her lead. And that's exactly what we've been doing for the past year. We sent her to therapy. We put her on antidepressants that made her even worse. We shipped her off to your sister when everyone suggested a change of scenery. We let her come home when she wanted to come home, even though I thought . . ." His voice trails away and I miss the rest of his sentence. Even though he thought *what*?

"I'm not having this conversation again," my mother snaps at him. "So drop it."

I hear the fridge door slam, an angry thump. "No, I won't drop it. You weren't there this morning, Mandy. You didn't see her face. How is she supposed to move on when every time she turns around, there's another reminder of the nightmare she went through? I get that you feel guilty for sending her away, but it was for the best. She should've never come home. She should've stayed there and graduated at Somerset Prep. She wasn't ready to come back and you know it."

Mom says something else but I don't stick around to hear it. I get back into bed, secure my earbuds, and hit shuffle on one of my longer playlists. I don't bother to close my eyes, or even wipe them dry. Sleep is out of the question now. It's hard to relax in the bedroom I've known all my life when my own father thinks I no longer belong here.

four   # Sophomore Year

"WE WON'T STAY LONG. AN HOUR OR TWO, TOPS. Come on, Aubs, don't be antisocial."

She glowered at me across the kitchen table, where we were icing the shortbread cookies we'd made earlier. Aubrey loved to bake, but we always did it at my house because her mother had a thing about unnecessary messes. "I'm not antisocial," she said, affixing a silver candy ball to the perfect icing swirl on her cookie. "I just don't see the point in going to the park at eight o'clock on a Saturday night. What's there to *do* there?"

I licked a blob of icing off my thumb and sighed. She was such an old lady sometimes. "Do? You don't *do* anything. You just *be*. Everyone hangs out there on weekends. Paige told me—"

"Paige hates me," she cut in, as she did whenever I mentioned my second-closest friend.

"She doesn't hate you." I said this as convincingly as I could, but my tone still rang false. Paige did kind of hate Aubrey, and I had a good idea why. Not only had Aubrey replaced Paige as my best friend back in middle school, she also had this mystifying bond with Paige's boyfriend, Travis. *I* didn't even understand their friendship, and whenever I asked Aubrey about it, she'd shrug and say something like, "Deep down he's really sweet."

If Travis Rausch was sweet, he only ever showed it to Aubrey. I wasn't convinced he even *had* a "deep down."

"Whatever," she said, grabbing another cookie to ice. "Where's Tobias? We need an impartial taste-tester."

I went upstairs to find my brother, happy to let the subject of Paige drop. I hated being caught between them.

Tobias was in his room, damp from his bath and dressed in Spider-Man pajamas. "Are the cookies ready?" he asked the second he saw me.

"Yeah." I stood in the doorway and pressed a hand on either side of the doorframe. "But to get to them, you'll have to get past me."

He gave me a gap-toothed grin and moved to duck between my legs. I crouched down to block him, but he squeezed past me and flung himself over my back, wrapping all four limbs around me. I rose slowly to my feet, acting like he wasn't even there, and carried him downstairs to the kitchen. We found Dad standing by the sink, cracking open a can of beer.

"Help me, Dad!" I mock-cried, reaching back to poke a finger into my brother's ribs. He wiggled, almost jerking me sideways into the stove. "I seem to have some sort of giant growth on my back."

"Uh-oh." Dad sipped his beer and leaned in to examine my "growth." "Looks serious. I think I might have to go out to the truck and get my pry bar. That'll take care of it."

Tobias giggled in my ear as Dad pretended to excise him from my back. Aubrey watched us from her seat at the table, a small, wistful smile on her face.

Later, after a large percentage of the cookies had been tested and approved, I started working on Aubrey again.

"Just for an hour," I begged. "It's a five-minute walk down the street, and we both have to be home by ten anyway." She didn't respond, so I brought out the ace I'd been saving for when all else failed. "I heard Justin Gates hangs out there sometimes."

A spark of interest flashed in her eyes. She and Justin had been semi-flirting at school for the past two weeks, smiling when they saw each other in the halls and accidentally-on-purpose walking by each other's lockers. While I was happy for her, I couldn't deny that ever since that day in the cafeteria,

I'd been thinking about him too. I kept it to myself, though. I wasn't the one he liked, and I didn't want Aubrey stop flirting with him out of loyalty to me. If the situation had been reversed, I knew she'd feel the same.

"Okay," she said with a long-suffering sigh, like she was agreeing only because I'd badgered her into it. "But I have to go home and change first. My shirt's full of flour."

My parents let me go with the usual warnings—no drinking, no smoking, no drugs, and text if I'm going to be later than ten. Aubrey's parents had all the same rules, but unlike my parents, they didn't bother issuing them more than once. They correctly assumed their kids would stay out of trouble without their reminding.

When Aubrey and I had dropped by her house so she could change clothes, we discovered Ethan playing video games in his eerily neat room. And before I could stop her, Aubrey somehow persuaded him to come with us to the park. I felt like throttling her. Who brings their little brother along on a spontaneous, sort-of-maybe date thing?

Aubrey. That's who. But she was nervous, and she and Ethan had always been each other's security blanket.

In any case, the three of us were now walking along the gravel path that snaked through Juniper Park, heading toward the stone fountain area, where everyone had gathered. The fountain was dry and had been since August, when some kids dumped in a few bottles of dish soap and made a huge, bubbly mess.

"Hey," Paige said as we approached. She was sitting on the lip of the fountain, her thigh pressed against Travis's and her fingers cradling a lit cigarette. When we reached them, she stood up and hugged me as if we hadn't just seen each other in school yesterday. As she pulled away, her gaze landed on Aubrey and Ethan. "Hey," she said again, but with much less enthusiasm.

Aubrey nodded at her once and then glanced around. A dozen or so people lounged around the fountain and on benches and grass, talking and laughing and smoking. Justin Gates wasn't one of them. Looking slightly dejected, she sat down on the fountain edge a few inches from Travis.

"How's it going, McCrae?" he asked her as Ethan and I sat on her other side. Travis called everyone by their last names. Probably even his parents.

"Oh, you know," Aubrey said with a shrug. "It's going."

Beside me, Ethan coughed into his hand. Paige's smoke was clearly aggravating his asthma. I bumped his shoulder with mine and leaned in to ask him if he was okay.

He nodded briskly. "I'm fine."

I turned back to Aubrey, who was now staring down at her phone. Even in the shadows, I could see the blush staining her cheeks.

"What?" I asked.

She stuffed her phone back in her pocket and looked at me,

panicked. "He texted me. Justin. Asked me what I was doing. I told him I was here and he said he's on his way."

"That's good, isn't it?"

"Yeah, but . . ." She grabbed my arm. "Is my hair okay? Do you see any cookie dough stuck in it?"

I inspected her long hair and pronounced it dough-free. She raked her fingers through the strands anyway, checking for herself. I caught Ethan's eye and made a your-sister-is-a-weirdo face. He smiled. Whenever Aubrey went into freak-out mode around us, Ethan and I banded together to make fun of her.

After a while, Travis and Paige and some of the others drifted over to the playground a few yards away. Aubrey had told Justin she'd wait for him at the fountain, so Ethan and I stayed to keep her company. By the time Justin finally showed up, Aubrey was practically vibrating with nerves. He walked across the grass toward us, flanked by two guys I'd seen around school. Neither of them was Wyatt, much to my—and Ethan's—relief.

Justin broke away from his friends and came to a stop in front of us. I saw a flash of white teeth as he grinned down at Aubrey.

"Prodigy," he said in greeting.

"Stop calling me that."

Her voice was more flirty than annoyed, and he grinned even wider.

"It's a compliment."

"I think you can do better," she said.

Justin laughed and all of a sudden I felt like a third wheel. He hadn't looked at me or said hi or even noticed my presence. Not that I expected him to, with Aubrey beside me, but still. I didn't want to sit here like an idiot and watch them flirt.

"I'll be right back," I told my best friend. She nodded, eyes locked on Justin's as if he'd evaporate if she looked away. I got up and motioned for Ethan to join me. The second we'd vacated the fountain's edge, Justin took my place.

Ethan and I headed across the gravel path to the playground.

"I don't like that guy," he said as we walked.

"You don't?" I assumed he meant Travis, who was sitting on top of the monkey bars, showing off for the small crowd below.

"He hangs around with that Wyatt jerk. Anyone who's friends with someone like that can't be a decent person."

For a moment I was confused, wondering when Travis became friends with Wyatt, and then it hit me that he was talking about Justin. "He seems okay to me."

Ethan smirked, letting me know my not-so-innocent thoughts were completely transparent. I elbowed him in the ribs, realizing as I did that I no longer had to bend down to do it. He really had shot up over the summer. Soon we'd be the same size and I'd lose my advantage over him. Not that I wrestled around with him anymore. That stopped last year sometime when it started getting awkward. Now I just punched him in the arm when he got out of line.

"Hey, Shepard, look at me!" Travis yelled when he saw me. He ignored Ethan, as most of Aubrey's and my friends did. He was simply *there*—quiet, unassuming—easily blending into any crowd.

"Travis," Paige said dully as she lit another cigarette. "Get down from there before you break your neck."

Travis arranged his legs around the monkey bars and crossed his arms. No hands. Were we supposed to be impressed with his heroic bravery? I'd seen little kids do that.

"Last year," said a guy sitting on a bench a few feet away, "someone walked across the top of the bars and slipped. Landed right on his nutsack and now he can't have kids."

Travis's jaw went slack and he slid down, landing with a thump on the gravel. "Fuck that. I value my manhood."

While everyone laughed, I examined the bars. They weren't very high, and they were definitely thick enough to hold a foot. A steady one. "I bet I could do it," I said to no one in particular. "Walk across."

Travis snorted. "Sure. At least you don't have a nutsack in danger of crushing."

"I'm serious."

He stopped brushing his hands off on his shirt and studied me closely, checking to see if I really meant it. Whatever he saw in my face made him grin. "Okay, then. I *dare* you to walk all the way across. You have to walk on the bars, too, not on the wood where it's wider."

"Oh God," Paige groaned. "You *had* to dare her, didn't you? Now she's actually gonna *do* it."

I would have done it without the dare, but I let them think that was the reason. I was Dare-ya Shepard, after all.

I kicked off my flip-flops and stepped toward the wooden stairs leading up to the platform.

"Dara, I don't think . . . ," Ethan mumbled from somewhere behind me, but I ignored him. What I was about to do required concentration.

Luckily, it was neither humid nor windy at the moment. The metal bar felt cold and dry against my palms as I boosted myself up.

"What is she doing? Dara, are you *insane*?"

Aubrey sounded breathless and alarmed, like she'd run over here to save me. I didn't look down or respond, too focused on positioning my feet on either side of the wooden frame. When I got my balance, I slowly stood up and rested my right foot on bar number one. Eight more stretched out before me, looking a lot thinner than they had from the ground.

"All the way across, Dare-ya," Travis called, followed by a grunt as someone—probably Paige—smacked him.

The slight, end-of-summer breeze ruffled my hair. A muscle twitched in my leg. I could sense everyone holding their breath as they stared up at me, waiting to see if I'd fall.

All I had to do was walk fast enough.

I moved forward without thinking, and before I even had time to panic I was on the last bar, crouching and wobbling and grabbing the wooden frame so tightly, I knew I'd spend the rest of the night digging splinters out of my palms. But it was worth it for the look on Travis Rausch's face.

"That was pretty badass, Shepard," he said with a tone of grudging respect.

I smiled as I lowered myself to the ground. Gravel dug into my bare feet, but I hardly felt it through the euphoria. Aubrey handed me my flip-flops and glared at me like she was sorry I hadn't fallen and broken a few bones. She'd never appreciated my stunts. Ethan gave me a tremulous smile, anxiety giving way to relief.

But it was Justin's expression that struck me the most. He looked at me like he'd suddenly remembered the girl whose aim he'd admired in the cafeteria a couple of weeks ago, before Aubrey caught his eye. Like I was someone interesting he should probably get to know.

Totally worth a few splinters.

five   **Senior Year**

DR. LEMKE HASN'T CHANGED A BIT IN THE PAST
year. He's still slim and tanned with smooth, parted hair that
reminds me of a Ken doll. He also still has that penetrating
blue-eyed gaze that makes me feel like my brain is being tele-
pathically dissected.

"How's school going?" he asks during our Monday afternoon session.

It feels strange to be back here, sitting on this leather couch
again. The last time I sat here, I was due to leave for Aunt
Lydia's house in a few days and Dr. Lemke had grilled me
about my reasons for skipping town. I couldn't give him any
concrete answers. Back then, my thoughts were cloudy wisps,

always slipping away before I could get a decent grasp on them.

My head is clearer now.

"It's okay," I tell him.

"Last summer, you expressed some concern about going back to Hadfield High and facing your peers."

I glance at my chart, which rests on the table beside him, unopened. He obviously studied it before I came in here. "Yeah," I say.

Dr. Lemke twists his wedding ring around and around on his finger, a quirk I suddenly remember drives me crazy. "How's the reaction been so far?"

"Pretty much as I expected, I guess." It's mostly the truth. That awful rumor managed to catch me off guard, but the stares, whispers, and awkwardness—all exactly as I anticipated. "I mean, it's not easy being back, but there's a counselor I can go to if it becomes too much."

"Good. It's important for you to have that support." He stops playing with his ring and grabs a pen, flipping open my chart at the same time. "So. Last time you were here, you weren't very open to discussing your reason for leaving after your friend's death. Do you think you're ready to talk about that now?"

And we're back to this already. "There were a few reasons. Three, to be exact."

"Can you tell me the first one?"

I hesitate, and Dr. Lemke's face drops slightly like he's expecting me to do what I did last year—clam up and refuse to discuss it. Part of me wants to—talking about those first few weeks after Aubrey's death isn't easy—but thoughts of my parents and their drawn, worried faces won't let me avoid it. They're paying a small fortune for these weekly sessions, and I owe it to all of us to get the most out of the experience.

"My family," I say.

"Your family . . ." He waves a hand, prompting me.

"They're the biggest reason I left." I scratch an itch on my nose and quickly return my arm to my side. "Mom and Dad and Tobias. They needed a break from me. I was making their lives miserable."

"You were suicidal." He says this like I need a reminder.

"I only thought about it." I say this like *he* needs a reminder. "I never would've actually done it. And I'm not suicidal any-more."

Dr. Lemke regards me for a moment and then nods. He knows I'm telling the truth. I haven't wanted to die since I hugged my parents and brother good-bye at the airport over a year ago, when I realized that losing me—even to my aunt and uncle—tore their hearts out. I couldn't put them through any more stress and anguish. And I knew, even then, I deserved to live with what I did.

"What's the second reason?" Dr. Lemke asks when I fall silent.

I cross my legs to stop them from jiggling. "Cowardice. I

wanted to go away and pretend it never happened. Start over somewhere else."

"And did you? Start over?"

My mind drifts back to my time there, living with Lydia and Jared. Attending Somerset Prep. My parents had sent me there out of desperation, hopeful that the new setting would rouse me from my debilitating grief. I gave in for much the same reason—because I was stuck, with no clue how to move forward. Maybe leaving it all behind could be the first step.

And it did help, for a while. No one there knew about me; I'd made up some elaborate lie about how the lack of satisfactory education in our public schools drove my parents to send me to Somerset Prep because my aunt taught there and could get us a discount on tuition. My aunt and uncle went along with it unquestioningly. I guess they didn't want any horrified stares or nosy questions either. But a person can only pretend for so long, and denying Aubrey was dead because of me just made me feel like a giant fraud.

She's dead, it's my fault, and there's no running away from it.

"I tried for a while, but eventually it followed me there," I tell Dr. Lemke. "That's why I came back."

"Can you expand on that a little bit?"

I look down and pluck at a loose thread in the couch cushion, wrapping it around my finger. "I was sort of in a bubble there," I explain. "I got so good at pretending to be fine, I convinced everyone it was true. I think I even convinced myself at one point. But I wasn't fine, not really. I was just avoiding dealing with it, and I could do that there because I was so far away from everything here, all the things and places that remind me of Aubrey. She seemed almost like a dream sometimes. A person I knew a long time ago."

Dr. Lemke jots something down on my chart. "How did that make you feel?"

"Guilty," I answer immediately. "I felt like I took the easy way out and ran away to avoid responsibility. I shouldn't get to do that."

He nods again and goes back to the ring-twisting. Since I became a human girl statue, I notice other people's gestures and tics all the more. Dr. Lemke's are especially dizzying. Nod, twist, nod, twist. "What was your third reason for going away?" he asks.

I see the graveyard, the coffin containing Aubrey's broken body slowly dipping into the ground. Red-rimmed eyes, not once meeting mine. "Ethan. Aubrey's brother."

"How did Ethan factor into your decision to leave?"

"I didn't want him to have to look at me every day. The person who . . ."

Killed his sister. I want to say the words out loud, but I know Dr. Lemke will probably latch onto it if I do. Those words make people uncomfortable. *Killed* is harsh, deliberate.

It makes me sound like a cold-blooded murderer instead of a girl who accidentally pushed her best friend in front of a truck. Fortunately, Dr. Lemke lets my sentence trail off without comment.

"And now? Do you still feel that way?" He sticks his pen into his shirt pocket.

I think about how quickly Ethan disappeared in the hallway the other day. He stuck up for me, but he barely looked at me and then left without a word. Seeing me probably brought back horrible memories for him. Seeing *him* wasn't exactly easy for me either, and he wasn't the one who did something horrible.

"Do you think it helped him heal, not seeing you every day?" Dr. Lemke continues when I don't respond. "Did it help *you* heal, not seeing him?"

I shrug, even though for me the answer is no. Escaping was a Band-Aid, not a stitch. The wound tended to reopen with the slightest movement.

"Well," Dr. Lemke says as he glances at his watch. My hour is almost up. "It's a good sign that you came back, Dara. It shows your willingness to face what happened and move on from it."

Now *I'm* nodding, even though the idea of moving on still feels impossible. Even my father thinks my chances are slim as long as I'm here in Hyde Creek, surrounded by reminders.

Dr. Lemke is right about one thing, though. I'm here to face what happened. I'm here to look into my friends' eyes, into my family's eyes, and see the impact of my mistake and the effect it had on those I care about. I'm here to take all their sadness and anger and blame.

I'm here for Aubrey.

The school scheduled me for a weekly appointment with Mrs. Dover, every Thursday morning before class. A check-in, they call it. Double the therapy, double the fun.

Afterward, I head for my locker, eyes sweeping the crowd for Ethan. I've only seen him that one time, but I've been on guard ever since, waiting for some kind of confrontation. Part of me wishes he'd yelled at me by the music room the other day, just so I'd know exactly where he stands. Where *we* stand. Right now, I'm still clueless.

When I swing open my locker, a piece of white paper, folded once like a greeting card, falls out and lands at my feet. It's not mine. It wasn't there yesterday after school. Slowly, I crouch down and grab it, unfolding it as I rise back to standing.

It's a childish pencil sketch depicting two stick figures, a tall one with straight hair and a smaller one with curls. The small one is flying through the air, mouth gaping open in a silent scream. Beside her is a pickup truck with oversized wheels. This truck is going to hit her and she knows it. The tall figure's stick arms are outstretched, like she just finished pushing the small one, and she has a great big smile on her face.

A smile. She's smiling. As if she's happy about what she did. As if she'd set out to do it from the very start.

My eyes prickle with tears, and I crumple the paper into a tight ball. I don't want to put it back into my locker. I want it away from me, so I shut my locker and carry the ball to the end of the hallway, where there's a trash can. My skin feels hot and cold at the same time. The moisture in my eyes blurs my vision, causing me to miss the opening of the trash can. I pick up the paper ball and toss it again, carefully this time. It goes in.

The hallway is starting to fill up, and people are looking at me like they're waiting for me to lose it. Did one of them put the picture in my locker? Is there someone nearby who's reveling in my tears and humiliation right now?

The bell is going to ring soon, but I don't move. I stay by the garbage because I'm not sure I can concentrate in class with that image in my head. The tall figure—*me*—smiling. Happy about what I'd done.

The sketch just confirms what I already know—there are people in this school who believe I'm a murderer.

A rush of dizziness makes my head swim. I need air.

Instead of turning left, back to my locker, I turn right and sprint down the stairs. At the bottom, there's a door leading to the back parking lot. I burst through it and into the sunshine, gulping fresh air like I'd just emerged from underwater. When the dizziness starts to fade, I press my back against the cool brick of the building, close my eyes, and try to pull myself together.

Several minutes pass before I feel calm enough to open my eyes. When I do, I see two boys in the parking lot a few yards away, sitting on the hood of a dusty black car. One of them is Hunter Finley, a senior. The other is Ethan.

I squint at them for a moment, trying to work out why they're hanging out together. All I know about Hunter is that he plays drums and is apparently really good. We travel in different circles, so I've never spoken to him before. Most guys like him, with his longish hair and beat-up leather jacket, act like they're too cool to associate with the rest of us conformists. Hunter is a hard-core rocker.

Ethan, on the other hand, is a band geek. Or at least he used to be. I'm not quite sure who *this* Ethan is.

They're talking to each other, too busy with their conversation to notice me by the door. I can't hear what they're saying, but I'm close enough to see them pretty clearly. Hunter is smoking a cigarette, every so often turning his head to exhale away from Ethan. I wonder if smoke still aggravates his asthma or if he can handle it better now. I wonder what's changed about him that he can sit next to one of the most badass guys in school and look like he belongs there.

An image of the younger Ethan springs to mind and it hits me again how much he's grown. Everything is different, from the shadow of stubble on his jaw right down to the way he fills out his jeans. There's a quiet confidence in the way he's sitting—back straight, palms pressed to the hood behind him, one foot on the bumper and one on the ground—that he's never shown before. The transformation is equal parts shocking, disturbing, and fascinating.

I'm so dumbstruck, it takes me a few seconds to realize the bell is ringing and Ethan and Hunter are now off the car and walking toward the door. Toward me. My first instinct is to panic and bolt for the door, but I resist it and stay put. It's time to face him head-on and take whatever he decides to throw at me.

I don't move or breathe as they approach. The dizziness returns full force, and my mouth feels like the desert. Suddenly I regret coming back here and subjecting myself to this. I must be out of my mind. This is worse than the stupid drawing in my locker. Worse than the staring and whispering and snickering. Worse than the guilt that still feeds on me like a parasite.

Ethan nods to Hunter, who nods back and disappears inside the school. It's just us now, alone for the first time in over a year. The first time since Aubrey died. He looks at me without expression, like he knows I've been standing here all along, watching him.

He takes a step toward me and I brace myself for what's coming. Because if there's anyone in this world who has the right to scream at me and call me names, it's Ethan.

But he doesn't. Instead, he moves closer and leans against

the wall next to me. A subtle woodsy scent that's both familiar and new hits my nostrils. Silence fills the space between us, and just as I decide to swallow my fear and say something, anything, he beats me to it.

"I'm glad you're back."

The words sound strange in his new deep voice, and they're the complete opposite of what I was expecting to hear. I wait for him to add a punch line or a disclaimer, something to let me know he didn't really mean what he said, but he doesn't do that either. I turn my head to speak, to say *thank you* or *I'm sorry* or both, but the bell rings before I can squeeze the words past my throat. Ethan nods like I said them anyway and goes inside, leaving me alone under the bright sun.

six

Sophomore Year

THE SAME NIGHT I TOOK THE DEATH-DEFYING sprint across the monkey bars, Justin finally asked Aubrey out. By the end of September, they were officially a couple.

Aubrey and I both refused to hang out with Justin's junior jerk friends at lunch, so most days, he sat wherever we did. I realized just how much he liked Aubrey the day he willingly joined us at a tableful of orchestra kids. Not that there was anything wrong with Aubrey's musician friends, but Justin was more of a sports guy. I was into sports now too, but I felt comfortable at their table. Ethan usually sat there, and Sierra Humphrey, who I'd been friends with for years.

But Justin was definitely out of his element. When the discussion evolved into complaints about the new orchestra teacher, I noticed his eyes glazing over. Maybe mine were doing the same, because suddenly he looked at me and said, "Have you ever been skydiving?"

I glanced over at him, thrown by the randomness of his question. "What?"

"Skydiving. Jumping out of a plane with a parachute strapped to your back. You've never heard of it?" His eyes sparkled as he teased me, setting off a warm tingling in my stomach.

"I know what skydiving is, and no, I've never done it. Have you?"

"Not yet, but I'm doing it next month for my birthday." He took a drink of his Gatorade. "My brother knows an instructor and he set it up for me."

"That's awesome," I said, brimming with envy. Skydiving was like the ultimate daring activity—barreling toward the earth at top speed while wearing a parachute that might or might not open. The thought of it gave me chills. "It'll be such a rush. I'd totally do it if I had the chance."

Aubrey's attention shifted back to us. "Do what?"

Justin turned to her. "I was just telling Dara about my birthday skydiving plans. She's all for it, unlike you."

She grimaced and bumped his shoulder with hers. He bumped her back, making her laugh.

"I'm afraid of heights," Sierra said, overhearing us. "I couldn't do it."

The rest of the table joined in the conversation, everyone discussing whether or not they were brave enough to jump. Well, everyone except Ethan, who was watching Justin and me with a slight frown on his lips. Maybe he was picturing me falling to my death and preemptively blaming it on Justin.

"I'll let you know what it's like," Justin said, nodding at me. "Providing I don't die."

I laughed. "Even if you do, I'd probably still want to try it."

Aubrey rolled her eyes. "I think you're both crazy."

The skydiving talk fizzled out after that. Aubrey and the rest of the orchestra people went back to griping about their teacher while Justin caught my eye across the table. He smiled and shook his head at me, like he was wondering if there was anything I wouldn't do.

Now that Aubrey was one half of a couple, at least one of her weekend nights was devoted to her boyfriend. I understood, of course, because I would have given up time with her too if it meant I got to spend it with a boy whose smile needed a warning label. While they went out on dates, I hung out with the girls from the volleyball team, which I'd joined at the beginning of the year. Or I spent time with Travis and Paige, who were together so much that neither of them minded sacrificing the occasional night of one-on-one time.

One Friday night in the middle of October, they invited me to go to the movies with them. Aubrey and Justin were seeing a movie too, but at a bigger theater a couple of towns away that had IMAX. I pictured them there, peering at the screen through 3D glasses, their hands accidentally meeting as they both reached for popcorn like some corny scene from a romantic comedy. More likely, Justin was making her laugh as she tried in vain to concentrate on the movie's plot.

Just like I was struggling to do now, sitting with Paige and Travis.

"You want another Coke?" Paige whispered when she caught me yawning during a high-speed chase scene. "More popcorn? I could go out and get more."

"Nah, I'm good." I shot her a smile. She was always extra attentive with me when I tagged along with her and Travis. *Unlike* some *friends*, her actions seemed to say, *I'll always include you in my plans.*

"You never offer to get *me* more popcorn," Travis said on her other side.

"Um, excuse me. You never offer to get me any, either."

The woman in front of us half turned to give us a dirty look, so I focused my attention on the female cop in the scene in front of me. She was totally badass, flipping men twice her size over on their backs and pointing her gun in their faces. It didn't matter that they were bigger and possibly stronger than her—she was brave and confident and in control.

"Do you think I could do that?" I asked my friends after the movie ended and we were waiting in the theater lobby for Paige's mom to pick us up.

"Do what?" Paige said, tapping on her cell phone screen.

I thought about the final scene in the movie, the way that badass cop rounded up all the criminals one by one, making the city safer with each arrest. "Be a police officer. Like the woman in the movie."

"Seriously? You mean, like, the kind who chases down drug dealers and kicks people's doors in and stuff?"

"Sure, why not?" I said, even though I was sure there were not-so-glamorous aspects to the job too. But that didn't deter me.

"Officer Dare-ya." Travis squinted at me like he was trying to picture me in uniform with a gun strapped to my belt. "Suits you, Shepard."

Paige snorted. "Yeah, like your parents would be on board with you doing something so dangerous."

She had a point. My parents claimed that each wrinkle and gray hair they had represented a bloodcurdling stunt I'd pulled. But the danger aspect was exactly what appealed to me—facing challenges, evaluating risks. Conquering and surviving.

"Someone's got to do it," I said, shrugging.

"Does Aubrey know you wanna be a cop?" Travis asked. He smirked like he was imagining her reaction.

"No. She'd probably try to talk me into becoming a librarian or something instead."

"She's not your mom," Paige said, rolling her eyes. "It's not her job to worry over you."

"That's just the way she is," I told her. "She has a soft heart."

"And she cares about people," Travis added.

Paige grunted like she had a popcorn kernel stuck in her throat and grabbed Travis's hand. Then she threaded her other arm through mine and pulled us both outside, where her mother was waiting to take us home.

"Proteins are made up of amino acids, not fatty acids," Aubrey said, peering over at the notes in my lap. It was the next weekend, and we were lounging on her living room couch, studying together for our upcoming bio quizzes. "Lipids are made of fatty acids."

I sent her a grateful smile and fixed my answer. "Thanks. I always get those mixed up."

She nodded like she could relate, even though Aubrey rarely got things wrong. She was in all advanced classes and made straight As. My watered-down course material must have seemed simple to her, but she never made me feel dumb for making mistakes.

Aubrey's phone beeped with a text. As she read it, her face broke into a huge smile.

"Justin wants to come over," she said breathlessly, her eyes sparkling in the glow of the table lamps.

"What, tonight? Now? But we're studying."

"I think we've done enough for tonight. It's Saturday. Mom and Dad won't be home until midnight or something. They'll never know, right?"

I gave her a who-are-you-and-what-have-you-done-with-my-best-friend look and frowned. "But I'm not . . ." I gazed down at my slobby self. In my sweatpants and ratty T-shirt, I wasn't exactly presentable for company. Especially cute male company.

Aubrey waved her hand like my attire didn't matter. Easy for her to say. She looked great in her leggings and long sweater, her curls loose and tumbling over her shoulders. "Do you mind if he comes over? He won't stay long, and then we can study or watch a movie or whatever you want." She seized my arm, her face lighting up like she just remembered the existence of a giant carton of cookie dough ice cream in the freezer. "Hey! I could ask him to bring a friend."

I raised my eyebrows. "Like who? Wyatt Greer?"

Her cheeks turned blotchy and she looked away. Over the past week or so, she'd seemed to have a change of heart about the junior jerks, claiming they weren't "that bad" and that I shouldn't judge all of them on the actions of one. I guess she had a point. Wyatt was a bully, yes, but Justin wasn't. He'd even apologized for whatever Wyatt had done to offend us, and acknowledged that he was a douche. Maybe not all the junior jerks were jerks, but that didn't mean I wanted to hook up with one when I hadn't showered yet today and there was a zit the size of Mount Vesuvius on my chin.

"Sorry," Aubrey said, hands rising to section her hair, coil it into a braid. "I just thought . . ."

Her face was completely red now, like she felt ashamed for preferring an hour or so with her new boyfriend over studying biology with me. This boy thing was all so new to us. No one had ever breached our safe best-friend bubble before, and neither of us was prepared for how one extra person would affect our relationship.

But Aubrey was happy, happier than I'd ever seen her, and with all the pressure in her life from parents and teachers and expectations, she deserved something fun for once.

"It's okay." I pushed her hands away from her hair and unwound the braid, fluffing her curls with my fingers until they hung loose again. "I don't mind."

Her smile was blinding. "Really? Dara, you are the best friend ever. Justin and I hardly ever get to be alone and—"

I held up my hand, cutting her off. I didn't want to hear about how they spent their rare time alone. Especially since they wouldn't *be* alone tonight. I'd be here, probably trying to blend into the furniture while they took advantage of a parent-free house.

Justin arrived fifteen minutes later—without a friend,

thankfully—and the three of us headed down to the basement to watch TV. Aubrey and Justin snuggled together in the middle of the couch while I sunk into the chair near the TV, feeling like an unwanted chaperone. Why had I agreed to this? Downtime with my best friend was so limited, and I'd always been protective of it. I was a little hurt that she didn't feel the same.

"You can pick the show, Dara," Aubrey said, handing me the remote like a peace offering. She was trying to make me feel included, but it was hard to feel anything but awkward sitting in a dimly lit basement while my best friend snuggled with a cute guy a few feet away.

I scrolled through the channels, even though it was pointless. They wouldn't have noticed if I turned on the French channel. Finally, I stopped on some cooking contest show and pretended to watch it while the happy couple murmured and giggled.

I stood up. "I'm going to make some popcorn."

"Okay," Aubrey said, blinking up at me. She got the same glazed-over look when she was in the middle of a complicated violin piece. "I'll help you."

"No, it's okay." I let my gaze rest on Justin. He met my eyes and gave me his brain-scrambling smile. For a moment, I wondered what it would feel like to trade places with Aubrey. To snuggle under the curve of his arm. To have his lips on mine.

It could've been me, I thought. *If only he hadn't chosen Aubrey.* I quickly shook those thoughts from my mind. They made me almost resent my best friend, an emotion I'd never felt toward her before.

"Are you sure?" Justin asked, snapping me out of my daze.

"Um, yeah," I said, flustered. My skin felt scorched, like I was suddenly running a fever. "I can manage by myself."

I bolted upstairs. The quiet, empty kitchen was a welcome sight, and my body temperature slowly returned to normal as I stuck a bag of popcorn in the microwave. Now that I was up there, alone, the guilt was setting in. A good person didn't fantasize about kissing her best friend's boyfriend. What if my feelings showed on my face? Then again, why would Justin even notice my face—or anything else about me—when he had Aubrey? Okay, so I did have some qualities she lacked—like height and boobs and pin-straight hair that never frizzed—but the only people who thought I was beautiful and special were my parents. And they didn't count. They weren't a boy I was 99.9 percent sure I had an illicit crush on.

The microwave beeped, interrupting my thoughts. I dumped the popcorn into a huge bowl and carried it through the kitchen, pausing at the door to the basement. I could hear TV voices and the faint tinkle of laughter. They sounded so happy, like they weren't missing me at all.

I hesitated for another few seconds, then backed away from

the basement door and turned left, toward the stairs leading up to the bedrooms. Aubrey and Ethan's house was a lot like mine—two-story, twenty years old—only theirs was bigger and more updated. It was cleaner too, so clean it didn't feel lived in. Unlike my house, which was dusty and jumbled and currently covered in chintzy Halloween decorations.

Ethan's bedroom door was open a crack, but I gave a courtesy knock anyway.

"What?" his voice barked from inside.

Surprised, I jerked back, almost dropping the bowl of popcorn on the floor. I recovered quickly and nudged open the door, revealing myself. Ethan was sitting at his desk, laptop open in front of him. When he saw me, his face turned red and he leaned forward to press pause on whatever video game he was playing.

"Oh," he said. "Hi."

I held up the bowl. "Popcorn?"

"Uh." His brow creased and he craned his neck to look behind me, like he was expecting more people. "Where's Aubrey?"

I edged into his room, which was, as usual, improbably neat for a teenage boy. "In the basement. Justin's here so I thought I'd . . . you know . . . give them some privacy?"

He grimaced and mumbled something, but all I could make out were the words *barf* and *phony*. I snorted. Ethan's contempt for Justin hadn't waned. In fact, it became more transparent by the day. Aubrey was still in the my-new-boyfriend-is-flawless phase and couldn't fathom the idea of her own brother not sharing the same opinion. But I understood where Ethan was coming from. After all, Justin *was* friends with the guy who'd slammed him into a locker a few weeks ago.

"Is it okay that I'm in here?" I asked, placing the bowl on the desk and knocking over a speaker. I righted it, then grabbed a handful of popcorn.

"Sure." He swiveled in his chair, his gaze following my movements as I crossed the room and sat on his bed. He seemed vaguely surprised, like he couldn't quite believe I was in his room. We'd hung out together before, just the two of us, but never on a weekend night and never in his bedroom. Usually, the only time we were alone without Aubrey was when we were both waiting for her.

I nibbled my popcorn, taking care not to drop any on the clean floor. Ethan's room was so *impersonal*. Aubrey's was the same. My room at home was a clutter of posters and pictures and nail polish and school work, but Aubrey and Ethan weren't allowed to put posters or pictures up on their walls. Each item they owned had its rightful place.

"Aren't you supposed to be practicing something?" I asked, nodding toward his violin and acoustic guitar cases, resting side by side against the wall by the window.

"I am, but Mom and Dad aren't home, so . . ." He shrugged

and spun back around to face the laptop screen.

I tossed a piece of popcorn up in the air and caught it in my mouth. "Slacking off, are you? Do you even like playing the violin?"

He twisted halfway around and looked at me. "Do you like cleaning your room? Going to school? Getting your teeth cleaned at the dentist?"

"Of course not. My parents *make* me do those things."

"Exactly," he said, and faced the computer again.

I stared at the back of his head for a moment. I knew their parents were rigid in their expectations, but the idea of them forcing Ethan to do something he had no interest in was excessively overbearing, even for them.

"Aubrey loves violin," I said, like that was somehow relevant to his situation.

"Lucky her," he mumbled, tapping on the keyboard.

An awkward silence hung between us, and suddenly I was desperate to lighten the mood.

My right hand was still half full of warm, buttery popcorn. I transferred it to my left hand, then chose the biggest kernel and lobbed it at Ethan's head. It bounced off his ear and landed on the keyboard in front of him.

"Hey," he said, wiping a splotch of fake butter off his ear as he turned to glare at me. "What the hell?"

I grinned and threw another piece at him, then another,

until finally he grabbed his own handful from the bowl on the desk and started flinging them back at me. A few minutes later, the bowl was empty and his room looked like a popcorn machine had exploded.

But Ethan's mood had improved, as had mine, so it was definitely worth it.

"You're cleaning this up," he said.

"No. I'm a guest in this house and guests shouldn't have to clean."

"Let's go get Aubrey and make her do it, then."

"Make me do what?" Aubrey appeared in the doorway, alone, her hair tousled from I didn't want to know what. "Dara, what happened to you? You went to make popcorn and then—" The lovesick fog lifted from her face and she noticed the mess on the floor. "What on earth happened in *here*?"

Ethan coughed. "Um, just a little accident."

"Well, make sure you clean it up before Mom and Dad get home." She sighed and looked at me. "Dara, do you want to make more popcorn? I want some that hasn't been on Ethan's floor."

"Sure," I said, hoping she and Justin had gotten their fill of each other while I was gone.

The second Aubrey turned to leave, Ethan picked up a piece of popcorn and flung it at me. I caught it and popped it in my mouth as I followed his sister out the door.

seven

Senior Year

I'M GLAD YOU'RE BACK.

I've spent the last five days turning those four words over and over in my head and I still don't understand. If I was sure of one thing during the past fifteen months, it was that Ethan hated me. He didn't look at me at the funeral. Didn't answer the letter I'd sent him the day after, describing how infinitely sorry I was. Didn't contact me at all in the month between Aubrey's death and the day I left for my aunt and uncle's house. Not that I ever blamed him for any of it. I robbed him of his sister. His rock. I didn't deserve his mercy.

The fact that he gave it to me anyway doesn't make me as happy as it probably should. How is it possible that he doesn't hate me? What's his secret? How can he even stand to look at me after what I did?

"Dara! Dinner."

I continue scrolling through the webpage I've been reading for the past two hours—the "RIP Aubrey McCrae" Facebook group, which for some reason still exists even though there haven't been any new posts since the one-year anniversary of her death last June. I don't know why I'm torturing myself with it. Actually, yes, I do. I think I owe it to Aubrey to witness the pain I caused, even when I'd rather turn away. So I read every one of those sad, melodramatic messages, even the ones written by people I've never even met before—who Aubrey never met. Dying young is a tragedy that belongs to everyone.

And then there are the posts about me.

They started appearing the September after Aubrey died, around the time school opened up again. Most of the comments are written by people I know, at least by name or sight. They're vague, but it doesn't take a genius to figure out who they're referring to.

I guess she's afraid to show her face.

Maybe she ran off to Mexico.

Or off a cliff.

Only the guilty run away and hide.

Apparently, the rumors have been circulating for a while. It's a little scary knowing there are people out there who believe I'm capable of something so evil. I never expected to be welcomed back with open arms, but I didn't expect to be labeled a murderer either.

I click X on the page and lie back on my bed, wondering if I can somehow get out of dinner tonight. I'm not hungry, and I'm definitely not in the mood for family time around the dinner table. But Mom insists on it. She won't let me hole up in my room anymore, because the last time she let me do it, in the weeks after the accident, I'd told her I wanted to die too.

I get up and go downstairs. My father and brother are already sitting at the dining room table, loaded bowls in front of them. My mom comes in with two more bowls and sets them down at our respective spots. Beef stew. Yum.

Dad gives me a timid smile as I sit down, but I don't return it. Ever since overhearing his conversation with Mom, I can barely bring myself to look at him. *He doesn't want me here. He wishes I'd stayed where I was.*

"How was school today, Dara?" Mom asks cheerfully as she butters a roll.

I poke at my stew and think about what I *could* say—that people still look at me like I'm dangerous and most of my old friends ignore me and I'm anxious every time I open my locker that there's going to be another drawing in there, even though it only happened the one time. But I've put them through enough already, so I say, "Fine."

Mom nods like I said something interesting and turns to Tobias. "How was your day, bud?"

Tobias grins, revealing his oversized front teeth, and launches into a story about his teacher, Mr. Kline, who apparently has a black belt in karate, and how he showed the class— after lots and lots of begging—a few of his favorite moves. As he recounts the incident, complete with extensive hand gestures, I can't help but smile. Missing my little brother definitely played a part in my decision to come home. Now that I'm back, though, I can see it's going to take a long time for him to warm up to me, if he ever does. He's wary of me now. I can tell he thought going away would fix me, turn me back into the sister who played with him like she wasn't afraid of hurting him somehow. He seems disappointed that it hasn't.

The minute dinner is over, I go back upstairs, open "RIP Aubrey McCrae," and pick up where I left off.

I have a couple of classes with Paige, but she's been avoiding me since my return, practically sprinting in the other direction if I so much as look at her. So I have no idea what to expect the next day when I happen upon her in the stairwell on my way to the cafeteria.

She's climbing up the same stairs I'm about to go down. I see her at the same moment she sees me, and we both pause on the steps. Panic flashes in her eyes as we stare at each other.

What is she afraid of? Me? Talking to me? Being seen with me? Whatever it is, finding herself alone with me in an empty stairwell is obviously freaking her out.

"Paige," I say. Nothing else comes after it, but it doesn't matter, because she doesn't seem to be listening anyway. She drops her gaze and starts moving again. "Paige, please," I try again as she gets closer. "Can we just talk for a—"

"No." She pauses next to me on the top step and raises her chin. The panic in her features has morphed into a dull anger. "I have nothing to say to you."

"Wait," I beg as she brushes past me. I want to follow her and grab her arm, but I don't. I stay planted on the stairs and address my next words to her back. "Paige, come on. We've been friends forever. We used to be close, remember?"

She stops on the landing and spins around to face me, her eyes wild and glassy. "Close? Yeah, we were such *close friends*, Dara. So close you didn't confide in me *once* during the whole Justin drama sophomore year. No, I had to hear about it through gossip after the fact. So close you didn't even bother to tell me you weren't coming back to school last year. I heard that secondhand too."

"I'm sorry, I—"

"Not to mention all the texts I sent you after Aubrey died that you ignored," she continues like I haven't spoken. "So don't even try to pretend like we were the best of friends. That stopped when Aubrey came into the picture. She was your number one from that moment on and you know it."

I climb the last step and move closer so I can tell her how sorry I am for not confiding in her like I should have. And that I didn't mean to put Aubrey before her. And that I ignored *all* my friends' texts and calls after Aubrey died because I wanted to forget everything about Hyde Creek, even them. But before I can say any of it, the door to the stairwell opens and Travis appears.

For a moment he takes in the scene, his gaze bouncing from me to his girlfriend's red, puffy face. He reaches us in one long step and takes Paige's hand, ushering her away from me.

"Travis," I say. My throat is so tight, his name comes out sounding strangled. We lock eyes, and my stomach jolts when I see the fiery anger in his.

"Don't talk to me," he says in a low, even voice. "Don't talk to either of us."

My mind scrambles for a response, but nothing comes. I doubt there's anything I can say that will satisfy him, anyway. Either of them. They're clearly done with me.

Paige tugs on Travis's arm. "Let's go."

His eyes stay glued to mine. "Why did you even come back here? Like, are you a sucker for punishment or what?"

"*Travis,*" Paige says firmly. "Come on. It's not worth it."

He clamps his mouth shut and gives me one last lingering glare before letting Paige pull him through the doorway. When they're gone, I grab onto the railing and squeeze until my fingers throb. Then I retrace my steps to the hallway.

Once I reach my locker, I'm not sure what to do next. My appetite is gone, so there's no point in heading to the cafeteria anymore. I consider going outside to hang out behind the school, but it's drizzling and even I'm not pathetic enough to stand all alone in the rain. That leaves the library, where I can at least sit down for a while. I start walking again.

"Dara."

The hallway is packed with chattering groups of friends, loud and chaotic, and at first I think it's Travis behind me, back to finish me off. I spin around, anticipating another blast of venom, and accidentally thump Ethan in the chest with my hand.

"Sorry," I say, jerking away from him.

He moves back too, out of reach of my flailing limbs. "It's okay."

Horror rises in me when I mentally replay what I said. *Sorry.* I just apologized for *smacking him*, of all things. Like that's the worst I've ever done. It's so insane, so absurdly inadequate, I actually start laughing. There's nothing joyous about it. It's the laughter of a person who's about ready to snap. The uncontrollable, erupting kind that usually precedes heavy sobbing and tears.

I can't cry. I *can't*. Not now.

Ethan's watching me with a slightly worried expression, like he's debating whether to yell for help. I take a few slow, deep breaths and squeeze my eyes shut. When I feel in control again, I open them and ask, "Was there something you wanted?"

He's still staring at me, one hand gripping the strap of his backpack and the other suspended in the air between us, like he's readying himself to catch me if I faint. *This* strikes me as funny too, that he'd even bother saving me from slamming my head off the floor, and I almost break up again. Ethan must sense it, because he shrugs and says, "Not really. You just looked upset and I wanted to make sure you were okay."

Make sure I'm okay. After everything, he's concerned about *my* welfare. I don't get it. I don't get *him*, and now that I have him here, in front of me, my need to understand is overshadowing everything else.

"Can we talk for a minute?" I ask.

He edges a little closer. "Sure."

"Not here," I say when I notice a few people watching us. Seeing Ethan and me in the same space is clearly noteworthy for those who know the details, and I really don't want anyone listening in on this.

I turn and walk away, hoping he'll follow. He does, and I lead us to an out-of-the-way alcove near a supply closet. The old Dara would take his arm and pull him into the alcove after me, but I don't touch people anymore. Instead, I wait until he steps in and leans against the wall opposite me.

"So," he says. "You're back."

"Yeah." I wonder if he knows where I've been, and why. My parents didn't tell many people, but gossip spreads like a flu outbreak here. But I don't want to talk about my homecoming right now. "What you said the other day, when we were outside . . . ," I begin. "How do you . . . how do you do that?"

His forehead creases, and I notice a tiny scar right below his left eyebrow that hadn't been there the last time I stood this close. "How do I do what?"

I swallow and lower my gaze to the front of his hoodie, which is gray and worn and gives off the familiar scent of the laundry soap his mother always used. Still uses, apparently. "How can you be glad to see me?"

He's silent for a long time. So long I'm afraid to look up again, in case I catch a glimpse of the same fire that was in Travis's eyes. Maybe Ethan didn't mean what he said. Maybe he really wishes I'd stayed away forever and he's going to tell me so right now.

"I just am," he says finally. "I know we haven't really talked since you got back, but it's not because I'm avoiding you or anything. It was just a little harder at first than I thought it would be. Seeing you again, I mean."

I nod. I know the feeling.

"I don't hate you, if that's what you're thinking," he goes on. "What happened was an accident. A horrible accident that could've happened to anybody. How can I hate you for it?"

The same way I do, I want to say, but I don't. I raise my

eyes to meet his again. He holds my gaze. He really believes what he said. Ethan's always been dependably honest—a pure, intrinsic kind of honest that doesn't just disappear overnight.

An accident. The words swirl around in my brain for a moment before slowly sinking in. Ethan is not like the people who wrote those Facebook posts. He's not like the person who put that horrible sketch in my locker. He's not like the people who think the worst of me.

He doesn't believe I purposely killed Aubrey because of jealousy over a boy. He doesn't believe I am a murderer.

I feel myself starting to lose it again, but I force the emotions back. At least I try to. In my struggle to remain calm and still, I almost miss what Ethan says next.

"You loved her as much as I did, Dara. You'd hurt yourself before you'd ever hurt her. I witnessed that firsthand, remember?"

A cloud passes over his face and I know exactly what he's remembering. He's thinking about Aubrey's last few days with us and everything we should have done differently. He's thinking about Justin Gates and how he almost tore all three of us apart. He's thinking about the pointless what-ifs, torturing himself with them just like I torture myself with mine almost every single day.

"Look," Ethan says, snapping us both back to the present. "I don't know your reasons for coming back here or why you'd willingly subject yourself to the ignorant assholes in this school, but if you're expecting the same treatment from me, I can tell you right now you're not going to get it. Okay?"

I'm so surprised by the forcefulness of his tone that I nod automatically. He nods back and leaves the alcove, glaring at a handful of nosy gawkers as he strides down the hallway. They quickly look away from him, like they're scared of what he might do.

I don't look away, though. I watch him go and remember how I used to think of him, like a lamb in a den of lions. But he's not that weak little lamb anymore. At some point over the past year, while I wasn't around to see it happen, he became one of the lions.

eight

Sophomore Year

"WHAT ARE YOU DOING?"

I jumped and almost dropped my phone on the floor. "Nothing." Aubrey had snuck up on me as I stood waiting for her at her locker. "Just researching something."

She dumped her backpack in her locker before leaning in to look at the screen. I watched as she took in the title of the page I'd been reading.

"'Training programs for public policing,'" she read. She glanced up at me, dark brows raised. "Why are you reading about police academies?"

"Because I want to be a police officer." I grinned and gestured dramatically at her. "Mother-hen face—activate!"

She stared at me, her features smooth. "Really? That's . . . great, Dara."

"You think?"

"I mean, yeah, I'll worry about you getting shot in the street or whatever, but it doesn't surprise me that you're interested in doing something dangerous." She nudged me and smiled, but something about her demeanor seemed off. Maybe she thought it was a horrible idea but didn't want to dampen my excitement.

"There's more to it than that," I said, sliding my phone into my pocket. "I've been researching it all week. Being a cop takes a lot of work and commitment. It's not all nonstop action like it is in the movies."

She nodded approvingly at my realistic attitude. "Makes sense. What do your parents think?"

"Well, they didn't exactly jump for joy when I mentioned it to them, but they said they'll support me." I closed and locked my locker. "Honestly, I think they were a tiny bit relieved too. My grades aren't good enough to get me into a decent college, and they'd never be able to afford four years of tuition anyway."

"My parents can't afford it either," Aubrey said, turning back to her locker. "But Ethan and I are both going to college. That's what scholarships and student loans are for."

I almost laughed at the idea of me getting a scholarship. And Aubrey and Ethan's parents had probably been saving up for years to send their kids to college. Their father worked in human resources for an IT company and their mother ran a catering business. They definitely made more money than my parents. Tobias and I would be lucky if Mom and Dad scraped up enough cash for one year of community college (or six months at a police academy).

So I'd never be a doctor. Or a civil rights lawyer, like Aubrey wanted to be. That was fine by me. I'd wear a shiny badge and serve the community in different ways.

"Are you okay, Aubs?" I asked. She was still standing in front of her open locker, swinging the door back and forth like she'd forgotten how to close it. "The thought of me carrying a loaded gun isn't *that* horrifying, is it?"

To my surprise, her big eyes filled with tears. I stepped closer and touched her arm.

"It's okay, Aubrey, really. I'll be fine. I won't even *be* a cop for another four or five years, at least. And my mom thinks I'll probably change my mind a hundred times before I graduate, so—"

She shook her head quickly. "It's not that. I'm just not having a very good day today."

"Fight with Justin?" I guessed. Nothing else, aside from maybe a B on her report card, had the power to get her down like this. She and Justin had been dating for a full six weeks now, and lately, tiny dents had begun forming in their "newly dating" armor. Justin took issue with Aubrey's insanely busy schedule and how little time was left over for him, and she took issue with his lack of understanding about her goals and priorities.

I actually appreciated where Justin was coming from, because I often complained about the same thing myself, but Aubrey was my best friend. If I had to choose sides, I would always choose hers.

"He's annoyed that I still haven't told my parents about him." She wiped her eyes with the edge of her sleeve. Aubrey was a quiet, discreet kind of crier, so no one in the crowd milling around us even noticed.

"Are you ever going to?" I asked, though I already knew the answer. Last year, when Sean Ryland—a guy she liked from orchestra—asked her to the Valentine's Day dance, her parents refused to let her go, claiming she was too young to date. I doubted that was the only reason. To Aubrey's parents, boys equaled distraction. Boys meant threats to her focus and potential.

Aubrey shut her locker with more force than usual. "I can't. They'd make me stop seeing him. You know that. They already took away my phone because they thought I was on it too much. Justin's pissed about that too, by the way. He thinks I should stand up to them."

Maybe you should, I felt like saying, but I didn't. I knew how she'd respond to that one too. Standing up to them would be pointless, and it was easier to surrender, toe the line, and keep them happy. She'd been living that way for years and I couldn't see it ever changing. Her parents weren't like mine. They didn't hear her out and provide feedback and tell her they'd support her in whatever she decided to do. They had plans for their children and fully expected them to follow through.

"He only says that because he's never met them," Aubrey continued as we made our way to the cafeteria. "Whenever I try to explain to him how strict they are, he thinks I'm either exaggerating or making it up. If he could just see for himself—" She slowed her pace and clutched my forearm with both hands. "*You* could tell him."

"What?"

"Would you talk to Justin for me, tell him how unreasonable they are and what would happen if they found out I'm dating him? Maybe he'd believe it coming from someone else. Plus, you know my mom and dad. You've seen what they're like."

"I don't really—"

"*Please*, Dara. He needs to understand why. I don't want to drag you into this, but I just . . . he won't listen to me. Please," she repeated, dropping her hands from my arm and looking up at me with wretched, bloodshot eyes.

I sighed. Aubrey didn't ask me for much. And she'd been so supportive about my career aspirations, I felt like I owed her one. "Okay. I'll talk to him."

She closed her eyes and let out a breath. "Thanks."

We shuffled into the cafeteria and got in line for today's

special: grilled cheese. The smell of slightly burned bread filled the air. My gaze immediately went to the junior jerks table, but Justin wasn't there. I turned back to Aubrey and caught her looking over there too, a slight wrinkle between her eyebrows.

After buying our sandwiches, Aubrey and I headed for a table by the window.

"Can you text Justin?" she begged once we'd sat down. "He's obviously not going to show up here. He's avoiding me."

I bit into my sandwich, which was cold and gummy. How was it even possible to screw up a grilled cheese? "You want *me* to text him?"

"Yeah. Ask him to meet you somewhere after school so you can talk. No, ask him to meet you somewhere after school so you can talk about *me*. That'll get his attention."

I watched her as I sipped my juice. Desperation looked really bizarre on Aubrey. "And where will you be? Hiding behind a plant and eavesdropping?"

She threw a piece of bread crust at me. "I have a lesson. So you'll do it, then? Get him to meet up with you after school?"

I popped the last of my sandwich in my mouth and took my time chewing so I didn't have to answer right away. Meet with Justin? Alone? It was exhausting enough trying to hide my attraction when we were around other people. Having his undivided attention would make it that much harder.

I could walk across monkey bars and climb to the highest

branch in a tree and aspire to a career involving walking into hostile crime scenes with barely a twinge of hesitation, but the mere thought of talking to Justin one-on-one had me sweating through my bra.

"Of course I will," I told her once the slimy glob of cheese finally made it past my throat.

Justin agreed to meet me outside by the lone, scraggly tree that had been randomly planted on the lawn near the school's front entrance. By the time I got outside, he was already there, sprawled on the grass with his backpack wedged behind his head like a pillow.

"Hey," I said, stopping near his legs. I wasn't sure if I should sit down next to him or wait for him to stand up.

Justin squinted up at me. "Finally. My ass is getting numb."

I stuffed my hands into my jacket pockets and smiled. "That's what you get for lying on the ground in the middle of November."

"I got tired of standing." He got to his feet and reached down for his backpack, slinging it over one shoulder. "Want to walk?"

I nodded and we set off toward the road. Justin walked home after school, like Aubrey and Ethan and me. He lived on the other side of town from us, however, so he usually went in the opposite direction when we reached the road. Today, though, he stayed with me, his shoulder brushing mine as we walked down the narrow sidewalk. I tried to ignore the way my stomach swooped each time we connected.

Danger. Danger. Stand down.

We turned onto the paved walking path that cut through the small patch of green space between Dwyer Street and Fulham Road. I shifted sideways until I was practically in the trees and said, "So. Aubrey asked me to—"

"Hey, check it out."

I clamped my mouth shut and followed his gaze to the fenced backyard of the house on our left, where there was a weather-beaten tree house resting in the branches of a massive oak. I'd taken this shortcut almost every day for more than a year, so this tree house had become part of the scenery, like the giant boulder about three feet off the path with the letters *SW+KL* spray-painted on it and the tiny squirrels that flitted up and down the trees. I barely even noticed it anymore.

But Justin never walked this way, so of course it caught his eye. Like me—like *most* kids—he'd probably always wanted a tree house but never got one.

"We should go in it." He stepped off the path and approached the chain-link fence separating the yard from the path.

I stopped walking and watched him as he gripped the top of the fence with both hands. "Um. It's someone's private yard. We can't just go in there. That's trespassing."

He turned to flash me a grin. "Are you saying you've never

trespassed on private property . . . *Dare-ya?*"

I crossed my arms and smirked. He was mocking me, clearly, but the accompanying smile reduced some of the sting. The truth was, I *hadn't* trespassed on private property before, but Justin didn't need to know that.

"Come on." He rattled the fence, testing its sturdiness. "No cars in the driveway and the house looks empty. No one will see us. Everyone works in this town."

I glanced around at the streets and houses, quiet in the waning sun. He was right. Hyde Creek was a blue-collar town—everyone worked. Almost four o'clock on a Tuesday afternoon was probably the safest time to break rules without getting caught.

I walked over to the fence, dug my boot into one of the links, and hoisted myself over, landing with a muffled thump on the dying grass. Justin, who was still on the other side, nodded with approval.

"I knew you wouldn't be able to resist," he said.

My skin glowed warm all over, despite the cold. He looked at me like he thought I was tough and fearless, like I could do anything. And in spite of the little voice in my brain telling me I shouldn't care so much about impressing him, I did.

"Well?" I said, then turned and sprinted for the oak tree. Behind me, I heard the clang of the fence as Justin scrambled over. He appeared beside me as I reached the tree.

"Ladies first," he said.

I examined the rickety ladder that stretched up through the tree house's floor. "Nice try. You go first and see if it's steady enough to hold our weight."

He raised an eyebrow. "And if I fall?"

"I'll make sure to move out of the way."

Laughing, he grabbed onto the ladder and started pulling himself up. I scanned our surroundings, making sure no one was spying on us. No one was, but I kept checking anyway so I wouldn't do what I really wanted to do, which was ogle Justin's backside as he climbed.

"Okay," he called softly from several feet above. "It seems pretty stable. Be careful on the ladder, though. Some of the rungs are loose."

I took my time, testing each rung before putting weight on it, and soon I emerged into the tree house. As my eyes adjusted to the dimness, I could see it had been months—or possibly years—since anyone had been up here. The platform was covered in dirt and dead leaves, and whoever once played up here had taken any toys or belongings back down with them. All that remained was a crushed juice box and a few scraps of faded paper.

"Whoa," I said as I crawled across the decaying boards to where Justin sat, facing the yard with his legs dangling off the edge of the base. I sat next to him, tensing as the branches creaked with the movement. Or maybe it was the tree house making that noise. Maybe we *were* about to plummet to the ground and die. "You can see the entire neighborhood from up here."

"I can't believe you've never sneaked up here before." He nudged my leg with his. "Miss Adrenaline Junkie."

The adrenaline was coursing, all right, and it was only partly due to being several feet above ground in a decrepit tree house. "There's a first time for everything," I said, then immediately regretted it when he gave me a wicked grin. My jacket suddenly felt like an electric blanket, burning against my body and making me sweat.

I decided to stop talking before I said something even more suggestive and inappropriate. Instead, I focused on the view in front of me. The sun was dipping lower in the sky, throwing shadows across the lawn below us. In the distance, windows began filling with yellow light as families arrived home from work and school. A dog barked a few houses away, and another, closer dog answered with his own series of barks.

"So," I said, swinging my legs into the empty air and bringing us back to the reason we were together right now, "Aubrey's parents are strict. She's not exaggerating when she says they'll stop her from seeing you. They will. If they ever find out, they won't just take away her phone and ground her for a week. They'll make her life hell . . . and yours too, if you don't back off."

He laughed. "You make them sound evil."

"Not *evil* . . . more like overbearing. Aubrey's under a lot of pressure at home." I shivered in the damp cold. "So try to be patient with her, okay?"

He rested his forearms on his legs and peered down at the ground, silent. Finally, after a long pause, he turned his head toward me. "Did she tell you to talk to me?"

I nodded. "She wants you to understand what it's like for her. She doesn't think you really get it."

"It's not that I don't get it, it's just . . ." He sighed and rubbed a hand over his face. "Her parents are only part of the issue, you know? I don't usually date girls like Aubrey. She's so damn *driven*. It's intimidating. Sometimes I feel like she's way too good for me."

"I know," I said. God, did I know.

"Like, she'd never set foot in this death trap of a tree house just because I suggested it. She's too sensible and mature for stupid shit like this."

"Gee, thanks."

He breathed out a laugh. "Not an insult toward you. I never said *sensible and mature* are the kind of qualities I'm looking for in a girlfriend."

My heart froze, followed quickly by my lungs. What was he saying? That *I* had the kind of qualities he looked for in a girlfriend? A little thrill shot through me, followed quickly by anxiety. I might have been attracted to Justin, but I could never be his girlfriend, even if he and Aubrey broke up. Nothing was worth hurting my friend like that.

"Aubrey really likes you," I told him, hoping my voice didn't sound as shaky as I felt. Maybe I was suffering from elevation sickness. I had to get back on solid ground.

"I really like her too," he said. "And I'll try to be more patient with her, like you said."

My heart resumed its normal rhythm. I could breathe again. "Thanks."

We managed to make it back down the ladder and over the fence without getting either injured or caught, then parted ways at the path. I walked the rest of the way home by myself, so confused and distracted that I almost missed the turn for my house.

By the time Aubrey called to grill me at nine thirty, I had myself convinced that I'd imagined the charged vibe with Justin in the tree house, because any other option made my stomach twist with unease. He thought I was fun, that was all. Entertaining. He liked Aubrey, maybe even loved her, and neither of us would do anything to hurt her.

"You got your phone back?" I asked.

"Yeah, but I'm only allowed to use it between nine and ten, and only after I've finished practice and homework." She paused for a millisecond before shifting to the main reason she was calling. "Did you talk to him? How did it go?"

Feeling better now, I settled in, fulfilled my best-friend

duty, and told her everything. Well, almost everything. I left out the part about the tree house, even though not mentioning it filled me with guilt. But at the same time I wanted to keep those moments for myself, stashing them away in the tiny, secret drawer in my brain only I could open.

nine

Senior Year

I'VE GOTTEN INTO THE HABIT OF LINGERING IN classrooms after the dismissal bell. Pointed looks from teachers, silently urging me to hurry the hell up so they can go home, are better than navigating crowded hallways and overhearing people laugh and make plans for their weekends. I always feel most like an outsider at the end of the week.

Mrs. Tippet, my math teacher, clears her throat loudly as I stand beside my desk on Friday afternoon, slowly gathering my notes together. I'm the last one to leave, as usual.

"Enjoy your weekend," she says when I finally start moving toward the door.

"You too," I mumble.

The mob in the hallway has thinned out considerably by the time I reach my locker. The place always clears out extra fast on Fridays. I used to clear out fast too, back when I looked forward to weekends. Back when I had friends and a social life. Something else I hadn't anticipated about coming back here—the loneliness. I wasn't exactly popular before, but people thought I was fun and generally liked being around me. I miss that sense of acceptance.

That's what I'm thinking about when I open my locker and a folded sheet of white paper falls out—my former social life. So it takes a moment to sink in that I've received another anonymous delivery.

My heart seizes as I unfold it, expecting more crude stick figures, but it's something even worse. Someone has photocopied two rectangular sections of newspaper, placed side by side on the sheet. I know immediately what they are. One is an article on Aubrey's death that was published in our local newspaper on June 12, the day after it happened. The other is her obituary.

My eyes land on the obituary first. I've seen it before, of course, but seeing it again now sends a jolt through me. My brain registers only fragments of sentences—"deeply saddened" . . . "sudden passing" . . . "always in our hearts"—because all I can really see is the picture at the top. It's a school photo, polished and posed, but it still looks like Aubrey. Her dark curly hair fills the frame, and she's smiling the way she always did in pictures—tight and closemouthed—like she was trying to hide crooked teeth even though she'd worn braces at thirteen and her teeth were straight and perfect.

My gaze skips over to the news article. I've read this one before. I've read all of them, over and over, but this one sticks out because it was the first of several published that week.

TEEN DIES AFTER BEING HIT BY TRUCK

A Hadfield High student was struck and killed by a pickup truck on Tuesday morning. The incident happened on Fulham Road in Hyde Creek at about 11:30 a.m. Police have not yet disclosed the name of the student, but several sources have identified her as 16-year-old Aubrey McCrae.

Hyde Creek Police Staff Sgt. Peter Blakely told reporters that witnesses at the scene saw two girls "messing around" on the sidewalk when the incident occurred. Investigators are looking into the possibility that horseplay led to McCrae tripping and falling into the path of the truck. She was run over and died at the scene.

All final exams at Hadfield High are canceled today, but the school will remain open for students who wish to come in and speak to the team of grief counselors on hand.

Horseplay. Such a dumb term. It makes me think of when I was little, perching on my dad's back as he crawled around the floor, giving me "horsey rides." Or playing with Tobias, swinging him around until we were both too dizzy to stand. I never, ever thought it would be used in a newspaper article to explain how my playful pushing resulted in my best friend lying under a truck.

Luckily, no one needs to worry about my "horseplaying" anymore. Now I keep my hands to myself. Now I am a statue.

I look up from the paper and glance around, but the hallway is still empty. Whoever is putting these in my locker isn't interested in sticking around to see my reaction. They don't want to be known. I consider taking the paper down to the office and shoving it under Mr. Lind's nose, but that won't solve anything. What can the principal do about it? Set up surveillance in the hall? Hold an assembly and ask the culprit to come forward?

I'd rather get the passive-aggressive locker mail.

Instead of scrunching it up and tossing it in the trash like the last note, I take out an unused green notebook and place it neatly inside. I'm not sure why I want to keep it. Maybe because I don't have the heart to destroy an image of Aubrey's face, even if it is being used to hurt me.

Outside, the sky is the bruised shade of an impending thunderstorm. I start walking, fast. Now that I take the long way home, bypassing the shortcut path leading to Fulham Road, there's a good chance I'll be drenched by the time I reach my house.

The clouds open up as I cross over to Bartlett, the street

that takes me around Fulham and turns what could be an eight-minute walk home into a twenty-two-minute one. But I don't mind. I yank the hood of my sweatshirt over my hair and keep walking, so entranced by the polka-dot pattern the raindrops are making on the sidewalk, I don't notice the car pulling up beside me until I hear my name.

I jump like someone shot me and spin around, startled to see an old silver Saturn idling at the curb. Even more surprising is that Ethan's sitting in the driver's seat.

"Need a lift?" he says, leaning his head out the window.

I'm so surprised, I respond with the first thing that enters my brain: "You *drive*?"

He gives me an odd look. "Yeah, I've been legally allowed to operate a motor vehicle since last April, so no need to act so horrified. My driving record is spotless." A fat drop of rain splashes off his forehead and he ducks his head back inside. "Come on. It's pouring."

I stand still for a moment, hesitant and dripping, then circle around to the passenger seat and climb in. The inside is blessedly warm and dry.

"I didn't mean to act horrified," I say, buckling myself in. "I just . . . I don't know."

He merges back onto the road. "No, I get it. I'm still that skinny little kid who's afraid of his own shadow, right?"

My lips twitch at this description, because it's exactly how I remember him. And this image—the one I carried with me the entire time I was away—is almost impossible to reconcile with this new one. But I don't want to embarrass him further, so I say, "Is this your car?"

He nods and flicks the windshield wipers to a higher speed. "I bought it last month. It's a piece of shit, but it gets me around."

I study the interior, taking in the scratched dash and the faded, threadbare fabric on the seats. This car is probably older than both of us. "*You* bought it? Not your . . ."

The word *parents* sticks on my tongue. As awkward as it feels to be around Ethan, it would be even more awkward to mention his parents, the same people who decided to slap me with a criminal-negligence-causing-death charge barely a week after the accident. They withdrew the charge before my court date—for reasons never explained to me—but still, I'd rather not open that Pandora's box right now.

"I bought it," he confirms as he brakes at a stop sign. "I saved almost every penny I made for the past two summers to cover the costs. You know the Douglas farm in Covington, that little town out in the middle of nowhere about forty minutes south of here?"

I nod. It's on the way to the beach my family used to go to every summer. Tobias always loved to see the cows grazing in the fields.

"I started working there the summer before last, after . . ." He trails off, and it feels like all the oxygen has been sucked out of the car. *Aubrey.* There's no room for her here, not yet. Ethan tightens his grip on the steering wheel and tries again. "Anyway, I needed to get out of the house, get my mind on something else, and Hunter mentioned his uncle was looking for some extra help on his dairy farm for a couple of weeks. He's worked there every summer since he was about twelve, so—"

"Wait." I hold up a hand to stop him, pinching the bridge of my nose with the other hand. I feel like I'm missing several huge gaps of information here. "Hunter Finley? The guy you were hanging out with in the parking lot that day? His uncle owns the Douglas dairy farm?"

"Yeah," Ethan says, like this is common knowledge. "He works there in the summers and he got me a job there too. We do stuff like repair fences and haul feed for the livestock. It's a lot harder than it sounds, but I love it. The first summer I only did two weeks, but this year I worked there from the middle of June to the end of August. And all I have to show for it is this hunk of junk." He pats the dashboard, the corners of his mouth lifting in a way that tells me he doesn't regret it one bit.

My mind struggles to compute everything he just told me. A year and a half ago, if I were to picture Ethan with a job, it would've been something involving a computer and lots of time indoors. Fresh air and cows never would've crossed my mind. At least this explains the wide shoulders, lean muscles, and bronzed skin.

"How did you meet Hunter?" I ask.

"He came up to me one day at Ace Burger while I was waiting for my order and told me he'd seen me play guitar at school." He smiles faintly, like this memory amuses him. "We started talking about music and stuff and he asked me if I wanted to jam with him and his band sometime. At first I thought he felt sorry for me because everyone felt sorry for me that summer, but it wasn't that. He just thought I was talented."

"You are," I say before I can stop myself. It's the truth.

Ethan turns onto my street and pulls up to the curb in front of my house. My parents aren't home yet, having recently decided I was mentally capable to be alone in the house for the hour or so between my arrival and theirs.

"So did you?" I ask, running a finger over the frayed strap on my backpack.

"Did I what?"

"Jam with Hunter's band?"

"I did." He leans back against the seat, raking a hand through his dark hair. Now that he's let the buzz cut grow out, his hair is almost as curly as Aubrey's, but not quite. His curls are looser, more like unruly waves. "And last May, when their lead guitar player quit to join another band, guess who stepped in?"

I blink at him a few times. He can't be serious. "You?"

He smiles at me the same way he used to do whenever he

kicked my ass at *Mortal Combat*—slow and mischievous and quietly proud. "There's that horrified expression again. We practice on Saturday and Sunday afternoons at Hunter's house. Come by and see for yourself if you don't believe me. Sixty-three Cambridge Drive."

I shake my head, overwhelmed. The car, the farm, the hair, the band . . . all these things together are too much. "You've really changed, Ethan."

His smile falters, even though I didn't mean it as an insult. Quite the opposite. From what I've seen so far, his changes are all good ones. "So have you," he says, and going by the way he looks away after he says it, he probably *does* mean it as an insult. None of my changes are positive.

Shame washes over me. What the hell am I doing, chatting with Ethan like nothing ever happened? I try to imagine what Aubrey would want me to do right now. What *she* would do, if she were the one who'd done some horrible, life-altering thing to Ethan. She'd apologize, of course, and do everything in her power to make it right again, even if there was no easy fix. She'd make sure he was okay and be there for him if he wasn't. She'd look out for him the same way she always did and expect me to do the same in her absence.

"Ethan," I start, but before I can say anything more, my father's truck pulls into the driveway in front of us.

Shit. He's home early. And here I am, right next to the boy whose space I'm supposed to be respecting. I consider ducking, but it's too late. He's spotted us.

"I haven't seen your dad in ages," Ethan says as my father gets out and walks toward us, his forehead scrunched in confusion. "He looks . . . tired."

"He's been extra busy with all the rain we've been having," I say, not wanting to get into my role in Dad's weariness. "You know, leaky roofs and everything."

Ethan doesn't respond because my dad is now standing beside the driver's side window, peering in at us and frowning like he caught us smoking crack or something. Ethan rolls down the window. "Hi, Mr. Shepard."

Dad studies him for a moment and then his gaze shifts to me. I give him a small, hopefully reassuring smile, which apparently satisfies him, because he goes back to eyeing Ethan. A year and a half ago, he would have grinned affably. He would've invited Ethan inside and offered him a snack and teased him about the girls at school. But my father's transformation is almost as bleak as mine.

"Come on inside, Dara," he tells me, then turns and walks away without saying anything else. Ethan and I watch through the rain-smeared windshield as he steps up to the house and disappears inside.

"Sorry." I rub my cheek, which feels warm and prickly like a sunburn. "I should go in."

I reach for the door handle, but Ethan touches my arm, stopping me. Our eyes meet and for a moment—a tiny, flickering moment—he's the old Ethan again, young and sweet and vulnerable. It hits me then, how much I've missed him.

"Music saved me," he says.

My hand, clutching the strap of my backpack, trembles a little. "What?"

"After Aubrey died. I know it sounds corny or trite or whatever, but music was all I had left. That and working on the farm . . . it kept me going. And then I started hanging around with Hunter and joined the band and . . ." He lets go of my arm but doesn't break our gaze, doesn't even blink. "It saved me."

I nod, but only because it's clearly important to him that I understand what he's saying.

"Thanks for the ride," I tell him. He doesn't stop me this time as I swing open the door and step into the rain.

ten

Sophomore Year

AUBREY WAS A NEW YEAR'S BABY, THE FIRST BIRTH of the year in our hospital. The honor came with gift certificates from local businesses and even a blurb in the newspaper. When she told me about it, a month or so after we met, I wasn't at all surprised. Right from birth, Aubrey had been destined to go first, at least when it came to our friendship. She got her period before I did, even though I'd developed earlier. She was the first to get a babysitting job and wear makeup and go on an overnight school trip. She was the first to start dating and the first to be kissed for real. But most aggravating of all, she was the first to turn sixteen and become eligible for the most coveted rite of passage of all—the driver's license.

We spent the last half of Christmas break studying for the written test. Well, Aubrey studied, and Ethan and I quizzed her. My sixteenth birthday was still six months away, and Ethan's wasn't for well over a year, but some early cramming wouldn't hurt either of us. I couldn't wait to learn to drive. Aubrey, on the other hand, was weirdly freaked out about it.

"Tell me again how many feet from a fire hydrant," she said as we trudged down her icy driveway on Wednesday morning, the day after her birthday.

"Fifteen," Ethan and I chorused. We glanced at each other and exchanged a smile.

"Right. I keep getting that and the stop sign distance confused. What the hell is wrong with me today?"

The question sounded rhetorical, so I kept my mouth shut and climbed into the backseat of her mom's car. Aubrey had persuaded Ethan and me to come along with her to the DMV for moral support, even though it was our last day of break before school started up again and we would've much preferred lazing around the house all day. But we agreed to go because Aubrey clearly needed the support. We were only about two minutes into the drive to town when I realized she wasn't going to get any from her mother.

"Most of the questions will be common sense," Mrs. McCrae said in the only tone I ever heard her use with her kids—terse with a hint of condescension. "If you studied properly, there's no reason you can't get everything right. I mean, look at all the idiots on the road. If they can manage to get a driver's license, anyone can. So, no excuses, okay?"

Aubrey nodded and turned to gaze out the passenger-side window. I was sitting behind the driver's seat, so I had a clear view of her left side. Her arm was bent and moving, and I knew she was anxiously braiding her hair. She wasn't all that nervous about the test itself, I realized. At school, she rocked every test she took. But at school, her mother wasn't waiting for her right outside the classroom, silently judging and eager to pounce.

"You'd better get over your nerves fast," Mrs. McCrae continued to lecture as we turned into the DMV parking lot. "I can't take off work again if you have to write this test a second time and neither can your father. This is it, so focus."

Aubrey nodded again, her throat moving as she swallowed. Beside me, I heard Ethan let out a quiet sigh. When I glanced at him, he was staring out the side window too. A lot of scenery watching took place when Aubrey and Ethan were trapped in a car with one or both of their parents.

Inside, Aubrey stood in line to get her test sheets while Ethan, his mother, and I found seats in the waiting area. Mrs. McCrae sat down first and immediately pulled out her phone. Ethan and I headed for the two empty chairs across from her, facing the testing area. As I sat down, I caught Aubrey's eye and mouthed, *You got this.* She smiled thinly back at me. Her face looked pale, and her hair fell in frizzy waves from being handled and twisted so much.

"Sit up straight, Ethan." His mom paused in her texting or whatever she was doing on her phone to peer at him. "You're in public, not at home on the sofa."

Ethan slowly pulled his long legs out of the aisle and then slid up on his seat until he was no longer slouching. Satisfied, his mother turned her attention back to her phone. Out of the corner of my eye, I saw Ethan cross his arms and then promptly uncross them, as if he wasn't sure what to do with his limbs. I didn't blame him. His mother made me feel self-conscious too.

My gaze found Aubrey again. She'd gotten her test and was heading toward one of the carrel desks lined up along the wall. If she was this freaked out during the written test, I hated to imagine what she'd be like during the actual driving part. She'd have to be sedated, which would result in a fail for sure.

"What is wrong with her?" Ethan muttered under his breath. "She looks like she has to go to the bathroom."

We both watched as Aubrey squirmed in her chair, her legs pressed together.

"She's nervous," I whispered back. "I don't think we're helping."

For a moment, I wondered if she wished Justin was there for moral support instead of us. Not with her mother around, of course, since she still didn't know he existed; but hypothetically, would she rather have Justin in the waiting room? He was the one who made her laugh now, who urged her out of her comfort zone. Lately, they were tighter than ever. He'd stopped riding her so much about her busy schedule, and he'd seemed to accept the whole secretly-dating-behind-the-parents'-backs thing. I liked to think our chat in the tree house a few weeks ago had something to do with his change in attitude, but maybe he just realized his girlfriend was worth the hassle.

A few minutes later, Aubrey hit her stride and stopped acting like she needed to pee. Reassured, I settled back into my hard plastic chair and dug my phone out of my coat. I'd missed two texts—one from my mother, and one from Justin.

How's she doing?

Usually, Justin only texted me when he couldn't get ahold of Aubrey and wanted to know if she was with me. This text was about Aubrey too, but it felt different, somehow. Like the beginning of a conversation. Or maybe I was reading too much into it. Fine, I typed back. I think she's almost done.

Is Ice Queen there?

I stifled a giggle. Ice Queen was his nickname for Aubrey's mother. Pretty astute for someone who'd never even met her. Yep, I replied. Frosty as ever.

Try not to look directly at her. She might turn you into an icicle.

A snort slipped out, and I pressed my lips together to prevent further outbursts.

"What's so funny?" Ethan asked, leaning in to get a peek

at my phone. "Who are you talking to?"

My thumb slid to the power button. The texting was innocent and friendly, but I still felt uncomfortable about it. Like I'd been doing something wrong. "No one."

He grinned evilly and made a grab for my cell. I shoved his hand away and tried to stuff the phone back into my coat pocket, but he managed to get his fingers around it before I could safely stow it. "Ethan," I said, laughing as I snatched my phone back, "quit being such a pest. You're worse than Tobias."

He nudged my knee with his. I nudged him back, then poked him in the shoulder. He raised a hand to poke me back, but I ducked out of the way before he could make contact. I was stronger than him, and faster, and still an inch or so taller too. I could take him in a fight.

"What has gotten into you two?" His mother's voice sliced through our scuffling. "You're behaving like children."

I let go of Ethan's collar, which I'd grabbed to keep him still while I smacked him in the head, and sat up straight. Mrs. McCrae was gaping at me in horror, as if she couldn't figure out why her children associated with the likes of me. She'd always looked at me that way, actually. Aubrey never admitted it one way or the other, but I often sensed that her mother saw me as a bad influence, too immature and ordinary for her talented, brilliant kids. Maybe she had a point.

Ethan and I mumbled halfhearted apologies, and the three of us went back to quietly waiting. Fortunately, Aubrey finished a few minutes later and made her way over, results in hand. We all stood up to greet her.

"Well?" I asked, searching her face. She still looked pale, but it was more of a relieved kind of pallor.

"I passed!" She waved the paper around and smiled. "*Almost* a perfect score. I only missed one question."

"Aubrey, that's amazing!" I pulled her in for a quick hug. "I knew you'd kill it."

"Congrats," Ethan said as they slapped hands in a celebratory high five.

Mrs. McCrae came up behind us, slinging her purse over her shoulder. "Which one did you miss?"

Aubrey's smile slipped a notch. "Oh. Um . . . one of the road sign identification ones. I got it mixed up with another one that looked really similar."

"Well," her mother said with an airy smile, "let's hope you don't make the same mistake when you're on the road."

My hand itched to clobber her. I knew Aubrey and Ethan were used to this sort of reaction from their mother, but it must have felt awful, having your parents focus on the one tiny thing you did wrong instead of the hundreds of things you did right.

"Can we go now?" Ethan asked, his shoulders settling back into a slouch. The festive mood had been completely sucked out of the atmosphere.

"I have to go get my temporary license," Aubrey said in an

overly bright voice, trying to recapture some of the cheer. It didn't quite work.

Mrs. McCrae's cell phone rang from inside her purse. She dug it out, glanced at the screen, and then pressed it to her ear as she walked toward the exit. Ethan and I stayed behind to wait for Aubrey, watching as the woman behind the counter directed her to stand in front of a green screen for the license photo. Aubrey obeyed, her mouth twitching like she wasn't sure if she should smile. Before she could make up her mind, the flash from the camera lit up the screen, capturing her moment of doubt.

eleven

Senior Year

I WAKE UP LATE SATURDAY MORNING FEELING sluggish and tired, like I hardly slept at all. This has been happening more and more lately. For most of last year, I suffered through insomnia. Now I can go to bed early, sleep a solid ten hours, and still wake up feeling like shit.

If I mention this to my parents, they'll probably think I'm depressed. And if they think I'm depressed, they'll ship me off to the doctor, who will put me on antidepressants like the ones I was on for six weeks after Aubrey died. The ones that made me so dizzy and foggy and nauseated, I had to quit taking them.

I'm sure there are better medications out there for me, the

perfect pill that will balance my brain's serotonin levels and make me feel happy. But maybe I don't get to feel happy.

I sit up in bed, my back aching with the movement, and inhale. The scent of bacon has started wafting up the stairs. If there's anything that will get me out of bed this morning, it's bacon.

Downstairs, my mother and brother are sitting at the kitchen table, eating pancakes and the aforementioned bacon. I head over to the counter and grab a piece off the paper-towel-lined plate. It's still hot, but I chomp into it anyway.

"Good morning," Mom greets me as she cuts into a pancake. "How did you sleep?"

"Fine," I say, then turn and snatch another bacon so she can't see the dark circles that greeted me in the bathroom mirror a few minutes ago. I look zombified.

"Pancakes are here on the table. Come sit down."

I stay where I am, leaning against the counter. "I'm not very hungry."

"Just one." She points to a chair with her fork. "A couple of slices of bacon isn't breakfast, Dara. You need to eat."

Irritation flares through me, but I keep my voice low and calm. "I'll eat something else later. Okay?"

Mom sighs. Tobias stops dipping his bacon into a puddle of maple syrup and glances back and forth between us, his freckled face strained. A chunk of his hair sticks straight up from sleep and I want so much to go over and smooth it down, smooth those worried creases out of his brow, but I don't do either.

"Okay, fine," Mom says, standing up with her plate. "But if you're not going to eat, then you're going to help me clean up this mess."

I open my mouth to tell her I wasn't the one who *made* the mess so I shouldn't be the one to clean it up, but the determined set of her jaw stops me. She's hell-bent on pushing me to do *something* this morning.

Wordlessly, I swallow my bacon and start loading the dishwasher. Mom wipes the stovetop while Tobias lingers at the table, slowly drinking his apple juice. We clean in silence for a few minutes, but it's a silence even heavier than the slab of greasy pork fat in my stomach.

Finally, Mom joins me at the sink and says, "So. How do you think school's going? In general, I mean. Are you starting to readjust?"

I scrape a glob of pancake batter off the spatula I'm rinsing. "I guess."

"Have you reconnected with any of your friends?"

Ah. And there it is. The question is delivered so casually, as if it had only just occurred to her. A week has passed since Dad came home and saw me in Ethan's car, and ever since then, I've been waiting for her to bring it up. My father obviously told her about it right away, but since Dad doesn't talk to me any more than he has to and Mom is still following Dr.

Lemke's be-patient-and-follow-Dara's-lead advice, I thought I might be off the hook.

I guess not.

"No," I say, twisting around to place the spatula in the dishwasher. I'm not lying. Sure, Ethan drove me home last Friday and updated me on his life, but that doesn't mean we've reconnected. It's not like we hang out at school or anything. We barely even see each other, and the odd time we do cross paths, we nod at each other like we're vague acquaintances.

Reconnection has definitely not transpired.

My mother runs her dishcloth under the tap for the tenth time, rinsing out soap that's no longer there. "What about Ethan?" she asks. The forced nonchalance in her tone has sharpened to an anxious edge.

"What about him?"

She folds the cloth and drapes it over the tap. "Well, he drives you home from school, so naturally I assumed you've become friends with him again."

"He *drove* me home from school. Once. And that doesn't mean we've become friends again."

"Mom?" Tobias says from the table, where he's still sitting, watching us and listening. "Can I have more apple juice?"

Mom doesn't take her eyes from me. "One sec, bud."

"So what if Ethan and I *did* become friends again?" I shut the dishwasher with a bang. "What difference does it make?"

She looks away, sweeping a lock of hair off her forehead.

"We discussed this before school started, Dara. Your dad and I think it would be best if you left Ethan alone for now. It's a sensitive situation and emotions are probably still running high . . ." She sighs and faces me again, leaning her hip against the edge of the counter. "We're also concerned that spending time with Ethan might undo some of the progress you've made this year. He's all wrapped up with Aubrey and what happened and—"

"Of course he is," I cut in. "He's her brother. Was. And a lot of things are wrapped up with Aubrey and what happened. Do you expect me to avoid every single thing connected to her? I can't live in denial anymore. I won't."

"Mom?" Tobias says again. "I want more juice, please."

"That's not what I'm saying. Look, I know you want to face things, and we're proud of you for that. We just think it might be beneficial for you to move forward instead of falling back into the life you had . . . before. Why don't you try making some new friends?"

"Friends?" I barked out a laugh. "You think I can make *friends* in that school, Mom? People look at me like I'm a ticking time bomb. They think if they so much as say hi to me, I'm going to freak out and push them in front of a truck."

She winces and turns pale. Okay, maybe I shouldn't have been so harsh. And I *do* understand her concern. Still, I can't seem to help myself this morning. Since the second I woke up, I've been frustrated and pissed off and spoiling for a fight.

"Dara, honey," she says gently. "I think we may need help

working through this. How about we schedule a family session with Dr. Lemke?"

"Why? So the three of you can band together and dope me up again so you don't have to deal with me? No, thanks."

Mom's cheeks go from ashen to bright pink. "Dara."

"I really, really need some more apple juice over here," Tobias says loudly.

Unable to contain my frustration, I whirl around to face my brother. "Get it *yourself*, Tobias!"

His face crumples, and I immediately regret lashing out at him.

"Tobias, I'm sorry," I say, taking a step toward him. Before I can get any closer, he jumps up from his chair and runs out of the kitchen.

I give Tobias an hour or so to cool off before I approach him again. He's sitting on the living room floor in front of the TV, playing a video game. I say his name, but he doesn't even look at me. "I'm busy," he says, his mouth set in a scowl.

I stand there for a minute longer, in case he changes his mind and decides to forgive me. When he doesn't, I return to my room and try to do some math homework. But I'm too agitated to concentrate on sinusoidal graphs right now, so I take a shower instead. That doesn't help either.

"I'm going for a walk."

Mom looks up from the pile of wet laundry she's tossing

into the dryer and studies my face. My shower didn't do much to improve my haggard appearance.

"Did you talk to your brother?" she asks.

"I tried to, but he's still mad at me."

She frowns. "He just needs some time."

This is Mom's answer for everything. Time, the ultimate cure-all.

"I'll be back in an hour or so," I tell her, backing out of the laundry room.

"Where are you going?"

"Nowhere. I just . . . need some air."

She continues to watch me, even as she shuts the dryer and turns it on. "Okay. Bring your phone."

I nod and then turn to leave before I open my big mouth to remind her that I'm seventeen, not seven, and that I can handle going for a walk on my own. After our altercation in the kitchen earlier, I probably shouldn't push it.

As I walk, I think about Tobias and start to cry. Why did I yell at him? He was only trying to stop Mom and me from fighting. Conflict makes Tobias feel anxious. When he was really small and our parents would have one of their rare arguments, he'd find me, crawl into my lap with his blanket, and sit there quietly until the bickering stopped. Just thinking about that now, the way he tucked his hard little head into my chest and relied on me for security, makes me feel ten times worse.

I miss the way it used to be, when my brother ran *to* me instead of running away.

My nose is dripping. I pause and dig out a tissue, wiping my eyes first and then my nose. A woman driving by in her minivan stares at me, the strange girl blubbering on the side-walk, but I'm used to being stared at by now. Curious looks from classmates and strangers, uneasy glances from my family and therapists . . . Being watched and evaluated is the most human contact I get these days.

In fact, since I came back home, the only person who hasn't either ignored me or treated me like a dangerous, unpredict-able zoo animal is Ethan. The same Ethan who has more rea-son than anyone to steer clear and judge me from afar.

We practice on Saturday and Sunday afternoons at Hunter's house, he told me in his car last week. *Sixty-three Cambridge Drive.*

I glance around to get my bearings. Cambridge Drive is only about a ten-minute walk from here. I resume my pace and turn left at the next stop sign, ignoring my mother's voice in my head. Just because my parents disapprove of my spending time with Ethan doesn't mean I have to agree. Do they think avoiding him will make my guilt magically disappear? Right. If that were the case, I would've just stayed at Aunt Lydia's.

As I turn onto Cambridge, my mind is suddenly engulfed in second thoughts. What if Ethan didn't mean what he said as an invitation? Sure, he gave me the address, but he probably wasn't expecting me to show up, especially not unannounced like this. I pause on the sidewalk and pull out my phone. The number I have for him is a year and a half old, but I send a quick hello text anyway, thinking maybe it's still active. Then I start walking again, my steps so small it's like I'm barely moving.

After five minutes, he still hasn't answered. I stop for a second time, wondering if I should turn around and go home. But then I think about what he said to me—that music saved him—and I want more than anything to understand how something so simple can do something so incredibly powerful. I need to see it for myself.

I take a breath and keep going.

Sixty-three Cambridge Drive is a white split-level with red shutters. I rub my damp fingers on my pants and ring the doorbell. Moments later, the door swings open to reveal a plump woman with a short blond bob and square-framed glasses.

She seems way too normal and maternal to be badass rocker Hunter Finley's mom.

"Hi," I say when she smiles at me expectantly. "I'm looking for Hunter and, uh, Ethan?" I say it like I'm not sure he's here, even though his car is parked along the curb in front of the house.

The woman's smile grows warmer. "They're out back, honey. Just pound on the door."

"Thanks." I step away and she smiles again before slipping back inside.

Out back. When Ethan said they practiced here, I pictured them in a basement or a garage, not somewhere behind the house. I go around to the backyard. Toward the far left corner, nestled a few feet from the tall privacy fence, stands a square beige structure that looks like an oversized shed. Is this "out back"? Even from several feet away, I can hear muffled drumbeats seeping through the building's walls. The rhythm matches the dull thump in my head I have from crying. The reminder of how awful my eyes must look—not to mention the rest of me—should send me running back toward the street, but it doesn't. The vibration of that barely audible music hums through the ground and straight into my feet, propelling them forward.

Seconds before I reach the shed, the door flings open, releasing a blast of sound and a guy around my age who I've never seen before in my life. I would've remembered. He's slim and striking with black hair shaped into a kind of halfhearted Mohawk and a sculpted, almost delicate face. He pauses at the sight of me and I try not to stare at his eyes, which look like chips of blue-tinted ice against the light brown shade of his skin.

"Hi there," he says, cocking his head at me. "Who are you?"

His voice is like honey over gravel. Lead singer, of course. I stuff my hands in my pockets and glance toward the still-open door. The music has been replaced by a collection of different voices. "I'm . . . a friend of Ethan's."

He smiles and takes a step forward, offering me his hand to shake. "I'm Kel. Ethan's in there replacing a string on his Ibanez. Should I tell him you're out here or did you plan on surprising him? Either way, you'll probably make his day."

I tug my hand out of his firm grip and stuff it back into my pocket. Confidence practically oozes from this guy's pores. He knows he's hot and he can tell I think so too. And I do, in the same way I might think a painting is pretty. I can appreciate the beauty in a technical, abstract way, but it doesn't really do much for me. I haven't been attracted to a guy since—

No. Not going there. A shiver runs through me and I push the memories back down.

"You guys are busy. I'll just—" I turn to leave, already deeply regretting showing up here unannounced. What was I thinking? That because music helped Ethan heal, it would somehow help me too? So stupid.

"No, wait." Kel holds up a hand to me as he leans his head in the shed door. "Hey, E. Leggy blonde here to see you." He flashes a grin over his shoulder after he says this, and I feel my face flush.

Ethan bounds out the door, his gaze immediately landing on me. His expression wavers between confusion and surprise. Before he has a chance to say anything, Hunter Finley steps out of the shed, followed by a cute red-haired girl with a nose ring. They join our growing assembly on the lawn.

"Hi," the girl says to me.

As I nod at her, it hits me that she sits two tables behind me in chemistry. Since I'm not exactly social at school these days, I'm able to spend a lot of time listening in on conversations around me. So I already know her name is Noelle Jacobs and that she moved here last year, while I was away. I also know she's been dating Hunter since the summer. What I *don't* know is whether she's aware of who I am. Her expression isn't telling me anything. She just looks friendly.

Ethan walks over to me, his features relaxing as he adjusts to the shock of my presence. "Guys, this is Dara. She's, um, an old friend of mine. We go way back."

I don't miss the sudden comprehension that flashes across Kel's face at the sound of my name. He's heard of me. He knows what I did. They all do. Something like that is impossible to hide from your friends, especially when some of those friends go to Hadfield High. They've probably heard the rumors too. Any second now, they'll start asking questions.

Don't be such a coward, I tell myself as they all stare at me. *Stand here and take whatever they want to dish out. If you can do it at school, you can do it here too.*

But then I look at Ethan and see the anxiety on his face, and my brief surge of bravery starts to falter. This isn't three nosy strangers cornering me by the music room. These are his friends. He shouldn't have to defend me to them.

"I'm sorry, I shouldn't have interrupted your practice." I

quickly turn from the group and head toward the street and freedom. This was too much, too soon. I should have tried reconnecting with him one-on-one before showing up here and making a fool out of myself in front of his friends.

"Dara, wait!" Ethan catches up and slips in front of me, blocking my path. "Don't leave. Please. I was just surprised to see you, okay? I didn't expect—"

"I know," I say, skirting around him.

"No. You *don't* know." He moves in front of me again, his hand lifting to touch my arm. Seeing the warning in my eyes, he quickly drops it. "Please," he says again. "Stick around for a bit. You still haven't met Corey, our bass player. His girlfriend's here too. Julia. You can't leave without meeting everyone and hearing us play."

My head starts thumping again, only now there's no rhythm to it at all. It's erratic and painful and I know it won't let up until I'm home, alone in my room.

"I have to go, Ethan," I say.

This time, when I brush past him, he doesn't try to stop me. This time, it's me who disappears just as fast as I arrived.

twelve **Sophomore Year**

AUBREY LOST HER PHONE PRIVILEGES AGAIN IN
February when her parents caught her texting outside the des-
ignated time frame they'd set up for her. Because of this, we'd
resorted to an old-fashioned method of communication—
leaving notes in each other's lockers.

> Studying in library after school but I'll be done by 3:45.
> Wait for me? Need to talk.

I examined Aubrey's latest note as I stood at my locker after
last class. Her familiar slanted scrawl looked slightly wobbly,
like she'd written it in a hurry. *What now?* I thought, shutting

my locker. She'd seemed fine the last time I'd seen her, three hours ago at lunch. Was she fighting with Justin again? God, I hoped not. If she begged me to intervene like she did last time, I'd refuse. I wasn't their relationship mediator.

Stuffing the note in my backpack, I made my way through the emptying halls to the library. I knew Aubrey was expecting me to head to the main doors, where we met most days before walking home together, but I was too curious and impatient to stand around waiting. Maybe seeing me would inspire her to finish studying faster.

When I entered the library, the first thing I noticed was the back of Aubrey's dark head, bent over a mess of papers on the table in front of her. And sitting next to her, twirling a pencil between two fingers, was Travis Rausch.

"What the hell?" I mumbled to myself as I approached them. They had their backs to me, so neither of them registered my presence until I plunked down in the chair across from Travis.

"Shepard," he said, his neck turning red like it did when he was embarrassed. "Where'd you come from?"

I glanced at Aubrey, who had paused in writing down what looked like an algebra formula, and then at the papers and work sheets scattered on the tabletop. "Since when do you two study together?" I asked. "You're not even in the same math class." Aubrey took advanced math, of course, and Travis and I were in the same regular, non-genius class.

"We were both here at the same time, so . . ." Aubrey shrugged and flicked a look at Travis, whose gaze stayed locked on the pencil in his hand.

They were acting weird. I wondered if Paige knew Travis was here, sitting mere inches from Aubrey. She hadn't said anything about it in biology last period. And Justin . . . I didn't think he'd like the idea of his girlfriend huddling together with another guy in a virtually deserted library, even if the guy in question was Travis.

"I gotta get home." Travis stood up and slapped his math book closed, then shoved it in his backpack along with the pencil. "See you tonight, McCrae."

"Sure thing, Rausch," Aubrey replied with a smile.

Travis grinned back and gave us a small salute as he turned to leave. Once he was gone, I leveled a what-the-hell-was-that look at my best friend. "'Rausch'?" I asked. Calling people by their last names was Travis's thing, not hers. How much time did they spend together if his quirks were already rubbing off on her?

Aubrey shrugged again. "I say it to tease him."

I picked up a paper and scanned its contents. Algebra formulas, like I'd thought—the same ones I'd learned last week in math class. "Do you think he has a crush on you?"

She frowned and took the paper from me, placing it on top of a small pile of others. "Who? Travis? Of course not."

I gave her a look. "Aubrey. Travis doesn't *study*. In fact,

I'm pretty sure he's failed every math quiz our teacher gave us so far this year. Yet here he was, sitting in here doing practice problems with you. Maybe he secretly likes you."

"No, Dara. He doesn't. Not like that. He's with Paige, and I'm with Justin." She gathered the sheets and her calculator and tucked them into her backpack. "And speaking of Justin, I really need to talk to you about something."

I was only vaguely paying attention. Something Travis said right before he left had just caught up to me. "Wait. What's going on tonight?"

Aubrey zipped her backpack and stood up. "Huh?"

"Travis said he'd see you tonight. What's tonight?"

"Paige didn't tell you?"

"Tell me *what*?"

Mrs. Kirkland, the librarian, shot me a dirty look as she strolled past, a silent warning to use my inside voice. I hooked my arm through Aubrey's and hauled her out of the library. "Tell me what?" I asked again once we were in the clear.

"We're going glow-in-the-dark bowling tonight," she said, gently extracting her arm from mine. "Paige and Travis and me and Justin and a few other people. She didn't mention it?"

I shook my head. It seemed like there were a lot of things being kept from me lately. "So it's a bunch of couples?"

She threw me a sideways glance as we walked down the hallway. "Yeah. Maybe that's why she didn't bring it up. You're always saying how much you hate being a third wheel. Or a fifth wheel. Or whatever kind of wheel."

"And *you're* always saying how much Paige hates you," I spat back at her. "Now you're best friends and going bowling together?"

Aubrey stared at her shoes, looking chastened. "She's not so bad. We've gotten to know each other a little better over the past few weeks."

I made a snorting noise and quickened my pace. Aubrey kept up with me despite her much shorter legs and we stepped outside into the frigid winter air together. The icy wind was like a balm on my flushed face.

"Sorry," I mumbled a few minutes later as we skidded down the slippery sidewalk. "I just feel a bit left out sometimes."

"I'm sorry too. I don't mean to make you feel that way." She was silent for a moment, biting her lip. "How about I skip bowling and we'll go to a movie or something instead? Just me and you."

I stuffed my mittened hands into my coat pockets. "No, thanks. I'd feel like your charity case. You should go bowling."

"Well . . . you come too, then. No one said you *couldn't* go. I mean, it's a free country. Hey!" She turned to me, her nose pink from the cold. "I saw Grant Livingston checking you out at lunch yesterday. Maybe he'd like to come with us too. That way, you'll have a bowling partner."

The bright eagerness in her expression drained most of my

anger. She was so desperate to find a solution that would please everyone and make things right again. The dread she felt at the thought of hurting me made it virtually impossible for me to stay mad at her for long.

"Thanks, Aubs," I said, "but Grant Livingston is like a foot shorter than me. And he wasn't checking me out; he was staring at the huge chocolate milk stain on my shirt."

She snickered. "You have an amazing talent for finding something wrong with every guy I suggest."

"That's because I have high standards."

"No, it's because you're holding out for Micah," she said, elbowing me in the side.

I smiled. Micah was my favorite member of Stop Motion, a boy band we loved. Sometimes I wondered if I was only attracted to guys I could never have. "At least he's taller than me."

The vibe between us felt more companionable as we turned onto the shortcut path through the woods. As we passed the tree house, I suddenly remembered the reason for Aubrey's locker note.

"You said you needed to talk to me about something?" I prompted her.

She studied my face as if checking to make sure we were okay again before she proceeded. I gave her a reassuring smile, urging her on.

"So," she said, clearing her throat. "Justin and I have been together for a few months now and um, well . . ." She burst into nervous laughter, her cheeks almost as red as her coat. "God, this is embarrassing. My mom's not the type to discuss this type of thing with me, so . . ."

Ah. Now I got it. She wanted my advice about sex. With Justin. There were so many things wrong with that, I didn't even know where to start. For one, the sum of my sexual experience consisted of a single, five-second kiss with a boy named A.J. the summer before ninth grade, and I'd only kissed him on a dare. Neither of us had enjoyed it. And two, the image of Justin doing *that* with anyone—let alone my best friend—made my chest throb like a toothache.

Everything in me wanted to sidestep this conversation, but I couldn't. Aubrey needed to confide in someone, and I was it.

"Is he pressuring you?" I asked. If he was, my opinion of him would plummet lower than the current temperature.

"No. I mean, not exactly. He . . . well, I know he wants to."

We emerged from the path and hooked onto the sidewalk along Fulham Road. I peered at Aubrey. "Do *you* want to?"

Her lips twitched into a tiny smile. "It's not just guys who want sex, Dara. Girls want it too."

I knew this, but that didn't mean I wasn't shocked to hear it come out of her prim and proper mouth. "Are you asking me if I think you should cash in your v-card?"

"No." The tiny smile blossomed into a full grin. "I'm

asking if you'll come with me to the clinic tomorrow morning so I can get a prescription for birth control."

I stared at her, wide-eyed, wondering when we'd progressed from sleepovers and cookie-baking to *this*. Maybe it would always be like this, Aubrey blazing the trail ahead of me and claiming all the "firsts" before they even had time to register on my radar.

But this wasn't about me and my apprehension about being left behind. It was about me being there as a friend for Aubrey. "Sure," I said with a shrug. "As long as I don't have to watch you practice putting a condom on a banana."

Aubrey threw her head back and laughed just as her feet met an icy patch on the sidewalk. She let out a squeal as she slipped, her arms windmilling in an effort to regain balance. I reached out to catch her, not letting go until the threat passed and she felt steady on her feet again.

thirteen

Senior Year

I'M GATHERING MY THINGS TOGETHER AFTER chemistry class when someone slides into the empty chair beside me. "Do you think he waxes it?"

Startled, I spin around and see Noelle Jacobs. She's staring toward the front of the classroom, a thoughtful expression on her slightly freckled face.

"What?" I say, so taken aback by her presence that I drop two pencils and an eraser on the table. People don't usually seek me out in class, either because they don't know how to relate to the girl who killed her best friend or because they think I did it on purpose.

"Haggerty." She nods to our chem teacher, who's erasing

the whiteboard. "There's not a single hair on that man's head. Not even any stubble. I bet he gets it waxed on a regular basis."

I examine Mr. Haggerty's smooth, hairless head and picture him at a salon with several wax strips pasted to his scalp. The image makes me want to giggle. "His nickname isn't Mr. Clean for nothing."

Noelle grins and gives an exaggerated toss of her own long, lustrous hair, which is the same red-orange shade as the changing leaves on the big tree outside the window beside us.

"Heading to the cafeteria?" she asks.

"Um, I was planning on it, yeah."

"Well, I think you should rethink your plans." She rescues my eraser from the edge of the table and hands it to me with another smile. "It's Friday, and on Fridays we go to Subway for footlongs."

"We?"

"Me, Hunter, and Ethan. And now you," she adds, standing up. "Let's go."

I stay where I am and gape at her, speechless. We don't even know each other. Still, I find myself kind of liking her, even though she's pushy and a little strange. Maybe it's because she doesn't seem afraid to talk to me. Or maybe it's because there's something about her friendly face that eases my loneliness a little. In any case, I stand up to follow her after only a moment's hesitation.

"Did Ethan ask you to invite me?" I ask as we leave the

classroom together. I can't imagine why he'd want me near his friends after the other day.

"No, but I asked him if *I* could. He gave me his blessing." Noelle glances at me, worried. "I'm not overstepping here, am I? You guys are, like, okay with each other, right?"

I'm not sure how to answer. Ethan and I haven't spoken since I showed up unexpectedly in Hunter's backyard. I've noticed him in the halls, though. Despite the horrifying history between us, I still feel drawn to him. He's a part of Aubrey—a living, breathing connection to her. Aside from me, he's the only person who truly knew her. The only person who truly knows *me*.

"We're fine," I say, partly because I don't want Noelle to feel awkward but mostly because I want it to be true. If Ethan thinks there's still a friendship left to salvage, then I owe it to him to at least try.

We find the guys outside, leaning against the same black car I saw them sitting on the day Ethan told me he was glad I was back. "Dependable family sedan" doesn't exactly fit the image of Hunter Finley, Rock God, so I figure it must be his mom's.

"Hey," Ethan says when we reach them.

Noelle wraps her arms around Hunter's neck and gives him a loud kiss. After she extracts herself, she looks over at Ethan. "I *told* you she'd come." Her gaze shifts to me and she adds, "He said you'd probably say no."

Ethan ducks his head, suddenly fascinated by a small scratch in the car's paint job.

"She had me at footlongs," I say, and everyone laughs. It feels so good, so *normal*, my first instinct is to do what I always do whenever something feels good or right—resist it. Withdraw. But I don't. Instead, I let the feeling snuggle up inside me, just for one quick moment. It's been so long since I made a joke, or laughed, I almost forgot about the warm, floaty sensation it produces.

We arrive at Subway ten minutes later. The place is teeming with Hadfield High students and filthy construction guys on their lunch breaks. For a panicked moment I wonder if my dad might show up, but he always brings his own lunch to work, so it's unlikely. Still, I can't seem to fully relax, standing here with Ethan and his friends. My social skills are rusty at best.

A table opens up and Noelle and I dive for it, leaving our orders with the guys. The line is so long, I doubt we'll get our subs in time to eat them here.

"How long have you known him?"

I tear my gaze away from a splotch of mustard on the table and focus on Noelle. She gestures over her shoulder to the guys, who are chatting while they wait. Once again, I get that surreal, time-warp feeling as I look at Ethan. Two seconds ago he was playing video games in his room and riding his bike down my street, and now he's hanging out with cool seniors and driving his own car.

"A long time," I tell her. "Since he was ten."

I wait for her to ask about Aubrey next, if I offed her like everyone's saying, but she doesn't.

"What was he like back then?"

My gaze skips to Ethan again, registering the wide, sturdy set of his shoulders and the way his black hoodie makes his eyes seem even darker. "Nothing like he is now," I reply honestly. "He used to be shy and kind of geeky and now he's this . . . guy in a band."

"Musicians," she says with a long-suffering sigh. "They're my one major weakness." She smiles and leans across the table, like she's about to divulge a secret. "They have good hands."

A laugh bubbles up in my throat, and I press my lips together to keep it inside. Noelle takes one look at my expression and cracks up. She's still laughing when the boys arrive with our lunch.

"What's going on over here?" Hunter asks as he claims the seat next to her.

I try not to look at his hands. Or at Ethan's, when he slides my meatball sub toward me.

"Nothing," Noelle says, tearing into her turkey wrap. "Dara was just asking about Realm."

For a moment I'm confused, then it clicks in that *Realm* is the name of their band. Recovering quickly, I chime in with, "Yeah, I was wondering if, um, the other guys lived around here."

Ethan shakes his head. "Corey and Kel live in Brentwood."

"Oh." This explains why I've never seen Kel around. Brentwood is a small town about ten miles south of here.

My face must look weird or something because Noelle narrows her eyes at me, suspicious. "Please don't tell me you fell for whatever line Kel gave you the day you came over. That boy hits on anything with a pulse."

"He's shameless," Hunter confirms, flicking a lock of shaggy blond hair out of his eyes. "We only keep him around for his voice."

"Resist him, Dara. Stay strong."

I wash down the food in my mouth with a sip of Coke. "No problem," I assure her. Falling under Kel's spell—under *any* guy's spell—is the last thing I need right now.

We finish eating with two minutes to spare. On the way back to school, Noelle asks me if I'm going to Hunter's house tomorrow afternoon so I can finally meet the rest of the band and hear them play.

"Maybe," I say, glancing at Ethan. He smiles and shrugs one shoulder. I still know him well enough to decipher his body language, so I know he's telling me he's fine with it, but it's totally up to me. I give him a tiny nod in response.

"She'll be there," he tells Noelle.

I wait until after lunch the next day to tell my mother I'm going out. When I add the words "with a friend," her entire body freezes and she stares at me like I just told her I made the honor roll.

"A friend? Who?" She snaps her laptop closed and sets it beside her on the couch.

"Just this girl from my chemistry class. We're going for a walk. No big deal." I plan to tell her about Ethan and the band . . . eventually. Just not today.

"This *is* a big deal, Dara. It's been a while since—"

She clams up as Tobias passes by the living room on his way to the bathroom. He and Dad have been outside all day, replacing rotten boards on the back porch. They've been doing this a lot lately, hanging out together, undoubtedly bonding over their mutual wariness toward me. Tobias hasn't spoken to me since I yelled at him—even though I apologized three times—and Dad continues to be confounded by me.

"We're just hanging out," I tell Mom, who's got this dopey grin on her face like she's imagining sleepovers and cookie-baking and study sessions—all the things I used to do with Aubrey. "I barely know her."

She opens her mouth to respond but the doorbell cuts her off this time. We both go to answer it.

"Hi," Noelle chirps. "Are you ready, Dara?"

I nod and grab my jacket.

"I'm Noelle," she says to my mom, and then sticks out her right hand.

Mom shakes it, her eyes doing a quick scan of my new

friend's bright hair and nose ring. "Noelle. What a pretty name."

"Well, I was a Christmas Eve baby, so . . ." She shrugs and unleashes a dazzling smile. My mom visibly relaxes.

"Have fun, Dara," she tells me. "Bring your phone."

I hold up my cell. "Got it."

Outside, Noelle and I head for the sidewalk in silence. Once we're a safe distance from my house, I say, "Sorry about that. My mom tends to hover."

She waves a hand. "I'm good with moms. They always seem to trust me immediately. It's the freckles, I think."

"You didn't have to come to my house, you know. We could've just met at Hunter's."

"I don't mind walking with you," she says with a smile.

I focus on my limbs, making sure they're a good distance from hers. Walking alongside someone on the sidewalk, with the street mere inches away, makes me nervous. Luckily, Noelle doesn't seem to notice. She babbles on, filling me in on her family (just her and her mom), why they moved here (her parents split up and her mother wanted to be near her relatives) and how she likes living in Hyde Creek (better than her old town). By the time we reach Hunter's backyard, I feel like I've been officially befriended. Pretty brave of her, considering what happened to my last friend.

There's no sign of music as we draw closer to the shed. The door is closed over partway and Noelle yanks it open, stepping in ahead of me. "I got her," she announces.

The interior is dark and it takes a minute for my eyes to adjust. When they do, I see a cramped space with thin blue carpeting on the floor and walls plastered with album covers and posters of band logos. On my left, Hunter sits behind an elaborate drum kit that eats up most of the square footage. Ethan crouches beside him, adjusting dials on an amp. Cradled in his arms is a steel-gray guitar I've never seen him play. The Ethan I knew before only played acoustic. *Classical* acoustic. And violin. This gleaming beast strapped to his chest is yet another addition to the long list of things he'd acquired while I was away.

A ratty tan couch sits along the opposite wall from the instruments, taking up the remainder of the space. On it is a skinny guy with messy reddish hair and an even skinnier brunette in skin-tight jeans. The guy is sprawled across the girl's lap, eyes drooping like he's high or suffering from an acute hangover or both, while she plays with her phone.

Ethan rises from his crouch to introduce me. "Corey and Julia," he says, motioning to the couple, who both glance up with the slightest show of interest. "Guys, this is Dara."

Corey smiles up at me. "How's it going?"

"Fine," I say, and then exchange a small nod with Julia. She looks bored, but I get the feeling she typically looks that way.

"Where the fuck did Kel go?" Hunter asks from behind the drums.

Ethan digs into the front pocket of his jeans and brings out a white guitar pick. "Inside to get a drink of water."

"That was twenty minutes ago."

"He's probably in there seducing your mom," Corey says as he lifts himself off Julia's lap. When he's fully upright, Hunter throws an empty water bottle at him. Corey catches it, snickering.

Noelle has claimed the spot next to Julia on the couch, so I sink down on her other side. The moment I'm somewhat comfortable, Hunter pounds out a practice beat that makes me want to cover my ears. Drums are *deafening* in this small space.

"Do the neighbors ever complain?" I ask Noelle.

"Nope. Hunter's dad built this thing from the ground up. It's almost completely soundproof."

"He built it just for Hunter?"

Her blue eyes crinkle at the corners. "It was either that or let him play in the house, and his mom says it's not worth the migraines."

The door opens and sunlight pours in, making us all squint. All I can see is the outline of Kel as he steps inside and heads directly for the red guitar resting on a stand near the drums. He picks it up, attaches a strap, and adjusts it across his chest in one fluid movement. It's not until he steps up to the mic stand that he finally notices me. His face splits into a grin.

Clearly, even knowing my role in Ethan's sister's death isn't going to deter him from trying to charm me.

The guys confer for a minute, then launch into a song that starts off with a lot of heavy bass. The rhythm is fast and frenetic and so piercingly loud, I can feel the vibration in my bones. After several beats, Kel leans into the mic. His voice is exactly like I imagined—rough and gravelly, yet melodic.

In my peripheral, I see Noelle's head bobbing slightly to the beat. Julia is still on her phone, oblivious to her surroundings. I'm not oblivious. This isn't my type of music, but there's something about it, something pure and unrestrained. The sheer volume and power of it occupies every sense, every thought, until there's nothing left but sound.

My gaze locks on Ethan. I almost forgot how effortlessly *good* he is, how connected he seems to whatever music he's playing. This is one thing that hasn't changed, even if the boy and the instrument are different. I watch the muscles in his forearms contract as his fingers fly across the strings. I see the raw joy infuse his face as he loses himself in the band's energy. And I remember again what he told me that day in his car: *Music saved me.*

I think I get it now.

An hour and five or six songs later, it's time for a break. Hunter and Noelle step outside for a smoke, and Corey and Julia head to the house to pee. Now it's just me and Ethan and Kel, who's lounging on the couch and strumming his unplugged guitar.

"So give me your honest opinion," Ethan says, unhooking the strap from the end of his guitar and sliding it off. "Do we suck or what?"

"I don't think so." I step away from the Metallica poster I've been examining and turn to face him. "But I'm not exactly an expert on rock and metal. Pop is more my thing."

"Yeah, I remember." He makes an expression of mock disgust, and I can tell he's thinking of all the times Aubrey and I tortured him with repeated blastings of whatever hit song we happened to be obsessed with at the moment.

"You guys sound good," I tell him. "Um, what do your parents think about all this?"

"About what? Me trading in my acoustic for an electric or me joining a band?"

"Either."

A huge smile lights up his face. "They *hate* it."

He looks so thoroughly thrilled when he says it, I can't help but laugh. Our eyes meet and he starts laughing too, and that's when I feel it. A tiny flutter of . . . something.

"You okay?" he asks when my laughter comes to an abrupt halt.

Luckily, the door swings open and saves me from having to answer. Ethan and I turn toward the sound, blinking against the sudden glare of daylight. At first I think it's Noelle returning, but as my vision adjusts I realize it's a different girl, one I haven't met. She's pretty, with shoulder-length dark blond hair and full, pouty lips. She's wearing a denim jacket over a cute floral dress—even though we're way past summer weather—and her legs are long and shapely.

"Hey, Lacey," Kel says without looking up from his guitar. "Nice of you to join us."

I assume she's with him, one of the many girls he probably invites here to swoon over him while he sings, so naturally I'm surprised when she walks up to Ethan and wraps her arms around his neck.

"Sorry I'm so late, babe," she says, and then proceeds to stick her tongue down his throat.

I stare. I can't help it. The way he's kissing this girl . . . Jesus. Not that I have much experience on this matter, but going by the way her fingers tighten on the back of his T-shirt, it seems his talents might stretch beyond guitar-playing.

Ethan detaches himself from the girl and looks at me as if I haven't been standing two feet away from him for the past several minutes. Maybe some brain matter leaked out through his mouth along with all that saliva.

"Um, this is Lacey," he tells me with a trace of embarrassment. "Lacey . . . Dara."

"Hey," she says, dabbing her mouth with the sleeve of her jacket. If she has any clue who I am, it doesn't show on her face. Maybe she thinks *I'm* one of Kel's groupies.

"Hi," I say.

An awkward silence ensues, during which we all look

anywhere but at each other. My phone chimes in my pocket, and I almost break a finger diving for it. It's a text from Mom, asking if I want to invite my new friend over for dinner. Normally I'd be annoyed at the intrusion, but at the moment I've never been more grateful for my mother's hovering in my life.

"I have to go," I announce to no one in particular.

"Already?" Ethan says. His arm hasn't moved from Lacey's tiny waist.

I nod and start toward the door. "Thanks for having me."

Kel shoots me a knowing grin and I want to kick myself for phrasing it that way. Instead, I lift my hand in a vague wave and book it out of there fast.

Outside, I run into Noelle and Hunter on their way back to the shed.

"Leaving already?" Noelle asks.

"My mom needs me at home," I tell her. It's easier to lie than explain to her what just happened inside. I don't even know for sure.

Noelle nods like she understands even though she doesn't, not really. I say good-bye to them and continue to the street, already missing the way that loud, rumbling music took over my body, pushing everything else away.

fourteen — Sophomore Year

THOUGH AUBREY AND I HAD BEEN FRIENDS SINCE sixth grade and logged many hours at each other's houses, her parents and mine never managed to bond. My mother thought her mother was "a piece of work," and my father thought her father was "high and mighty." Aubrey and I never discussed it, but I knew her parents thought my parents were "tacky and limited." So imagine my surprise when my mother came in my room one Sunday afternoon at the end of March to tell me she'd just gotten off the phone with Mrs. McCrae.

"What did she want?" I asked, looking up from the collage I was making for art class. Mom had the small wrinkle between her eyes that meant she was either worried or annoyed.

"She has some concerns about Aubrey." She sat beside me on the edge of my bed. "Apparently, she's been sneaking around with some boy behind her parents' backs."

My blood froze. *Crap.* "Um, why does she think that?"

"Because she was driving by the park yesterday and saw them together. Holding hands and kissing." Her eyes narrowed and she peered closely at my face, which probably glowed like a stoplight. "She thought I should be in the loop, in case you're hiding things too."

God, I loathed Mrs. McCrae. "I'm not, Mom. I swear. I don't have a secret boyfriend."

"But you knew Aubrey had a secret boyfriend?"

"Well, yeah. She's my best friend." I traced my finger over my collage, which was supposed to be a representation of all my favorite things. So far, all I had was a picture of Aubrey and me, a magazine cutout of an actor I liked, and bubble letters spelling out my name. "I don't get what the big deal is, anyway. Why can't she have a boyfriend? Would you freak out if *I* had one?"

"Depends on the boy, but no, I wouldn't freak out. I can't speak for your father, though."

I snorted. Dad often joked that the first thing he'd do when I brought a boy home was take him down to the basement and show him his rifle collection.

Mom reached down to pick some paper scraps off my carpet. "The problem with Aubrey's parents is they're scared to let their kids be kids. And if you expect perfection out of your children and make them feel like they can never mess up . . ." She shook her head. "It's only a matter of time before they rebel."

"Aubrey's not *rebelling*," I said. "It's not like she ran off with a biker gang or something. She and Justin are just, you know, hanging out."

This earned me another narrow-eyed look. "Is that all?"

My mind flashed with an image of the small boxes of birth control pills the clinic doctor had given Aubrey a few weeks ago. She'd hidden them on the top shelf of her closet, behind her old porcelain doll collection. Every night, she had to dig around up there and then swallow a pill with the bottle of water she kept on her nightstand. Then I thought about the twinge of jealousy I felt when she told me she was no longer a virgin.

So it definitely wasn't *all*, but no way in hell would I discuss my best friend's lack of virginity and the crush I had on her boyfriend with my mother. I could barely even admit one of those things to myself.

"That's all," I said in what I hoped was a convincing tone. It must have been, because the wrinkle between Mom's eyes all but disappeared. "Did Mrs. McCrae tell you anything else? Is Aubrey grounded?"

Duh, I thought. Why did I bother asking? Of course she was grounded. They'd probably taken away her phone and laptop and locked her in her room with a tray of stale bread and lukewarm water. Maybe I'd never see her again.

"She didn't get into any of that. I think the main reason she called was to make sure I'm parenting *my* kid." Mom stood up and tossed the paper scraps into my overflowing trash can. "You know you can talk to your dad and me about anything, right? Even if you think we'll disapprove, don't ever be afraid to come to us. Okay?"

"Okay," I said.

She gave my hair a gentle tug and left the room. Not even a minute later, my phone started dinging with texts.

Can you come over?

She won't come out of the bathroom.

Not sure what to do.

My stomach dipped. They were all from Ethan, who rarely texted me and never asked me for help. I texted back, Your parents home? If Aubrey was grounded, it meant grounded from everything except school and violin.

No.

I looked down at my collage, which was due Tuesday and nowhere near finished. Then I thought of my best friend, crying in the bathroom while her brother stood outside the door, helpless.

Be there in 10 mins.

Downstairs, I told my parents the truth—Aubrey was upset and needed me. It was enough. Dad drove me over so I wouldn't have to walk in the biting cold. To my relief, Mr. and Mrs. McCrae's cars were still gone when I arrived.

Ethan swung open the door before I even had a chance to knock. His face was drawn with worry.

"Where is she?" I asked, slipping out of my heavy coat.

"Upstairs bathroom." He ran a hand over his buzzed hair. "She's been crying for . . . I don't know, at least forty-five minutes, and she won't open the door. She yelled at me to go away."

His tone held a combination of hurt and surprise. Ethan and Aubrey weren't the type of siblings who fought and called each other names, like Tobias and I sometimes did. Aubrey rarely got angry with him or pushed him away, and I could see on his face that it had shaken him.

"Ethan." I wrapped my fingers around his forearm and jostled him a little so he'd look at me. "She didn't mean it."

He nodded quickly. "I know."

I wasn't convinced he did, but I'd worry about him later. His sister needed me more.

Upstairs, I knocked lightly on the bathroom door, trying the knob with my other hand. Locked. "Aubrey," I said, knocking again. "It's me. Open up."

A loud sniffle filtered through the door, followed by the sound of toilet paper unrolling. I listened as she blew her nose, then knocked a third time.

"Go away."

Her voice sounded nasally and rough, and so unlike Aubrey it made my heart thump. I glanced behind me to where Ethan was leaning against the opposite wall, watching me. He looked slightly relieved that I'd gotten the same response.

"Aubrey," I said in a don't-test-me voice. "Open this door or I will break it down."

My threat was greeted with complete silence. Either she didn't believe I had it in me (I did), or she was considering the potential damage to both the door and my body if I *did* have it in me. Fortunately, her practicality won out and she opened the door before I got the chance to follow through.

"Are you okay?" I asked the second I saw her red, puffy face.

She ignored my question, which was admittedly stupid, and sat down on the edge of the bathtub. I edged into the room while Ethan stayed put outside, waiting. The cloud of estrogen wafting out of there was probably making him uncomfortable.

I sat next to Aubrey, my foot crushing one of the balled-up tissues scattered across the tile. For several minutes we just sat there, not talking, Aubrey's occasional sniffling the only sound in the room.

"I'm not allowed to see him anymore."

Again, my heart jolted at the tone in her voice. She sounded beaten. Hopeless.

"I tried to keep up," she went on, pressing a fresh wad of tissue to her eyes. "I thought I could do it all . . . school, homework, violin . . . and still have time left over for him. But there was never enough time, so I kept choosing him. I started neglecting all the other stuff and I was too stupid and preoccupied to realize my parents would eventually notice I was slacking off. They don't notice everything, but they do notice that."

I wrapped my arm around her slumped shoulders. "Aubrey . . ."

"They grounded me for a month. A *month*. They took away my phone and my laptop and I'm not allowed to go anywhere or do anything unless it involves school or orchestra. I'm a prisoner."

Fresh tears rolled down her cheeks and she sopped them up with the soggy tissue. The Kleenex box on the counter was empty, so I handed her some more toilet paper. She tossed the used pieces on the floor with the others and folded the clean stuff into a smaller square.

"As soon as Mom left for work, I called Justin on the landline." She took a deep, hitching breath. "He was *pissed*. Told me he was done with all this crap. He doesn't think I'm worth it and I don't even blame him."

"He told you that?" I asked, rubbing her back. "That you're not worth it?"

"No, but I'm sure it's what he thinks. Who wants a girlfriend with psycho parents? It's too much hassle. All this drama . . ." She leaned into me, her small body trembling against my side. "I don't even think you could talk him down this time, Dara."

The despair in her voice made me want to find Justin and kick his ass for hurting her. Then she started sobbing again, and the urge passed. Seeing her like this, completely shattered at the prospect of losing him, made me realize exactly how much he meant to her. I felt guiltier and more ashamed than ever for feeling even the slightest hint of attraction toward him. Or envy toward her.

From now on, I told myself, I'd be the image of appropriate. I wouldn't secretly watch him, or think about him, or revel in any accidental touches. I'd see him for what he was—the boy my best friend had fallen in love with. And instead of feeling jealous of her, I would channel my resentment into helping her outwit her parents so she could have a life outside the narrow space they'd restricted her to.

"Don't worry," I told Aubrey as she cried against my shoulder. "It'll be okay. Your parents probably won't back down any time soon, but Justin will. And when he does, I'll do whatever I can to help you guys, okay? You *are* worth it, Aubs, and he knows it. He'll come around. If he doesn't . . . well, he's just as psycho as your psycho parents."

She pushed out a breathy laugh and sat up straight. Her eyes were swollen and bloodshot, but significantly less drippy. "Thanks, Dara. You always know the perfect thing to say to make me feel better. I'm sorry for crying all over you."

"No worries. It's part of my job description." I lifted my foot off the damp tissue and cringed. "Uh, you might want to get rid of this mess before your parents get home. It looks like a trash can threw up in here."

"Just a sec."

She stood up and went to the door, opening it all the way. Ethan was still standing in the exact same spot, waiting for us to emerge. Aubrey headed straight for him and pressed her forehead into his shoulder.

"Sorry for yelling at you, Eth," she told him. "I didn't mean it."

His hand came up, hovering over her for a moment before resting on her hair. "I know."

Our eyes met over her head. I knew we were both thinking the same thing—no matter how hard she pushed us away, Aubrey would always come back to us eventually.

fifteen

Senior Year

"YOU'RE LOOKING BETTER, DARA."

I adjust my feet on the floor, making sure they're straight and still. "Better how?"

Mrs. Dover perches on the end of her desk, fingers curling around her usual purple coffee mug. "Healthier. Your cheeks have more color, and it looks like you gained some weight. In a good way, of course."

She's right—I *have* gained weight. My clothes fit me now instead of falling off me, and my face is fuller. I'm still not as rounded as I used to be, or as strong, but at least I stopped looking like I'm either sick or on drugs.

"Your grades are good too," she goes on. "Have you been thinking about college? Mr. Lind mentioned something about you wanting to be a police officer. I could help you look into it, if you want."

"Maybe later," I say vaguely. "I'm still kind of dealing with the everyday stuff right now."

"Of course." Mrs. Dover straightens her skirt over her legs. "I saw you in the hallway the other day. You were walking with another girl, talking to her and smiling. That's good too, Dara. This is all good stuff."

I shift a little in my chair. Hearing her say things like that makes me anxious, like I'm going to screw up any progress I've made and disappoint her. Disappoint everyone. "That was Noelle," I tell her. "We're . . . she's a new friend. I guess."

"Wonderful." She smiles at me. "There *are* people around here who will accept you for you. I'm glad you found one of them."

Uncomfortable, I shift again. I don't know if Noelle accepts me or not. We've only known each other for a couple of weeks and for all I know, she could have befriended me out of pity. Or morbid curiosity. Or because she has a death wish.

"Have you connected with anyone else?" Mrs. Dover sets down her mug and moves behind the desk, folding gracefully into her chair. When I don't answer right away, she starts sifting through a pile of papers, giving me some extra time.

"Ethan," I say when she looks up at me again.

She slides the papers to the side. "Aubrey's brother?"

Something occurs to me after she says this. Does she know him? Is she his counselor too? Then I remember she's only assigned to seniors, not juniors, and I relax somewhat. "He . . . I think he still wants to be friends. We've hung out a few times."

"That must be difficult for you. For both of you."

I nod. "My parents think I should be giving him some space."

She pulls out the typical psychoanalysis question: "And what do *you* think?"

I study my hands, clasped and motionless on my lap, and consider her question. Maybe I *should* keep my distance. Maybe bringing him back into my life is a huge mistake. Maybe this horrible thing between us is too big to overcome and I'll end up losing him too. Maybe losing him will be the thing that destroys me completely.

Maybe I deserve to be destroyed.

But I don't share these thoughts with Mrs. Dover. Instead, I say, "I think they're wrong. I mean, it would make more sense if he hated me for . . ." I swallow and glance up at her. She's watching me patiently, listening. "But he doesn't. He's *glad* I'm back—he said so. And I don't *want* to avoid him. I want to show him that I came back here to hold myself accountable for what I did. Even if it's hard."

Mrs. Dover nods in her calm, understanding way. "Have you talked to Ethan about this? Why you came back?"

I shake my head. Ethan and I have never discussed my year away. We also haven't talked about Aubrey or Fulham Road and what it all means for our future as friends. It's easier to talk about the band, or music, or our preferred toppings at Subway . . . topics that aren't so loaded that simply mentioning them feels like ripping the pin out of a grenade.

"Well, maybe you should," she says, like it's a simple thing. And maybe it is.

"Yeah," I agree, even though just thinking about that conversation makes my palms slick with sweat. "Maybe I should."

After several days of searching for Ethan around school, I finally spot him on Tuesday afternoon, sitting outside alone on the concrete stairs leading to the gym's outdoor exit. His hood is up, protecting his face from the brisk October wind, but I can tell it's him by the way he's sitting—feet apart, elbows resting on knees, head bent over his phone.

He doesn't look up until I'm standing right in front of him. When he does, his pensive expression lifts, and he tugs out the earbuds I just now noticed are jammed into his ears. "Hey," he says, flipping down his hood. His dark hair blows across his forehead. "Haven't seen you in a while."

"Yeah." I gesture vaguely behind me. "Are you waiting for someone or . . . ?"

"Oh. Yeah, I'm waiting for Hunter. He's got basketball practice in the gym, but he's probably going to be a while yet."

He slides over a few inches and nods to the space beside him. "Want to sit down?"

I sit and tuck my backpack next to my feet. "Hunter plays basketball?"

He wraps his earbuds wire around his phone and stuffs both into his pocket. "Not all musicians are stoners, you know. Some of us are also part jock."

"I know." I adjust my behind on the hard concrete. "But when you look at Hunter, you don't think jock. He wears a leather jacket and smokes like a chimney."

Ethan laughs. "Yeah, the smoking holds him back a little on the court. Sometimes he wheezes even worse than me."

"How's your asthma these days?"

"Not as bad as it was."

I glance over at his angular profile and feel a pang of something close to protectiveness. It's like Aubrey has somehow possessed me with her mother-hen qualities and is imploring me to inquire about her little brother's welfare.

"So," I say, going with it. "Lacey seems nice."

He gives me an odd look, probably because he knows as well as I do that I've only spent two minutes in Lacey's presence and therefore can't really comment on her personality. "She's okay," he says.

Okay? He's dating—not to mention kissing and who knows what else—a hot girl and she's *okay*? "How long have you guys been together?"

He shrugs and peers straight ahead toward the back parking lot. "A couple of months, I guess. She goes to school with Kel and Corey and Julia. I met her through them. We're not serious or anything."

"Do you think—" I clamp my lips together, hesitating. Even though I sought him out today for this very reason—to talk about some of the hard stuff—the words aren't going to come easy.

Maybe he senses what I want to ask, because he looks at me and says, "Do I think what? Just say it, Dara."

I let out a breath. Beside us, I can hear the muffled *thump-thump-thump* of a basketball and several pairs of sneakers squeaking against the gym floor. I concentrate on that until my heart stops racing.

"Do you think Aubrey would've liked her?"

To my relief, Ethan laughs again.

"No," he says firmly and without hesitation. "She's kind of shallow, and she's always late. For everything. She also cracks her knuckles."

I shake my head, a giggle tickling the back of my throat. "Oh, God. She'd *hate* her." Nothing annoyed Aubrey more than constant lateness, and nothing grossed her out more than knuckle-cracking. She would've loathed Lacey on the spot.

"To be fair, I think she would've hated pretty much anyone I dated," he says, reaching down to scoop a pebble off the bottom stair. "She'd probably think no one was good enough for me, just like I thought no one was good enough for her. Especially that douchebag Justin."

My breath hitches in my chest, and I have to force myself not to reach out and touch his arm, stop him right there. Justin, like Fulham Road, is a piece of the past I'm not quite ready to confront. "I don't want to talk about him right now."

Ethan nods, looking mildly guilty. "Sorry. So, um, what was it like living with your aunt and going to private school?"

Even though he just provided me with an opening to the exact thing I want to discuss, my pulse speeds up again. "How did you know that's where I was?"

"I asked around." He bounces the pebble on his palm. "It wasn't exactly classified information."

I want to ask him why he'd inquired about me to begin with, but I push the question aside for now. "It was . . . different. I went because my parents thought I needed a change of scenery."

"I get that." He tosses the pebble toward the gravel path below the stairs. It lands a few feet away, blending in with all the others.

"I want to tell you why I came back," I say, without lifting my gaze from the ground.

"Okay."

I keep silent for a moment, my thoughts whirling as I work out how to start. Sometimes, when I try to explain my reasoning to Dr. Lemke or even to my parents, it seems like they don't fully understand. But Ethan might. He's the closest to the situation, and we've always had a bond. We get each other. Or at least we did when Aubrey was still here, linking us together.

I take another breath, block out the incessant thumping on the other side of the gym door, and let the words spill. "My first few months at Somerset Prep, I kept to myself. I was a loner. I didn't want friends, so I went out of my way not to make any. I was still messed up, obviously, and it was like people could smell it on me. Everyone left me alone. I was the sad, quiet, new girl who never spoke to anyone or did anything. No one there knew about me, about what happened with Aubrey, and I didn't *want* them to know. I liked being anonymous."

I pause to glance at him. His face is tilted down and he's staring at the space between his feet, but I can tell he's listening carefully.

"There was this girl," I continue. "Molly Slater. The teachers at Somerset always arranged us in alphabetical order, so she and I were always grouped together. We shared a table in bio. She was this nice, bubbly, outgoing type . . . sort of like Noelle. She was always trying to break me out of my shell, make me laugh. I was lonely, I guess, so I let my guard down after a while. I started hanging around with her and her friends, just doing stuff like going to the movies and the mall. And it was . . . nice. I felt kind of normal again. My aunt and uncle were happy. My parents were thrilled. They assumed I'd want to stay and do my senior year there too."

Ethan nods, still with me. I wrap my arms around my knees and keep talking.

"One day last summer I was sitting in a coffee shop with Molly and a few other girls, and we were laughing about something. I don't remember what. And all of a sudden, while I was laughing, someone walked by who wore the same perfume Aubrey used to wear. Did you know smell is the most powerful memory trigger? One second I was there, drinking iced lattes with these girls, and the next second it was like every memory I had of Aubrey went flooding into my brain all at once. And I realized I'd barely thought about her at all that day. I'd started going minutes, even hours, almost forgetting what happened. The guilt I felt over that almost knocked me over right there. How dare I forget, even for one second, what I did to her, what I did to your family . . ."

Ethan's fingertips brush my wrist. "Dara."

"No." I shake him off. "Let me finish."

He drops his hand and sighs, clearly wanting to speak but willing to let me get this out of my system first.

"I left two weeks later," I go on, my voice quivering. "I knew I couldn't stay there. No one knew about me at Somerset. Aubrey had never been there, so there weren't a thousand reminders of her. *You* weren't there, or your parents. I could drive through town with my aunt without worrying about driving past a spot where I'd done something horrible. Living there made it too easy to move on and I shouldn't *get* to move on. If I do, it's like I'm forgiving myself, and I can't do that. So I came back to where I can never escape it."

Ethan is silent for a few moments, either waiting to make sure I'm finished or arranging his own whirling thoughts. When he finally speaks, it's with an edge of exasperation.

"You're not the only one with guilt," he says. "I feel it too. Even my stupid parents feel it, even though they'd never admit it. And the guy who hit her? He definitely feels it, probably even more than us. We all played a part in it. None of us can forgive ourselves. It's not all on you."

"But if I hadn't pushed her, she'd still be alive."

"If she hadn't tripped, you mean."

I swallow hard. "I'm the *reason* she tripped, Ethan."

"Well, I convinced her to go talk to you, so I'm the reason she was there in the first place."

"None of it would have happened if it weren't for me."

"It wouldn't have happened if she hadn't been walking in that exact spot, right at that exact moment," he countered. "Or if I hadn't encouraged her to go after you. Or if the driver had been paying closer attention. There's no point thinking about what might have been. It happened. It was a stupid, random accident, and we can't go back and change it."

A gust of wind slams into me, making my legs tremble. I hug them closer to my chest and peer over at Ethan. He's staring straight ahead, his jaw clenched tight and twitching. For the first time since I got back, I've pissed him off. This wasn't what I had in mind when I sat down.

"I still don't understand how you can treat me like noth-ing's happened," I say softly.

"What do you want me to do, stone you to death?" His jaw relaxes and he drops one foot to the bottom step. "I *was* mad at you for a while, right after it happened. Does that make you feel any better?"

It does, actually. And it explains why he didn't contact me or answer my apology letter.

"I was mad at everyone. I got over it, though. Then I just missed you." He gives me a sideways glance, like he can't believe he said that out loud. "I missed both of you," he amends quickly.

Suddenly I'm extremely aware of my body, his body, our proximity, and the strange, charged air between us. Being around him still hurts, but opening up to him about why I came back has helped a little. The more time I spend with him, the easier it gets.

If *easy* even exists between us anymore.

"You coming over to Hunter's this weekend?" Ethan asks, switching topics again. His face is red and I don't think it's from the wind. "We're booked to play an all-ages showcase at the community center in a few weeks and we need to start nailing down a set list."

The thumping and squeaking noises from inside have stopped. Hunter will be out soon and Ethan will go back to his other life, where he's the cute, guitar-playing boy who dates hot girls instead of the poor, tragic boy who lost his sister.

I grab my backpack and stand up. "Maybe," I tell him. Even though Noelle's invited me more than once, I haven't gone back there since the day I witnessed Ethan making out with Lacey. Since then, every time I picture his hands on her waist, or his mouth moving against hers, I get that odd fluttering in my stomach again. Like I'm hungry or anxious, even when I'm neither. Seeing him with a girl revealed a whole new side to him that I'm not sure how to process.

"What?" Ethan says, and I realize I'm still standing in front of him, staring. "Why do you keep looking at me like that?"

I busy myself with my jacket zipper. "Like what?"

"Like you haven't known me for six and a half years. Like you're not sure who I am."

"I'm not." My face heats and I start edging away, toward the parking lot and the road beyond. "It's just weird sometimes, seeing you like this. All grown up, I mean."

"Still think of me as the annoying little brother, huh?"

No, I don't think I do. Not anymore. "I need some time to get used to it, I guess."

"Okay." He flips his hood back up. "But don't take too long."

sixteen

Sophomore Year

AUBREY'S MONTH-LONG GROUNDING WAS HARD on both of us. While she stayed chained to her house, banned from technology and interaction with the outside world, I kept myself as busy as possible with my other friends and volleyball practice. When I didn't have plans, I'd mope around the house, bored and lonely. One Saturday about three weeks into Aubrey's grounding, I started getting on my mother's nerves so much that she forced me to go with my father to Home Depot just to get me out of the house.

Tobias came too, and the two of us trailed behind Dad as he strolled down each aisle, his face the picture of relaxed bliss. I didn't know if he even intended to buy anything; Dad just liked being there, among the tools and flooring, breathing in the scent of fresh-cut lumber. I didn't mind it myself, but I wished I was still back home, wearing sweatpants and watching YouTube.

"Dad, I need to pee," Tobias said after we'd been browsing aimlessly for a while.

Our father glanced up from the paint swatches he was comparing and said, "Can it wait a second, bud? I need to find someone who can tell me where this paint is, because I don't see it anywhere on the shelf."

Tobias crossed his legs and hopped up and down. "No."

It never changed. We could be anywhere in public—a store, the park, the beach—and Tobias would need to pee. His bladder was the size of a walnut.

"I'll take him," I said. I was getting bored, anyway. Picking out paint was about as exciting as watching it dry.

Tobias and I headed for the front of the store, where we assumed the bathrooms were located. In the kitchen fixtures aisle, he darted ahead of me, making a beeline for the assembly of display kitchens set up a few feet away. Full bladder forgotten, he tossed me an evil grin and disappeared behind a partition. I quickened my pace and swung around the corner, ready to grab him, but he wasn't there. I passed through two more sample kitchens and finally found him in the third one, playing with the knobs on the (thankfully-not-hooked-up) stove.

"What's for dinner?" I said as I sneaked up behind him.

He let out a yelp and took off again. Laughing, we chased each other through the kitchens and then spilled out into the main aisle, where I almost collided with a man pushing a shopping cart. Tobias took advantage of the diversion and zipped around a corner. I apologized to the man and took off in the same direction.

"Kids! No running in here!" called a woman in an orange Home Depot apron as we ran past.

Her reproach made Tobias pause for a moment, and I used the opportunity to close in on him. "Gotcha." I wrapped both arms around him and lifted him off the floor, proving once again that I was the faster, stronger, smarter one. The little imp.

"Stop," he said, wiggling out of my grasp. "You're gonna make me pee my pants."

I set him down and took his hand, holding on tight so he wouldn't run off again before we reached the bathroom. He didn't even try, so he was obviously busting. Before he went in the bathroom, I peeked inside, like my mother taught me, to make sure there were no creepy men hanging around in there. Then I waited for him right outside the door.

"Race ya back to the paint," Tobias said two minutes later as he swung open the door and bolted past me. Cursing under my breath, I hurried after him.

I only made it about ten feet before I skidded to a stop,

almost plowing down an old lady this time. "Sorry," I mumbled in her general direction. My attention was completely focused on the sight in front of me: Justin, standing near the customer service area at the front of the store. Aubrey's Justin, who'd been avoiding her since the day her mother caught them in the park and grounded her.

An unexpected burst of anger swept through me. I had no interest in talking to the guy who'd caused my friend so much unhappiness, so I continued to follow Tobias, who I could still see up ahead, sprinting toward the paint section and our waiting father. Hopefully Justin hadn't seen me.

"Dara! Dara, wait up."

Damn it. I stopped and spun on my heel. Justin was walking toward me, a thin sheaf of papers in his hand and an expression of firm resolve on his face. *Damn it damn it damn it.*

"Hey," he said, coming to a stop in front of me.

Under his jacket, he wore a dark blue button-down shirt that made his blue eyes look almost indigo. I did my best not to notice. "What are you doing here?"

He held up the sheets of paper. "Dropping off résumés. I'm trying to secure a summer job. What about you?"

"Oh, I just hang out here sometimes. You know, for fun."

His eyebrows shot up at my tone. "I take it you're pissed at me?"

I looked away. *Of course* I was pissed at him. Aubrey had chosen *him* to be her first, and then, when their relationship hit a rough patch, he dumped her. He didn't fight for her, didn't try to work through it, didn't tell her he'd stick by her no matter what. He just gave up. So yes, I was mad, because Aubrey *was* worth the trouble and only an idiot wouldn't see that.

An employee pushing a trolley squeezed past us, making me realize we were blocking traffic. Justin realized it at the same time and moved out of the aisle, motioning for me to follow. We stopped near a display of hardwood floor cleaner, our bodies barely a foot apart. It amazed and horrified me that even though I was mad at him, and even though my best friend was in love with him, my stomach still tingled when he stood this close. Stupid, traitorous body.

"You're not being fair," he said in a low voice.

"How am I not being fair? You're punishing her because she happened to get stuck with parents who are assholes. *That's* not being fair."

"It's not really any of your business."

I crossed my arms over my chest. "Yes, it is. Who do you think stays with her when she's crying in the bathroom at school after you refuse to talk to her? She's my best friend and you hurt her."

"Well, she hurt me too," he snapped.

A middle-aged couple sauntered past us, discussing what shade of grout they needed to buy. When they were gone, Justin focused on me again, his gaze intense. I felt exposed and slightly uneasy.

"She refuses to stand up to her parents, even when it involves me," he went on. "She lets them run her life and I got sick of dealing with it. If that makes me a dick, then I guess I'm a dick."

I understood now why Aubrey got so damn frustrated sometimes when they fought. "You agreed to be patient with her. Remember? That day in the tree house?"

Was that *amusement* flickering in his eyes? What could possibly be funny about this?

"Yeah, I remember." He sighed and rubbed a hand over his face. "Look, I'll stop avoiding her, okay?"

I gave him a pointed glare I'd learned from my mother. "And you'll talk to her? Let her explain?"

"I'll call her tonight. How's that?"

"She lost her phone privileges, so you can't call her. But you *can* talk to her at school on Monday instead of running in the other direction like a coward."

He flashed his perfect smile at me. "Done."

"And don't tell her about this conversation," I added. "Forget you even saw me today."

His gaze flicked down to where my arms rested over my chest. "Impossible."

I felt a different sort of fluttering in my stomach, one that made me want to back away from him. *Did he . . . ? Yes, I think he did. Justin Gates just checked out my boobs.*

I couldn't believe his gall. Did he honestly think he had any kind of chance with me? Crush or no crush, there were some lines I'd never cross.

"Dara?"

I jumped and looked toward my father's voice. He stood a few feet away, a can of paint dangling from each hand, and his eyes latched onto Justin. Tobias was next to him, holding a package of paint rollers.

Justin's smile faltered as he took in my very tall, very strong, very bearlike father. "Gotta run," he told me, then turned and walked away before I had a chance to introduce them.

Dad wasn't the nosy, overly interested type, so he waited until we were buckled into the truck before asking any questions.

"Who was that?"

The words sounded casual, but I detected a trace of suspicion underneath. "Justin. Aubrey's boyfriend, remember?" Ex-boyfriend, really, but I wasn't about to get into that.

He grunted. Dad was fond of Aubrey, but he didn't concern himself with the details of her personal life.

"Do they kiss each other on the lips?" Tobias asked from the backseat.

I rolled my eyes. "You asked me that before, Tobes, and the answer is still none of your business."

"Well," Dad said, twisting around to check behind us as he pulled out of the parking spot. "Aubrey's boyfriend or not, I can't say I was pleased with the way he was looking at my fifteen-year-old daughter."

Face burning, I dug out my phone and pretended to text someone so I wouldn't have to respond.

seventeen   **Senior Year**

"WE HAVE TO DO SOME COVERS."

"Dude, it's a *showcase.* As in, you showcase your originals."

"Our set is eight songs. At least half of those should be covers. Audiences like covers."

"Audiences like good fucking songs and that's what we play."

"And some of the good fucking songs we play are covers."

Kel scowls and puts down his guitar. I'm getting whiplash trying to follow this dispute between him and Hunter. So far, I've determined that Kel wants to play all original songs at their upcoming all-ages showcase—probably because he's the one who wrote them—and Hunter thinks covers will go over better with the audience. I've also determined, after sitting in on band practice for the past two weekends in a row, that the two of them butt heads like goats every time they're together.

"Jesus," Corey says as he detangles himself from the cord attached to his bass. "No wonder Marco quit."

I lean closer to Noelle, who's sitting beside me on the couch. "Marco?" I whisper.

"The guy Ethan replaced," she whispers back. "He didn't get along with Kel either."

I nod, unsurprised. Kel has an ego the size of Hunter's drum kit.

"What do you think, E?" Kel turns to Ethan, looking for back-up. "Covers or originals?"

Ethan reaches down to flick off his amp, and my ears ring in the sudden quiet. The set they just finished was long and especially loud. Everything sounds slightly muffled now.

"I think we should open with covers, do some originals, and then close with more covers."

Kel's quiet for a moment, considering this, while Hunter sends Ethan a quick, exultant grin.

"You see?" Corey says to Noelle and me. "This is why it pays to have at least one really smart person in a band."

Realizing he's been overruled, Kel mumbles something about needing a drink of water and leaves. As soon as he's gone, the tension hovering over the shed begins to lift.

"Guess we're taking a break then," Corey says, and lowers himself until he's lying on his back on the floor beside the drums. He puts his hands behind his head and closes his eyes, like he's sunbathing on the beach.

Hunter shrugs and emerges from behind his kit, stepping over Corey's prone form. Noelle gets up to join him, and the two of them head outside for a smoke, even though it's cold and raining. Julia's not here today, so it's just Ethan, Corey, and me left inside the shed.

Ethan sinks down beside me on the couch, his guitar still nestled in his arms. He strums it almost absently, like it's an extension of his body he barely even notices anymore.

"When did you get this?" I ask, running my finger along the guitar's smooth gray paint.

He looks at me, still strumming. Without power, the strings give off a soft plinking sound.

"Oh, it's not mine," he says. "It's Corey's—he just lets me use it. I almost bought a guitar like this one at the end of summer, but I went for the car instead." He pauses to tighten one of the strings. "Maybe next year."

I lean against the back of the couch and watch him, my limbs heavy. The electric heater in the corner pumps out warm air, and raindrops tap a steady rhythm against the small window behind us. For the first time in I don't even know how long, I feel contented and relaxed. And guilty, of course, for giving in to the feeling.

"What's that song?" I ask, trying to decipher the melody in the chords.

Ethan smirks. "The annoying station you listen to would never play something like this, so you probably wouldn't know it."

I have an urge to punch his shoulder for that remark, but my hands remain still. Our conversation on the school steps helped alleviate some of the weirdness between us, but I'm not *that* comfortable with him yet. Not as much as I used to be, anyway. Then again, a lot of things are different now.

"Recognize this one?" He angles his body until he's facing me and starts a new song.

The opening chords do sound familiar, but I'm having a hard time concentrating because his knee is now pressed against mine. And neither of us is pulling away.

"I think so," I say, forcing myself to focus on the melody. "Guns N' Roses, right? My parents used to listen to them. When they were *teenagers*," I add with extra significance. "In the *eighties*."

"Are you questioning my taste in music?" He glances up at me, smiling. "Because it's not like you have much room to judge. Just saying."

"Well, excuse me for being current," I shoot back. "I was born in this century."

"Um, so was I."

I let it go and watch the muscles and tendons shift in his left hand as he presses hard on the strings. His fingers glide across the fret board like they know it not only by feel, but also by heart. They belong there.

"Do you still play violin?" I ask, trying to ignore the way our legs are still touching and that the heat from his body is now spreading into mine.

"E plays *violin?*"

Startled, I look over at Corey, who hasn't moved from the floor or made a sound the entire time we've been talking. I kind of forgot he was even here.

"No," Ethan says firmly, shooting me a look like I just ruined his rock star cred or something. "I mean, not anymore. I gave it up a year and a half ago."

"Too bad," Corey says. "Could've really added something to our sound."

Ethan shakes his head and lifts his guitar, propping it carefully against the wall next to the couch. He stretches his fingers like Aubrey used to do after a particularly long solo.

"Is that painful?" I ask, nodding toward his left hand. His fingertips are pink and slightly dented from the strings.

"Not anymore. The skin is tough as leather there. Feel."

I lean over and run my own, softer fingertip over his callused ones. As I do this, our shoulders graze and my hair tumbles forward, brushing against his chest. Did the tempo of his breathing just accelerate, or am I imagining it?

"Leather," I agree, pulling back quickly.

The door flies open, making us both jump. Kel walks in, followed by Hunter and Noelle . . . and Lacey. She runs a hand through her rain-damp hair as she takes in the scene in front of her. Her eyes lock on Ethan and me, sitting close together on the couch. Before I can even stand up and offer her my spot, she strides over and plops down in his lap, her calves pushing into my knee. I move over until she's no longer touching me.

God, I think as she winds her arms around Ethan's neck and acknowledges me with a friendly-yet-territorial smile. *Why doesn't she just pee on him?*

"Hey, guys, guess what?" Corey says as he scrambles to an upright position. "E plays *violin*."

"*Played*," Ethan corrects. "And I wasn't even very good."

I stifle a laugh. He took lessons for years and scored second chair in orchestra his freshman year. Even though he never had a passion for it, he was better than good. Musical talent runs through his veins, just like it ran through Aubrey's.

"You never told me that, babe," Lacey says in a pouty tone.

He shrugs and glances at me, embarrassed. It hits me then—he's hiding his past from these people, or at least editing it. Hunter knows almost everything because he's lived here for years and goes to school with us, but the rest of them—with the exception of Noelle—live in a different town. They must know about Aubrey, but only in a vague sense, and they obviously have no clue what Ethan was like before.

"We practicing or what?" Kel says gruffly as he adjusts

his mic on the stand. He's still not over the whole originals-versus-covers debate, apparently.

Lacey groans and tightens her grip on Ethan, like she dreads the thought of turning him back over to the band. I can't help but notice he doesn't seem to feel quite as possessive over her. His grip on her waist is much looser, more obligatory than natural. I remember what he said about her, that she's shallow and always late and has an annoying knuckle-cracking habit. And despite being pretty and normal and tiny enough to sit on his lap without crushing him, she's just "okay."

Lacey slides off him, finally, and he catches my eye again as he gets up and grabs his guitar. I hold his gaze for a second before looking away. The weirdness is back again, wedging into the space between us, and the comfortable, playful vibe from a few minutes ago is gone.

Now feels like the perfect time to make my exit. I mumble an excuse about my mother needing me at home and get up to leave.

"Wait." Ethan sets his guitar down again, this time on its stand. "It's raining out. I'll drive you home."

Kel shoots him an annoyed look. "But we're just about to—"

"She lives like four streets away. It'll take five minutes." He glances at Lacey, whose mouth turns down into a disapproving frown. "Be right back," he says to the room, and motions for me to go ahead of him to the door.

I say good-bye to everyone and, ignoring the perceptive glint in Noelle's eyes, step out into the chilly rain with Ethan.

"Thanks," I say once we're safe in the car. "You didn't need to ditch practice to take me home."

He shakes some raindrops off his bare arms and starts the car. He immediately spins the heat dial to full and we both shiver as cool air blasts out of the vents, followed gradually by warmth.

"I don't mind," he says. "Needed a little fresh air anyway."

I don't know how to respond, so I don't. He doesn't elaborate either, so we spend the rest of the two-minute drive in silence.

"Thanks," I say again once we're parked several feet down from my house. Both my parents' vehicles are in the driveway, but Ethan's car is half obscured by our neighbor's bushes so I doubt my family would see us even if one of them did happen to look out the front window.

Ethan nods, staring straight ahead. His hands tense on the steering wheel like he's trying to strangle it to death, and I'm about to ask him if he's okay when he lets go and reaches for me, pulling me against his chest in a rib-crushing hug.

I can't speak. I can't move. He's solid and warm and he smells so familiar, like his house on laundry day. Like Aubrey's room. My eyes well with tears and my arms ache to circle his torso and hug him back, but they don't move from my sides. They're paralyzed. *I'm* paralyzed.

"Sorry." He drops his arms and pulls away, looking everywhere but at me. My heart constricts when I realize why—his eyes are wet too.

"It's okay." My fingers grope for the door handle. "Um, I should probably go in. Thanks for the ride."

"Sure."

I manage to get out of the car and shut the door without looking at him once. My legs feel weak and shaky as I walk up the driveway to my front door. What the hell just happened? I can't even remember the last time Ethan hugged me. Maybe when he was about eleven, before he started acting shy around me.

My brain is so muddled as I enter the house, it takes me several moments to notice my parents. They're in the living room, sitting side-by-side on the couch and watching me.

Shit.

I quickly blink the tears out of my eyes and wipe them on my sleeve before facing them. Mom looks concerned and Dad's expression is downright stony.

"Dara," Mom says. "Come in here and sit down, okay?"

It's not a suggestion; it's an order. Legs still trembling, I go in and perch on the edge of Dad's recliner. They both study me, taking in my red eyes and undoubtedly pink face. I must look like I just endured a traumatic event. Which I sort of did, if unexpected hugs from your dead best friend's little brother count as traumatic.

"What did I do?" I ask, even though I know by now they saw me outside with Ethan. They were probably watching for me, checking to see how I got home after being gone for hours with Noelle or at the library or whatever fabricated story I told them before leaving the house earlier.

"Where have you been all afternoon?" Mom's tone is careful, curious. She's going to do the interrogation, obviously. It's always been like that. Mom asks the questions and doles out the punishments while Dad stands quietly beside her, backing her up and occasionally acting as the peacemaker. Only now, instead of looking like he feels sorry for me, it seems like he wants to yell at me, but is afraid to start because he might never stop.

Screw it. May as well give him a reason.

"I was over on Cambridge Drive, listening to Ethan's band practice."

The worry wrinkle appears between Mom's eyes. "Ethan is in a band?"

"Yeah. They're really good."

She glances at Dad, but he doesn't meet her eyes. His head is lowered, jaw muscles working like he's grinding his molars into powder. Mom sighs and refocuses on me.

"I thought we decided spending time with Ethan was a bad idea."

"*You* decided."

Dad glances up, surprised by the bitterness in my voice.

But he doesn't call me on it, so I keep talking.

"He's not holding me back, or whatever it is you're worried about. I thought you'd be happy I'm getting out of the house and spending time with friends again."

Mom shakes her head. "Dara, that's not the point. Ethan's a good kid, but maybe he's not the best person for you to be leaning on right now."

"Why not?" The shakiness in my body has been replaced with adrenaline. I'm sick of them treating me like I'm made of delicate tissue—one little tear and I'm ruined forever. "Tell me, please, what is *so* damn terrible about the idea of me hanging out with Ethan."

They stare at me for a long moment. I've clearly surprised them. This is the most life I've shown in well over a year.

Mom places a hand on Dad's knee and leans toward me. "Okay. I'm just going to say this straight out. It's his parents."

"His parents? What are you talking about?"

"Shortly after the accident, when you were . . ." She flicks a glance toward the ceiling and my bedroom, where I'd holed up for days on end, dazed with grief. "Your father and I went to the McCraes' house to apologize in person for everything that happened."

"You did?" I say, still confused about where she's going with this. I look at Dad for clues, but he's glowering at the floor again. "What did they say?"

"They—"

"They told us to go away," Dad cuts in, lifting his head to look at me. "And then they threatened us with legal action if you ever tried to contact any of them again."

The adrenaline drains out of me, leaving me exhausted. "Was this before or after they charged me with criminal negligence?"

"Before," Mom replies. "But I think they would have done that even if we hadn't shown up there."

I sit quietly for a minute, my mind spinning. Had Ethan's parents read the letter I'd mailed to their house the day after the funeral, even though it was addressed to him? Was it the last straw for them? Maybe they threw it away before Ethan could see it. Before he could read the three lines that had taken me hours to write: *Ethan, I know sorry will never be good enough, but I am. You have every right to hate me. I wish it had been me instead.*

I meant every word of that letter, and the thought of them keeping it from him pisses me off.

"Why didn't you guys tell me this before?" I ask, my annoyance seeping into my voice.

"Because we didn't want to add to your stress over starting school," Mom says. "Also, it wasn't really an issue then. You two weren't even in contact. But now . . ."

"What? You think his parents will try to do something if they find out he's been hanging out with me?"

Mom's throat moves as she swallows. "They were just so

hell-bent on making you pay for what happened. Anger like that doesn't just disappear, Dara. And how do you know Ethan isn't still angry too? He didn't get in touch with you once while you lived with Lydia and Jared, right? Why is he back in your life all of a sudden?"

Now it's my turn to stare. What is she getting at? "He wants to be friends," I say, remembering the feel of his arms around me, the softness of his T-shirt against my cheek. No one who hugged me like that could be mad at me. Or if he is, he's doing a damn good job of hiding it. "Ethan is *nothing* like his parents, okay? He doesn't blame me for what happened."

"Are you sure?" Dad asks.

The way they're looking at me, like I'm some kind of delusional mental case, makes me want to scream. They haven't spoken to Ethan in ages; they have no idea what his intentions are or how he feels about me. "No," I bite out. "You're totally right. He's manipulating me into trusting him. And then, when I least expect it, he's going to lure me out on the street and push me in front of a truck in revenge."

My father's face becomes a deep shade of purple and he springs off the couch, pointing a finger at me. "Don't you *ever* speak to us that way. We're just trying to help you."

The resentment I've been nursing for the past few weeks spills over and suddenly I'm standing too. "What do you care, Dad? You didn't even want me to come home, remember?"

That shuts him up. It shuts everyone up, for a moment.

The only sound in the room is Dad's loud, angry breathing. I've seen him furious before, like the time someone behind us was texting and slammed into the back of our truck, but his fury has never, ever been directed at me. I'm not sure what to do with it.

"Okay." Mom stands up slowly and touches Dad's arm. "Let's all take a breath. Screaming at each other isn't going to solve anything. That's why I think we need to sit down calmly with Dr. Lemke and work through this."

"Dr. Lemke isn't magical," I snap at her. "He can't fix everything."

I can sense my father gearing up toward another outburst, but I don't stick around to hear it. Instead, I escape to my room and almost trip over Tobias at the top of the stairs, where he's obviously been stationed for the past several minutes, eavesdropping. He looks at me the way he always does now—like he's scared of me—but I don't stick around for that either. I close myself up in my room, stick in my earbuds, and numb my brain with sound.

eighteen

Sophomore Year

"HEY, GUYS! GUESS WHAT?" PAIGE SQUEEZED between Aubrey and me as we headed toward the cafeteria. Ethan, who'd been walking on my other side, ducked behind me to avoid colliding with a trash can.

"What?" I said, grabbing Ethan's arm and pulling him back beside me.

"My mom and stepdad are going out of town this weekend."

"And?" Aubrey prompted.

"And . . ." She smacked her gum for a few seconds to create suspense. "I'm having a party Saturday night. One last blowout before we have to start studying for finals."

Aubrey frowned. "Your parents are leaving you alone in the house?"

Leave it to Aubrey to focus on the practicalities.

"No. My brother will be there."

"He won't mind you having a party?"

Paige shrugged. "He doesn't care. I think I can even convince him to buy us liquor."

"He won't tell your parents?" Aubrey asked as we entered the cafeteria. Immediately, she scanned the room for Justin. Things with her parents hadn't changed, but Justin had kept his word to me and stopped avoiding her at school. They weren't back together, but they'd been talking a lot more lately. He seemed open to working things out with her, which made me wonder if I'd imagined him checking me out at Home Depot. I hoped so.

"No way," Paige said confidently. "Believe me, I have some dirt on my brother I can totally use as blackmail material."

I didn't even want to know. "So is this our invitation?"

"Of course, dork. Aubrey, you can invite Justin. It's for juniors too. I think some seniors might even show up." She paused and looked at Ethan, her eyes carefully assessing him like he was an interesting new addition to the cafeteria she just now noticed. "You come too, Ethan. You're tall enough to pass as a sophomore."

Red blotches appeared on Ethan's cheeks. "Oh, uh, maybe. Yeah."

Paige smiled, waved, and jogged off to join Travis by the vending machines. Aubrey, Ethan, and I continued to the food line.

"You *are* going, right?" I asked Aubrey, recognizing the pinched look on her face. Already, she was worrying about getting caught at a party filled with underage drinkers.

"I guess so." She stood on her tiptoes, craning her neck to see over the crowd. I knew she'd spotted Justin when her face relaxed into a slight smile. "I'll be back," she told us before darting into the crowd.

I peered at Ethan. "Are you actually going or did you just say you were because you think Paige is cute?"

He smiled mysteriously.

"She has a boyfriend, you know," I said in a mock-stern voice. Ethan didn't go to parties, and he certainly didn't talk to girls, unless I counted as one. It surprised me that he was even considering going.

"Don't worry," Ethan said as we shifted forward in line. "She's not really my type, anyway."

I turned to him, all set to ask what type he *did* like, when it suddenly hit me why Paige had looked at him like she'd never really noticed him before today. The change had been gradual, building over the past few months, but now it was glaringly obvious.

Ethan was starting to get cute.

*　*　*

Getting to the party on Saturday night involved some planning. My mother totally bought the watching-movies-at-Paige's-house story and even offered to drive us over there, but I didn't want her to get tipped off by loud music or extra cars in the driveway. Instead, Aubrey and Ethan came to my house first and then the three of us walked the short distance to Paige's.

"When are your parents going to start letting you drive their cars?" I whined to Aubrey as the early-June wind tangled my hair, which I'd spent twenty minutes brushing to perfection. "You've had your license for ages now."

She rolled her eyes. "Maybe when I'm ninety and on my deathbed."

"They don't trust her," Ethan put in. "They think she might get a taste of freedom and never come back."

"Maybe they're right," Aubrey mumbled as we turned onto Paige's street.

Right away, I was relieved we hadn't let my mom drop us off. Cars spilled out of the driveway and lined the curbs, and some guy was walking across the lawn with a six-pack in each hand. Aubrey and I exchanged a here-we-go look and followed beer guy up to the front door.

Not bothering with the doorbell, we let ourselves in. Paige's house was a medium-sized split-level, and it seemed like everyone was on the upper floor, hanging out in the kitchen and living room. The three of us headed up there, shouldering through the mass of sweaty bodies. I recognized a lot of people from our class, but there were older people too, juniors and seniors who didn't discriminate when parent-free houses and copious amounts of alcohol were in play.

"There's another fridge in the garage," Paige was telling the guy who'd carried in the six-packs as we squeezed into the kitchen. She spotted us and grinned. "Hey, guys! You made it."

I reached out to hug her, careful not to flatten her perfectly curled hair. She wore a tiny skirt and an even tinier sparkly tank top, the type of outfit that would look borderline obscene on me. Paige's natural skinniness—along with Aubrey's petite figure—always made me feel extra bulky when we all hung out together. I hated being the tallest and most well-endowed of my friends.

"You guys want a drink?" Paige asked as Travis sidled up beside her and wrapped his arms around her waist. He greeted us with a nod, his eyes glassy and unfocused. Clearly, he'd been taking advantage of the party supplies.

"Um . . ." I glanced behind me to discover two pairs of dark brown eyes locked on my face. Aubrey had that pinched expression again, and Ethan seemed curious, like he was waiting to see if I'd cave under peer pressure even though I'd told them on the walk over I was definitely not going to drink.

"No, thanks," Aubrey answered for all three of us, then

caught Travis's eye. "Have you seen Justin?"

"Downstairs," he said with a smirk. "He's working his way through a case of Bud."

Aubrey sighed. Apparently, before they started dating, Justin used to get hammered with the junior jerks almost every weekend, and sometimes he still did. Aubrey hated it.

"I'd better get down there," she told me, turning in the direction of the stairs. "He's probably waiting for me."

Or maybe, I thought, he was drowning himself in beer because he *didn't* want to see her or get back together with her or any of the other things Aubrey was hoping for tonight. "Find us later," I called after her as she left the kitchen.

"Should we go downstairs too?" Ethan asked.

"Nah." I shook my head. "Let's give them some distance."

Relieved, he leaned back against the counter, his gaze following a trio of sophomore girls in tight jeans as they passed by the threshold to the kitchen. I nudged him with my elbow and he looked back at me, wide-eyed and innocent.

"What?" he said.

I snorted and ran my hand over my hair, trying to smooth out the tangles the wind had made. It probably looked like a rat's nest. "Nothing." I patted his head, surprised at how high I had to reach to get to it. We were officially the same height. "I'm gonna go fix my hair. Stay out of trouble while I'm gone, okay?"

"Can't make any promises."

I wagged a finger at him and edged out of the kitchen. The hallway leading to the bathroom was mobbed with sweaty bodies, and it took at least ten minutes for my turn to arrive. Ethan was probably wondering about me.

Or not. When I got back to the kitchen, he was nowhere to be seen. I turned and started in the other direction, occasionally smiling at people I knew. As I entered the living room, a hand shot out and seized my arm.

"Dara!" shouted Levi Mosley. Without letting go of me, he turned to Shane Dobbs, who was standing next to him, and said, "She'll do anything if you dare her first."

"Excuse me?" I pulled my arm out of his grasp.

"Relax," he said, digging in the front pocket of his hoodie and pulling out two handfuls of packaged, premixed shots, the kind I'd seen near the liquor store checkout when I went there with my dad. "Everyone thinks these are nasty. I *dare* you to down one without making a face or spitting it out."

I bit my lip, hesitating. Aubrey would be pissed if I drank after assuring her I wasn't going to, and my parents would *kill* me if I came home with my breath reeking of liquor. But damn it, a dare was a dare. I took one of the shots out of his hands and peeled back the aluminum seal without even reading the label first. Then, after throwing a quick glance behind me to make sure Aubrey and Ethan weren't anywhere in the vicinity, I tipped the shot into my mouth.

It tasted like lemons and cough syrup and burned my

throat like acid. Still, I used every ounce of willpower I had to swallow and keep my face perfectly smooth. Levi and Shane were watching me carefully, eyes twinkling like they were expecting me to hurl any second. When I didn't, they looked at each other and laughed.

"Told you," Levi said while Shane appraised me, his gaze settling on my chest.

Eyes watering, I handed the empty shot back to Levi and shoved back into the kitchen, heading straight for the fridge. I needed something to get this sour taste out of my mouth. Something cold, sweet, and fizzy. But the only drinks in there were milk and orange juice and bottled water, none of which would do much to cleanse my taste buds. Then I remembered Paige's parents kept an ample supply of Coke cans in the garage fridge.

I expected to find Aubrey when I got downstairs, but she wasn't there. Justin was, though, sprawled on the family room couch with a can of beer. A few of the junior jerks—including Wyatt—surrounded him, guzzling their own beers while they pulverized animated zombies with game controllers. I walked past them without saying hello and down the short hallway that led to the garage.

Away from all the voices and laughter and pounding music, this section of the house felt eerily quiet. I squinted as I entered the bright garage, which, for as long as I'd known Paige, had never actually held a car. Her parents used it for storage, mostly. One entire wall consisted of metal shelves stacked high with labeled boxes, while the rest of the space was taken up by a workbench with tools hanging on pegboard above it, bicycles, a chest freezer, and what I'd come in there for—the extra fridge. I made a beeline for it, desperate to rinse the nasty bitterness from my tongue.

I grabbed a Coke and immediately popped it open, sipping it as I closed the fridge door. The crisp sweetness cut the sour aftertaste within seconds, and the scorched feeling in my throat and stomach finally abated.

Someone had propped open the garage door with a toolbox, allowing for an unobstructed path to the beer fridge, so I didn't realize Justin had followed me inside until he actually spoke.

"Whatcha doin'?"

I jumped, almost choking on a mouthful of Coke, and whirled around. Justin was moving toward me, his gait slow and deliberate like he was trying to remember how to walk straight. He couldn't possibly have come for more beer. It looked as though he was well past his limit.

"Getting a drink." I held up my can as proof, then added, "Where's Aubrey?"

He came to a stop in front of me, his entire body swaying slightly to the left. "That's not a drink, Dare-ya," he said, ignoring my question. His bleary gaze traveled down my body, pausing at my cleavage before continuing to the can in my hand. "You need a *real* drink."

My stomach prickled with unease, but I smiled through it. "Already tried that. I think I'll stick with Coke."

He blinked at me for a moment before running a hand over his face. "You're so fucking distracting," he mumbled.

My heart thumped in my chest, so hard I wondered if he could hear it. What did he mean? What did I distract him *from*? Aubrey? The thought made me so uncomfortable that I turned away from him, facing the fridge instead. The can of Coke in my hand was still half full, but I grabbed the fridge handle anyway, pretending to need a fresh one. But I didn't get that far, because before I could pull open the door, Justin was right behind me, his chest inches from my back.

"It's not all in my head," he said, his beer breath rustling my hair. "I see the way you look at me."

My legs wobbled, and for a moment it felt like my grip on the door handle was the only thing keeping me upright. Justin was drunk, so drunk, and it was clouding his judgment, lowering his inhibitions. That was all. In the morning he wouldn't even remember saying these things to me, and I'd never remind him. I'd walk away now and pretend it never happened.

"Justin . . . *stop*. Please." I let go of the fridge and started to turn, pushing against him with my shoulder so he'd move back, give me some room. But he didn't. Instead he pressed closer, running his hand along my hair and then down my bare arm, his fingertips grazing the side of my breast.

I gasped at the contact, and my Coke slipped from my hand and dropped to the concrete floor, sending sticky brown droplets flying. The noise snapped Justin out of whatever had possessed him and he backed away, allowing me to slip out from between him and the fridge.

"What the hell are you *doing?*" I hissed at him, but he wasn't even looking at me. He was looking past me, his gaze focused on something beyond my right shoulder. I spun around to see what had caught his attention and came face-to-face with Ethan.

He was standing just outside the doorway, his face red with either anger or embarrassment. Maybe both. I wondered how much he'd seen, how much he'd heard, and my face flamed to match his.

Justin glanced at me once, his eyes foggy and confused. "Sorry," he muttered. Then he left without another word, brushing past Ethan like he was a decorative plant, no threat at all. Ethan glared after him for a moment before turning back to me, his expression softening.

"Are you okay?"

I opened my mouth to say yes, but nothing came out. My legs felt like someone had replaced my bones with cooked spaghetti, and I stumbled over to the chest freezer, lowering my body until I was sitting on the dirty floor in front of it. The coolness of the freezer seeped through my shirt, making me shiver.

Ethan walked over to the fridge, stepping over the spilled Coke on the way, and got me a fresh can. He handed it to me before sinking down beside me on the floor.

"What do you need?" he asked, his gaze skimming over me like he was checking for injuries. "Should I go find Aubrey?"

"No," I said quickly. He raised his eyebrows at my tone. "I mean, not right now. I don't want her to know about this yet."

"Seriously? He was touching you and you were telling him to stop. Aubrey will understand that it wasn't your fault."

I wasn't so sure. If Justin had noticed the way I looked at him, maybe Aubrey had too. What if she blamed me? What if she uncovered the deep, hidden place in my heart where I'd locked away every smile, every word, every secret desire I'd ever felt for the boy she loved?

I concentrated on the can in my hand, forcing back tears. "What he said wasn't entirely off base, okay? The way I felt about him *wasn't* all in his head. You know that. You're observant."

"So? He still had no right to touch you." He shifted closer and lowered his voice. "I hope you don't think you asked for that."

Deep down I knew Ethan was right, but another part of me—the part that was still in shock—insisted on downplaying the situation. "He had a lot to drink. People do stupid things when they're drunk. Things they don't mean."

"Why are you defending him? Drunk or not, he's still

an asshole. I should've smashed his teeth in when I had the chance."

"Ethan," I said, shocked. He'd never hit someone in his life. When did he get so bloodthirsty? "Please, just . . . let me handle this on my own. I want to give Justin a chance to explain himself before I tell Aubrey about this. Okay?"

"If he even remembers in the morning," he muttered. He let out a noisy breath and tipped his head back against the freezer. "So, what, we're supposed to walk out of here and pretend like nothing happened?"

"Just until I figure this out." I gripped his knee. "Please, Ethan. Do this for me."

He stared at me, unblinking, a mix of uncertainty and anger simmering in his eyes. After a few moments, he swallowed and looked away, toward the sticky brown stain on the floor.

"Okay, fine. I'll stay out of it." He slid his foot over, resting it against mine. "For you."

nineteen

LUNCHTIME HAS BECOME SOMETHING THAT I count on. With the exception of Subway Fridays, Ethan and his friends spend the hour either hanging out in the science wing near Hunter's locker or—on nice days—in the parking lot by Ethan's car. They never go to the cafeteria, and since the first day I tagged along with them to Subway, I started avoiding the cafeteria too, opting instead to hang out with them. Every day, Noelle meets me at my locker and then the two of us head to wherever the guys are waiting. I like the consistency of it, the routine. It's comforting to have something to look forward to each day. To have friends in my life again.

Today, though, the usual lighthearted atmosphere feels

subdued. Ethan barely touches his lunch, and his leg jiggles like my mother's does when she's had way too much coffee.

"You okay?" I ask softly. We're in the science wing today, and he's sitting next to me on the floor across from the lockers. I can almost feel the tension radiating from his body.

He stops fidgeting and crosses his arms over his chest. "I'm fine."

Across from us, Hunter swallows a mouthful of sandwich and says, "Stage fright."

Surprised, I look at Ethan again. Tomorrow night is the band showcase at the community center, and through all these weekends of practice, he's never once expressed any apprehension about it. Seeing him like this is a relief, in a way. He may seem confident on the outside now, but inside he's still the same Ethan who used to get nervous before orchestra concerts.

"Are you like this every time?" I ask him.

"He barfed for three days before our last show," Hunter says, smiling. Noelle, who's sitting next to him eating some kind of pasta from a thermos, reaches over to smack his arm.

"I'm fine," Ethan says again, like a mantra.

We all slide our legs in as a group of people approach. One of them, a guy named Seth who's in my Global Geography class, looks at Ethan and me and raises his eyebrows. This isn't anything new—people sometimes take notice when Ethan and I hang out at school, probably because the sight of us together is so unexpected—but Seth is known for being a bit of a loudmouth. Ethan watches him warily, unfolding his arms and placing his hands on the floor like he's preparing to jump up if Seth says one word. But he walks by without comment, and Ethan relaxes somewhat, his warm arm brushing against mine. Goose bumps rise on my skin. I rub my arms, telling myself it's just chilly in here.

"Don't worry about tomorrow night," Noelle says, picking the conversation back up without missing a beat. "We'll all be there for moral support. Right, Dara?"

I stop rubbing. "What?"

"You *are* coming, right? You've been sitting in on practices for weeks now. You *owe* it to the band to be there."

"I do?"

Going to their show isn't something I planned on doing. Realm isn't even scheduled to go on until eight forty-five or something, and I don't go out at night anymore. Also, I don't do crowds. They never used to bother me, but now they make me feel claustrophobic, panicky. What if I had an anxiety attack in front of everyone?

I glance at Ethan and he smiles shakily at me, his face pale. Maybe I do owe it to them, or at least to him.

"I'll have to think of something to tell my parents," I say, giving in.

Noelle grins. "Do I need to show off my freckles again?"

I shake my head. Dealing with my parents is something I need to figure out for myself.

*   *   *

The next night, I wait until the very last minute to announce that I'm going out. This time, it's only my father I have to get through. Mom left at five thirty to meet her girlfriends for dinner and a movie.

Once I'm ready, I head downstairs and stand in the entrance to the living room, where Dad and Tobias are watching one of the *Star Wars* movies. "I'm going out with Noelle," I say. "I'll be home by midnight."

Dad tears his gaze away from the TV and looks at me, not quite meeting my eyes. Two weeks have passed since the fight with my parents, and my father and I have barely interacted since. "Where are you going?"

"The community center." Points for honesty. "There's an all-ages show."

Dad's gaze slides back to the TV. "And your mother knows?"

"No," I say, moving away from the doorway. "But you can update her when she gets home."

Before he can say anything more, I make a break for the door and step outside. The air is crisp and cold and smells like snow, even though we haven't gotten any yet. The slight breeze seeps through my thin jacket as I walk to the end of the street, where Noelle has promised to pick me up. She's there already, sitting behind the wheel of her mom's red Toyota. Julia is in the passenger seat, so I climb in back.

"Oooh, I like your hair," Noelle says when she sees me. Julia, of course, is texting. I don't think I've ever seen her without her phone in her hand. I'm not even sure what color her eyes are, because she never looks up.

"Thanks." My hair does look better since I got it trimmed and started conditioning again. Earlier, I flat-ironed it until the strands hung down in a smooth sheet. "Where's Lacey?" I ask as we pull away from the curb.

Julia snickers, the first sound I've heard from her since I got in the car.

"Ethan broke up with her," Noelle says, meeting my eyes in the mirror. "About a week ago."

"Really?" I say, shifting in my seat. Lacey wasn't at band practice last weekend, but aside from that, nothing seemed amiss. Ethan hasn't been acting brokenhearted or depressed. In fact, he didn't mention her even once this week. Not to me, anyway. Then again, he's been acting sort of cagey around me since he hugged me in his car. "That's too bad."

"Yeah." She watches me for a moment before returning her focus to the road.

The community center is near the middle school, and luckily we don't need to take Fulham Road to get there. When we arrive, the parking lot is full and I can already hear the distant thump of music coming from inside. It gets louder as we approach.

I stick close to Noelle and Julia as we pay admission and

go inside. The place is teeming with people, mostly teenagers, but I see a few who look college-age. At the far end of the room, dozens of bodies surround a small stage, which is currently in use by a band that sounds part metal, part operatic. The sheer volume coming from the speakers makes my eardrums quiver, and I know I'm in for at least a day of hearing loss after this.

"I just texted Corey," Julia yells over the music as we wind through the mob. "They're in the back room next to the bathrooms."

The three of us crane our necks, searching for a bathroom sign. Noelle spots it first and veers left, motioning for us to follow. I try to keep up while simultaneously doing everything humanly possible not to bump into people. It isn't easy. My stomach tightens with rising panic.

Several minutes later, the crowd spits us out into a long, dimly lit hallway. The bathrooms are clearly marked but the "back room" isn't, so we keep going, following the sound of voices to the only open door. As soon as we step in the room, the knot in my stomach loosens. This area is busy too, but unlike the frenzied crowd we just came from, the vibe in here is definitely quieter and more relaxed. It's like some sort of holding room—bands waiting their turn onstage, lounging around on plastic chairs and tuning unplugged guitars.

Julia and Noelle head straight for their boyfriends, who are across the room talking to another band. Kel is nowhere to be found, which doesn't surprise me, because he's always disappearing and keeping the other guys waiting. But I stop wondering about Kel and his whereabouts the moment my gaze lands on Ethan.

He's slouched in one of the plastic chairs near the corner of the room, one foot propped on another chair in front of him. His guitar rests against his stomach, but he's not strumming or tuning like everyone else. He looks relaxed and peaceful and infinitely less nervous than he'd been since yesterday.

I make my way over and claim the chair next to his. "How's it going?" I ask, giving him a quick once-over. His face has regained some color, and he's no longer fidgeting.

"Better now," he says, still smiling.

"Why? Did Hunter slip you some tranquilizers?"

Before he can answer, Kel plunks down in the chair on my other side and says, "Nope, not tranquilizers. Beer. We all slammed a few in the parking lot about an hour ago."

I turn to stare Ethan down. So *that's* why he's so calm. I want to ask him how much he drank, but that would make me seem mother-hen-like, so I resist. I'm not his big sister and I don't want to be.

"Two," he says. "I only had two."

I shrug like it's none of my business how many beers he slams in the parking lot. His eyes flick to Kel's arm, which rests on the back of my chair. He's not touching me, thankfully, but I can feel the heat of his skin on my back. It's not entirely unpleasant, but I still don't want him touching me.

A chubby guy with greasy red hair and a clipboard in his hand appears in the doorway. "Realm," he barks. "You're up next. Ten minutes."

Ethan drops his foot from the chair and sits up straight, his face going white again. Two beers only go so far. My fingers itch to touch him, to squeeze his hand, to do *something* to let him know he'll be okay, but all I can do is catch his eye and smile. He smiles back tremulously and stands up to join the rest of the band. They all walk out together, and Noelle, Julia, and I follow close behind.

For some reason, I expect it to be like a real concert, with the band walking out onstage and playing with barely a pause in between. But high school bands don't have roadies and sound guys, so it takes several minutes for them to adjust their sound before they can start. When they finally do, it's even louder than the last act.

"Come on," Noelle screams in my ear. "Let's get closer to the stage."

Closer to the stage means heat and pressing bodies and not enough air. Bad idea. "I think I'll hang out back here."

Noelle tilts her head at me. "You sure? I'll stay with you, then."

"No." I nod toward the stage. "Go stand where Hunter can see you."

"If you're really sure . . ."

I nod again, and she squeezes my elbow before disappearing into the throng with Julia. Once they're out of sight, I find a vacant pocket of space at the back of the room and lean against the wall. Even though I'm as far away as possible from the stage, I can still see the band. Or at least their heads. A portion of the audience is in my line of sight too, and most of the girls seem to be watching Kel. Not all of them, though. Some of them—the ones who probably think Kel is too pretty and prefer the ruggedly good-looking type—watch Ethan.

And despite trying to convince myself otherwise, I'm one of them.

It's hard to tell from back here, but I think he's found his groove. He's not puking, anyway, and he definitely looks less terrified. By the end of their set (originals sandwiched between covers, like he suggested), he's even smiling. The audience claps and cheers as they leave the stage, and I'm relieved for them. They did great.

I lose track of everyone when the crowd near the stage starts to disperse. Suddenly, I'm trapped against the wall as people file toward the exit a few feet away from me. I stay perfectly still, waiting for an opening and trying not to panic. A girl steps on my foot, then shoots me a glare like it's my fault. That does it for me. Crossing my arms over my chest, I zigzag my way toward the bathroom and slip inside. This room, too, is mobbed. I back out again and stand next to the door, prepared to wait it out. I can hear the next band gearing up on stage.

Five minutes pass before I finally see Ethan. He's at the other end of the hallway, emerging from the back room. As he approaches, I notice his face is even whiter than it was earlier.

"Hey," he says when he reaches me, and that's when I hear the telltale shortness of breath, which I know is one of the warning signs.

"Are you all right?" I ask, alarmed. I've only seen him have a full-blown asthma attack once, when he was about twelve, and it was scary as hell.

"It's nothing." He leans against the wall beside me and coughs. "The band on now is using a smoke machine and my lungs didn't like it. But I'm fine."

"Did you take some medicine?"

He nods. "That's what I was just doing. I keep it in my guitar case."

This makes me smile. "Very badass."

"I know, right?" He tries taking a breath, and his face visibly relaxes when he discovers he can. "So what did you think of our set?"

The color is returning to his face, along with the high of success, and I remember how all those girls looked at him while he was up there onstage. And how instead of feeling protective or slightly amused, like Aubrey would have, like I *should* have, I felt a little annoyed.

What the hell does that even *mean*?

"It was great," I say, staring down at my shoes. The left one has a scuff from when that girl trampled me. "You were great."

"Yeah?" He shifts closer as if he's trying to hear me better, even though it's not as loud over here and he can obviously hear me fine.

"Yeah."

All night I've avoided human contact, but for some reason, standing this close to Ethan doesn't bother me at all. I look up, meeting his eyes, but I don't get the chance to say anything more, because at precisely that moment, a fistfight erupts in front of the bathrooms.

It must have started in the men's room, but now it's spilled out into the hallway, where there's a tiny bit more room to maneuver. A dark-haired guy has a grip on a blond guy's shirt, and he's using his free hand to pound on his face. The sound is dull and sickening. Blood spurts out of the blond guy's nose, and the pain clearly enrages him, because he charges the other guy and knocks him to the floor. A girl screams. It's total mayhem.

"Shit," Ethan says when the guys roll toward us, fists flying. "Come on, let's move."

He takes my hand and attempts to pull me away, but I'm rooted to the spot. Frozen. There's blood all over the floor, blood staining the blond guy's shirt, blood on the other guy's knuckles. I can't tear my eyes away. I can't move.

Blood, oozing onto the pavement, soaking into the fabric of her skirt—

Ethan squeezes my hand, trying to snap me out it. When that doesn't work, he lets go and steps in front of me instead, facing me with his arms on either side of my head, locking me in. For a moment I'm distracted, wondering why he's positioned himself like he's guarding me from a bullet. But then I hear the two guys scuffle past, still grappling like they're in a wrestling ring and not on a dirty community center floor. One of their flailing limbs bumps into Ethan, and I instinctively grab the front of his T-shirt, pulling him closer. We watch as the two guys tumble out into the main area, where they're almost immediately intercepted by three big guys and a security officer.

And as quickly as it began, it's over. The spectators who'd gathered to watch the fight rush out to catch the rest of the action, leaving the hallway virtually empty. All that's left is an extremely irritated man who's grumbling about the mess on the floor, and Ethan and me.

As the shock of the last several minutes wears off, I'm suddenly aware that we're still standing very, very close together. And that I haven't let go of his shirt. And that the horror I felt from seeing the blood is gradually being replaced by a different kind of fear.

"You okay?" Ethan asks. His cheek is inches from mine, and I can feel his breath on the side of my neck.

"I think so." My fingers loosen on his shirt, but I still don't let go.

He pulls back to look at me, and I feel something shift. He doesn't need to explain how *he's* feeling—I already know. Just like I know the quickening of his breath isn't because of his protesting lungs. It's because of what he's about to do, and because he knows, just by the way I tighten my hold on him, that I'm going to let him.

Even so, I'm surprised when he actually does it.

His lips are hesitant at first, testing, as if he's waiting for me to change my mind and flee. But I keep as still as I've ever been, so still he probably feels like he's kissing a mannequin. He lowers one hand from the wall and cups the back of my head, bracing me as his mouth becomes less gentle. And for a moment I get lost, a dormant part of my body waking up and taking over, making me forget where I am and who I am and even who I'm with.

But when he stops kissing me and pulls back, either to take a breath or check in with me, I catch a glimpse of his eyes, dark and familiar, and the reality of what I'm doing hits me with a jolt. It should feel weird, kissing my dead best friend's little brother in a creepy, bloodstained hallway. And it does, a little. Probably because it *is* weird.

I know this, just as I know that kissing him is bound to complicate things even more, but I still don't move or say a word. Ethan doesn't say anything either. He just stares at me, helpless and maybe a little guilty, his hand sliding down to rest on my neck. A shiver runs through me.

"Sorry," he says, finally. His arms drop back to his sides. "I just—you have no idea how long I've wanted to kiss you."

The thing is I think I *do* know, even though I've never admitted it to myself until right this second. Maybe I've always known.

A deafening screech of feedback filters into the hallway, reminding us there's still a concert going on just a few feet away. I unclench my fingers from Ethan's shirt and he steps back, his eyes still fixed on mine.

"We should probably get back out there before we end up missing the whole thing," he says, offering me his hand.

I look at it and feel a rush of affection for him so intense, it literally hurts. But there are other feelings now too, layered in between. Exhilaration. Hesitation. Desire. All the things I felt when he kissed me.

I take his hand and together we slip back into the crowd.

twenty

Sophomore Year

THE DAY AFTER PAIGE'S PARTY, AUBREY SHOWED up unannounced at my door with her arms loaded down with baking supplies.

"The auction, remember?" she said when I gave her a blank look.

Right. Our school was having a pie auction the next day to raise money for a local children's charity, and Aubrey had signed us up to make lemon meringue. I'd completely forgotten we'd made plans to bake at my house today.

My stomach tightened as we hauled everything into the kitchen. I was counting on not hanging out with her again until after I spoke to Justin. Or until after he told her himself.

I didn't want to talk about it now, when my brain was still muddled about what happened in the garage and what it might mean. I'd been feeling sick ever since, wondering if Ethan had said anything or if Justin had said anything or if Aubrey had somehow figured it out on her own. But she was acting the same around me as she always did.

"Here." Aubrey pushed a carton of eggs toward me. "Can you separate the eggs? Four should do it. Put the yolks in one bowl and the whites in another."

I nodded and got out some small bowls. We worked in silence for a few minutes, me separating and her mixing the dry ingredients. The radio was on, tuned to our favorite pop station, and normally I would have been relaxed and content, there in the warm kitchen with my best friend. But everything felt tainted now, secrets rising up between us like a brick wall.

I could tell her right here. She'll probably get mad and maybe even hate me—or worse, blame me—but at least she won't continue to give her heart to a guy who doesn't deserve it.

"Aubrey," I said as I handed her the bowl of egg yolks.

"Hmm?"

I watched her as she stood at the stove, whisking the pie filling until it reached the perfect consistency. One dark curl had escaped her ponytail, and she used her wrist to push it off her face. She looked so peaceful, humming along to Beyoncé as she worked. It reminded me of old times, back when our friendship still felt safe and uncomplicated.

"Um . . ." I looked away and grabbed the hand mixer. "You want me to whip these egg whites for the meringue?"

"Sure." She gave the filling one last stir and glanced at me. "Is something wrong? You're never this quiet."

I focused on the eggs, whipping them into frothy peaks. "I'm fine, just . . . tired from the party."

We finished the pie together and stuck our creation in the oven. While it baked, we tackled the kitchen mess.

"So," Aubrey said as she peeked in the oven at the pie, checking its progress. "Justin called me this morning."

I froze in place, heart leaping into my throat. Oh God, he'd told her. He'd told her, and she wanted to wait until I'd helped her with the pie before she stabbed me in the heart with a butcher knife. "Okay," I said, willing my voice not to shake.

"I didn't answer it. I was in the shower." She shut the oven door and turned around, her gaze focused on the floor. "What if he called because he wants to work things out?"

"Is that what you want?" I asked carefully. "I thought you were mad at him."

Last night during the walk home, she'd told Ethan and me what had happened when she went downstairs to talk to Justin. Minutes before he'd followed me into the garage, he and Aubrey had gotten into another argument about her parents and she'd stormed outside to get away from him. And instead of following her and trying to make things right, he'd followed me and made everything wrong instead.

"Yeah, I'm mad, but . . . this is my fault too, you know. Most of our problems are because of my parents. Which is really stupid, when you think about it." The timer went off and she turned back around, sliding oven mitts over her hands. "Maybe we just need to try harder to make it work," she went on as she set the pie on a cooling rack. "No more hiding. My parents will just have to deal with it. I'm sixteen . . . they can't keep me locked up in a tower like a princess."

I sat down at the table, my stomach churning like I'd eaten that entire perfect-looking pie in one sitting. If working things out with Aubrey was what Justin had in mind, there was no way I could let that happen. I could no longer ignore the fact that she'd given her heart and trust to a guy who had treated those gifts like they were nothing.

Sometimes I feel like she's way too good for me, he'd told me in the tree house back in November. He was right—she was.

"Are you sure, Aubrey?"

"Am I sure about what?"

"About Justin," I said, hesitant. "Do you really want to get back together with him?"

She pulled off the oven mitts and tossed them on the counter, her eyes never leaving mine. "What do you mean?"

I bit at a hangnail on my thumb. "I just think you could do better."

She continued to stare at me, her forehead scrunched in confusion. "You're the one who said he'd come around.

Remember? You're the one who said you'd do whatever you could to help us be together."

My brain was begging me to shut up, but I couldn't seem to help myself from adding more kindling to the fire. "I know, it's just . . . maybe you're not *meant* to be with him. What if you're having all these problems for a reason?"

"So you're only meant to be with someone when it's easy? When it's hard, you should just give up?" She shook her head and looked at me like I'd suddenly grown horns. "Do you really believe that?"

I didn't, usually, but obviously this was a special case. "I don't want you to get hurt," I told her. "I want you to be happy."

"That's exactly the point, Dara," she said, her tone sharp. "I'm *trying* to be happy. For once, I'm thinking about what *I* want. You don't like Justin? Fine. You don't need to. In fact, since you obviously have such a low opinion of him, we'll make sure to steer clear of you if we decide to get back together. Will that help?"

"I didn't mean—"

"No, it's fine. I get it. You think he's a loser. I'm glad it's finally out in the open." She picked up the pie, supporting the bottom with her palm. Even though it was obviously still hot from the oven, she didn't even flinch. "I think I hear my mom's car outside. I have to go."

I stood up, my eyes stinging with tears. "Aubrey, wait."

She lifted her chin and walked out of the kitchen, pie balanced securely in front of her. I didn't follow. A few seconds later, the front door slammed shut behind her.

I stood frozen in the middle of the kitchen, wiping my eyes with my sleeve as the radio played upbeat songs that only made me want to cry more. When I could no longer stand it, I shut off the stereo and went to my room, wondering how I'd managed to make things even worse.

twenty-one

I DON'T SEE ETHAN ALL WEEKEND. HE TEXTS ME once on Saturday morning, letting me know there's no band practice until next week so they can recover from the showcase and catch up on other things. That's the extent of our contact. I assume he feels conflicted about what happened in the community center hallway, like I still do. Afterward, we'd gone back out and listened to the rest of the bands, both of us acting like nothing happened. But it did happen, and I can't think about anything else. I spend most of the weekend in my room, alternately reliving the kiss and beating myself up for it. When I imagine Aubrey asking me to look out for her brother in her absence, I doubt this is what she'd have had in mind.

Monday morning, Ethan is waiting for me at my locker. My throat goes dry while the rest of me breaks into a sweat. I have no idea what I'm going to say to him.

"Hey," he says as I approach. He attempts a smile, but it doesn't reach his eyes. "Uh, how are you?"

I concentrate on my combination lock so I don't have to look at him. Here, in broad daylight, that kiss feels like it happened to other people. People who aren't us. "I'm fine."

He lets out a sigh and leans in until his face is inches from mine. "About what happened the other night . . ."

He smells so good, like soap and fresh mint. My fingers fumble on the lock and I have to start over.

"I wanted to apologize to you," he presses on. "It was—I didn't plan it or anything."

"You've already apologized." I finally get my locker open and start gathering what I need for my morning classes.

"I know, but I wanted to do it again. I also wanted to tell you that the reason I stayed away from you this weekend is because I was afraid I'd screwed everything up." He pauses to take a breath. "But I had to see you today so I could make sure we were, you know, still good."

The thought of *him* giving *me* space almost makes me smile. I turn and meet his eyes. The way he's looking at me, so earnest and concerned, feels like a fist around my heart. The last thing I want to do is hurt him. "We'll always be good, Ethan."

His entire body relaxes, and I know I've said the right thing, the exact words he needed to hear today. Like me, he spent the weekend wondering if we'd ruined the connection between us that, despite everything, still exists. Apparently, it's stronger than we thought.

"I also wanted to ask you a question." He tries for another smile, and this time it sticks. "Do you want to do something after school? Go grab a hot chocolate or a coffee or whatever? Just us this time."

Everything in me wants to say yes, even the tiny, freaked-out part that's wondering if "just us" is another term for "date." The idea of dating Ethan seems improbable to me, but for a second I find myself wondering what it would be like. At the same time, I'm relieved to have an excuse to say no. I don't feel ready to define whatever it is we are now.

"I have a doctor's appointment this afternoon," I tell him. It's not exactly a lie. Dr. Lemke *is* a doctor . . . of psychology. "Another time, maybe?"

He nods, his eyes never leaving my face. "Definitely. Another time."

We continue to stare at each other, the air between us thickening with a different kind of tension. The kind that warms my stomach and makes my heart flip painfully in my chest. The kind that makes the rest of the world, or at least the rest of the school, fall away.

But not for long. I catch a flash of movement out of the

corner of my eye and it suddenly dawns on me that we're being watched.

Travis and Paige are walking hand in hand past my locker, alternately looking at us and whispering to each other. I've gotten used to people staring at us, so it barely even registers for me. Ethan's not as immune though, because the moment he realizes we have an audience, his eyes go flat and his mood darkens like someone flipped a switch in his brain.

"Is there a problem?" He turns slightly toward Paige and Travis, shoulders squared and arm muscles tensed.

Travis laughs like Ethan said something funny. Paige's cool gaze bounces back and forth between us, her eyes widening as she takes in our nearness. Ethan shifts until he's slightly in front of me, shielding me like he did Friday night.

"Nope," Travis says with a smirk. He tugs on Paige's hand, and the two of them continue down the hallway without another word. I watch as they pause to join a cluster of people waiting by one of the classroom doors. Travis says something to the guy standing beside him, then he looks back at Ethan and me, a half smirk still on his lips. Is he talking about us?

It hits me then. All those nasty rumors going around about what happened between Aubrey and me . . . what if Travis is behind them? He and Aubrey were close, and he knew at least a little bit about the mess with Justin. What if he actually thinks—?

"Dara?" Ethan's voice cuts through my thoughts. "Don't

let them bother you. They're just being idiots."

"I'm fine." I quickly turn back to face him. His features have returned to their normal, nonthreatening state. "So," I say, forcing a smile as I go back to sorting through my notes. "When did you become so intimidating?"

He laughs. "Sophomore year, I guess, when school started up again and everyone was scared to talk to me because they didn't know what to say. Oh, and the fights may have had something to do with it too."

"Fights?"

"What, you didn't hear about that?" A muscle twitches in his jaw. "First thing I did when I walked into school last year was punch Justin Gates in the face."

My math book tumbles to the floor, followed by everything else on the top shelf of my locker. I ignore it. "Ethan, you didn't," I say, even though I know he did. I wouldn't have believed it two years ago, or even last year, but I believe it now. "Did he hit you back?"

"No, but Wyatt Greer did." He touches his eyebrow. "That's how I got this scar."

"Wait. You picked a fight with *Wyatt Greer*?"

He stoops down and starts gathering my things off the floor. "He was harassing some freshman kid in the parking lot one day. I wasn't going to let him get away with that."

I shake my head as I crouch down beside him. So, not only had he given up violin and joined a band and gotten hot while

I was away, he'd also taken up brawling. Good to know. An image of Aubrey flashes through my head, her mother-hen face jacked up to maximum.

"Why do you have this?"

I glance up to see Ethan holding a piece of paper. The same piece of paper I stowed in my green notebook a couple of months ago, the one featuring Aubrey's obituary and the first article about the accident. It must have slid out when everything fell. Two seconds ago I was thinking about her, and now here she is again, declaring her presence like she's afraid of being forgotten.

"Oh . . ." I take the page from him and stand up, wobbling as all my blood rushes to my head. "I found it in my locker one day."

Ethan straightens up too and hands over the rest of my stuff. "Someone put that in your locker? Why?"

"I don't know. To torture me, I guess?" I don't want to tell him about the first piece of mail, the pencil sketch of me pushing Aubrey, and that I'm wondering now if Travis is somehow behind both. "Anyway, it doesn't matter. I painted myself as a target the minute I decided to come back here, right? I deserve every shot I get."

Before I can react, his hand captures mine and holds on tight. "No, you don't, and I wish there was something I could do to make you see that."

The bell rings, the shrill sound of it breaking through the

intensity of the moment. Without another word, Ethan drops my hand and walks with me to the end of the hallway, where we each go our separate ways.

I pop my head into the kitchen, where my mother is catching up on some work at the table. "I'm going out," I tell her. Not waiting for a reply, I duck back out and continue to the front door.

"Dara! Dara, wait a second." She catches up to me in the entryway. "Where are you going?"

I give her a look. It's Saturday afternoon. She knows very well where I'm going. She doesn't like it, but she knows. "I'll probably be home in time for dinner."

"Wait," she says again when I reach for the doorknob. "I need to talk to you."

Sighing, I turn to face her. "Mom, I'm not going to stay away from Ethan just because you're afraid of what his parents might—"

"I talked to Dr. Lemke yesterday," she cuts in. I shut up and stare at her. "He said you want to cut back on your sessions."

I nod, wondering what else they talked about. "Going once a week isn't necessary anymore. Maybe we could switch to monthly or something."

"I'm not sure that's wise, Dara."

"Maybe not," I say, "but it's my life, and I'd rather not

spend the rest of it in therapy, talking about the same things over and over."

Mom's sigh is much longer and wearier than mine. "As for your friendship with Ethan . . . Dr. Lemke thinks it might be good for you. I'm not sure I agree with that either, but I'm willing to follow your lead and let you heal in whatever way feels right to you."

"Okay," I say slowly. "Thanks."

She crosses her arms and watches me expectantly. I know she's waiting for me to act thrilled and say *I told you so*, but the truth is, my reconnection with Ethan doesn't always feel right. Sometimes, when I think about Aubrey and how much she loved him and leaned on him, a different kind of shame overtakes me. Is it selfish of me to want him in my life? To want him in ways I probably shouldn't? He's *Ethan*. Aubrey's little brother, who I've teased and defended and treated like my *own* little brother since we were preteens. Sure, he's gotten all cool and cute and tall, but he's still the same old Ethan.

Only he's not, really. The old Ethan didn't give me goose bumps. The old Ethan didn't make my breath go shallow just by looking at me.

It makes me feel guilty, enjoying these feelings, but I do.

"Okay," Mom replies, then surprises me by wrapping me in a hug. She squeezes extra tight, like I'm about to do something brave and life-threatening, like go off to war. I don't resist the contact. She obviously needs the reassurance.

*   *   *

"I'm fucking starving," Corey announces a few hours later as he winds the cord for his bass into a thick black coil. "You think your mom would cook us up some spaghetti or something?"

Hunter shoots him a look over the top of his cymbals. "You're always starving. And no, my mother is not your personal chef."

"I bet we *could* have a personal chef, though. Someday. When we're rich and famous."

"Dream on."

Ethan catches my eye and shakes his head like it pains him to put up with these boys. I bite my lip, stifling a laugh. Now that the showcase is out of the way, band practice is much more relaxed. Even Kel's in a good mood. Julia and Noelle are both busy today, and if I'd known that before coming over I probably would've stayed away too. But now that I'm here, I'm glad I didn't. The lighthearted vibe is contagious.

"Let's order pizza, then," Corey suggests.

Hunter puts down his drumsticks. "I'm in. Let's go pick it up. I could use some fresh air. And a smoke."

"I'm in too," Kel says, collapsing beside me on the couch. He slides over until his leg is flush with mine. "What do you like, Dara?"

"Excuse me?" I glance over at Ethan. He's kneeling in front of his amp, facing away from us, but I can see his back stiffen.

Kel blinks, giving me the full benefit of his icy-blue eyes. "On your pizza," he says with mock innocence. Hunter's right—this guy is utterly shameless.

I shift away from him. "Surprise me."

He grins as if my words are a personal challenge and stands up, joining Hunter and Corey by the door. When Hunter realizes Ethan and I haven't joined them, he turns back to look at us. "You guys coming?"

Ethan's gaze finds mine. This is it. I feel like I'm standing at the edge of a cliff, staring down at the choppy water below, and it's time to make a choice. I can turn back right now, forgetting I was ever here. Or I can take a risk and jump.

My decision must be evident on my face, because he goes back to playing with his amp and says, "No, go ahead. We'll stay here and clean up."

I catch Corey's smirk out of the corner of my eye and it makes me wonder how much they know. Did one of them see us last Friday night in the hallway? Does Ethan confide in his friends about these sorts of things? I don't know, and I don't think I want to.

Once the guys are gone, Ethan seems to take much longer than usual to organize his belongings. Maybe he's weighing the same options—turn back or jump. The tension between us is palpable, and I'm honestly not sure if it's a good tension or a bad one. It feels good, but a little scary at the same time.

Finally, Ethan places his guitar in its case and locks it, the sound of the clasps like gunshots in the small space. I watch him, aware as I always am now of the breadth of his shoulders, the clean lines of his face, the unconscious way he pushes his hair off his forehead, like he's not quite used to having it there yet. Suddenly, I want more than anything to push it back for him, feel the soft strands between my fingers. But I've become so accustomed to avoiding human contact, to resisting the urge to touch, I'm not even sure how to do it anymore.

As if sensing my inner battle, Ethan turns around. His eyes flick between me and the small section of carpet between us, like he's asking permission to cross it. When I don't look away or make any other gesture to discourage him, he moves over to the couch and stops in front of me, still on his knees. Slowly, he takes both my hands in his and eases me toward him, so close that my legs have nowhere else to go but around his waist.

It takes me a few moments, but I eventually gather the courage to pull my hands out of his and rest them gently on his shoulders. He stays completely still, his gaze fastened on my face. But I can't look at him, not yet, so I keep my eyes on my right hand as it slides from his shoulder to his collarbone to his chest, where it stops just over his heart. It's pounding almost in sync with mine.

"Dara."

I raise my eyes to his. The strain in his face matches the tone in his voice. I lean in and brush my lips along the edge of his jaw, hoping to smooth the tension away, but my touch has the opposite effect. His fingers dig into my hips, and he draws me even closer as his resolve crumbles completely.

This kiss isn't like the first one, fumbling and tentative and awkward. I'm no expert, but even with my limited experience, it's obvious he's good at this. So good that for the first time in a year and a half, I forget about keeping still. My arms circle his neck and my body melts into his and all I can think about is how good it feels to be so close to another person.

Until the shed door swings open, that is, hurling me back to earth.

"Hey, E, did you want—oh, shit. Sorry."

Ethan and I detach ourselves and squint in the direction of the doorway. Corey stands there watching us with a mortified expression.

"I'm gonna . . . back away slowly now," he says, and he does just that, closing the door behind him.

Ethan rests his forehead against my shoulder and laughs. At some point in the past however many minutes, we'd ended up reclined back on the couch, legs entangled and hands underneath each other's shirts. I quickly extract my hand and hold it clenched at my side. My body tenses beneath his, and he can obviously feel it, because he leans back to look at me, his smile fading into concern.

"We still good?"

I nod and scramble into a half-upright position. He lifts himself off me and takes my hand, helping me the rest of the way. Once again, I find myself not being able to look at him, so I finger-comb my hair and adjust my shirt instead.

"I'm sorry," he says, still slightly breathless. "Again."

"You don't need to apologize. I wouldn't be here if I didn't . . . want it." Like the last time we kissed, it feels like something that happened to other people. Like it's not even real. Maybe that's why I keep coming back here, and why I let this happen not only once, but twice. Because in those moments, I can pretend to be someone else, just a normal, happy girl who's finally found a boy to love. The girl I could have been, if life had kept to the path it was on instead of veering off into tragedy.

"I've been in love with you since the first time you came over to hang out with Aubrey," Ethan says softly. "You knew that, right?"

A lump forms in my throat and I swallow, forcing it back. "God, Ethan, this is so messed up."

"Yeah, it's kind of weird for me too. I mean, after everything."

After everything. Meaning, after I caused the death of his sister, the person who meant more to him than anyone. *Weird* doesn't even begin to cover it.

I rest my head against the back of the couch, suddenly exhausted. "Do your parents know you've been hanging out with me?"

"No." He threads his fingers through mine. "But I don't

exactly keep them up to date on my personal life. They didn't know about Lacey either."

"You know they don't want me near you, right?" I tell him about my parents dropping by his house a few days after the funeral and the reception they got. "Did they give you my apology letter?"

"What apology letter?"

I knew it. My head pulses with anger and I avert my face, not wanting him to see it. Who knows what would've been different if he'd seen that letter a year and a half ago? Maybe I wouldn't have wasted so much time assuming he hated me.

Once again, Ethan notices the sudden tension in my body. He leans in and presses his warm shoulder against mine. "They're assholes, Dara. They've always been assholes. Besides," he adds in a gentler tone, "I don't need a letter from you to know how sorry you are."

If he says one more sweet thing to me right now, I'm going to burst into tears. His kindness makes my heart ache. I look down at our intertwined hands and try to picture us as a normal couple instead of two people whose lives are connected by tragedy. A tragedy *I* made happen. I think about our parents' disapproval and the shocked looks at school and what Aubrey would think if she were alive to see us. Everything is stacked against us, and yet here I am. Travis was right—I'm totally a sucker for punishment.

The shed is growing darker by the minute. It's definitely

past time for us to get off this couch and head up to the house for some pizza, yet neither of us makes a move to leave. I stay focused on our hands, linked firmly between us.

"I think I did know how you felt about me," I say. "Deep down. It's just . . . you were my best friend's little brother and I was . . . in denial, I guess. Why didn't you tell me years ago?"

"I hid a lot of what I felt back then." He skims his thumb along my palm. "But I'm done with hiding. Life's too short for that."

twenty-two   **Sophomore Year**

FIRST THING MONDAY MORNING, I HEADED straight for the second floor and Justin's locker. He was there, laughing and talking to his friend Will like he didn't have a care in the world.

"I need to talk to you," I said, sidling up behind him. I nodded briefly at Will, a silent apology for interrupting.

Justin glanced over his shoulder at me. If I hadn't been paying such close attention, I might have missed the flash of *oh, shit* on his face. He looked back at Will and shrugged, like he had no idea what this was about, and grabbed his backpack. I led him over to a less populated spot by the Multimedia classroom.

"Can we make this quick?" he asked. "I have to get to class."

Two days had passed since Paige's party. Two days of worrying and second-guessing and wondering if I was somehow to blame. Not once had I really gotten angry with him or what had happened. But now, with him looking at me like I was ruining his morning . . . I was suddenly *furious*.

"Did you tell Aubrey yet?" I said through clenched teeth.

"Tell her what?"

"What do you *think*?"

He glanced around like he was afraid to be seen with me and then met my gaze again. "Look. I don't really remember what happened the other night, but going by the way you're glaring holes through me, I'm guessing it wasn't good."

"No, it wasn't good," I said. "It wasn't good at all. You seriously don't remember what you said to me? What you . . . did? How convenient."

He looked away, his body shifting uncomfortably. "I remember a little."

"Whoa, that was quick. Two seconds ago you didn't really remember and now you remember a little. Maybe in five minutes or so your memory will return completely and you'll remember every single moment, like I do." I moved closer to the wall as a group of people brushed past us. When they were gone, I asked him again, "Did you tell Aubrey?"

"Did *you*?"

"No." I didn't want to add that she was mad at me for

something else and hadn't spoken to me since she left my house with her pie yesterday. "I figured I'd give you the opportunity to explain yourself first. Which you obviously haven't had the balls to do."

His jaw tightened. "Okay, so I messed up. I get that. But telling Aubrey about this isn't going to help anything. I know you think I'm an asshole and maybe I am, but I do love her. One stupid mistake doesn't have to ruin everything."

I almost told him he should have thought of that before getting drunk and groping me, but I was afraid someone nearby would hear me. "Tell her," I said in a low voice. "Or I will."

I spun on my heel, eager to make a quick getaway, and smashed directly into the person behind me. When I saw who it was, my cheeks flooded with warmth.

"Everything okay, Shepard?" Travis asked, glancing between Justin's face and mine. Clearly, he could see he'd interrupted an argument. How long had he been standing beside us? How much had he heard?

"Yeah." I adjusted my expression to look normal. "Everything's fine, Travis."

"Okay," he said, uncertain. He eyed us both again before continuing down the hall.

I started to follow him, but then changed my mind and turned back to Justin. "I'll give you one more day. One. Think you can remember *that*?"

Done with him, I spun around again and walked away.

twenty-three

CHEMISTRY HAS BECOME MY FAVORITE CLASS. Not because I like the material, but because it's the only class where I feel like I'm on the verge of fitting in again. And it's all due to Noelle.

Every time we have a lab or group project, she always chooses to work with me. Since she acts so normal and friendly around me, more of my classmates have been following suit. In this class, I'm not the girl everyone's afraid to talk to for fear of saying the wrong thing. Having a friend makes me more accessible; if someone as nice and cool as Noelle feels comfortable around me, then maybe I'm okay after all.

If only I could convince myself of this. Months of agonizing grief and guilt have made me question every good thing that comes my way.

"Noelle," I say during chemistry class on Wednesday. We're supposed to be filling out a worksheet, but Mr. Haggerty (aka Mr. Clean) is outside in the hall gabbing with another teacher and everyone's taking advantage of his absence to talk. "Do you know about me?"

She stops doodling on the worksheet and gives me a baffled look. "What do you mean?"

"Do you know about—" Uneasy, I concentrate on a scratch on the table, running my finger over it. "Do you know what happened with Ethan's sister? How she was killed?"

Noelle's eyes go wide and she blinks at me once before looking away. "Oh. Uh, yeah. I saw a few newspaper articles online. And Hunter told me about it too. The real story, I mean, not what some of the idiots around here *think* happened."

Several emotions hit me at once and I can't tell which is most powerful—relief or surprise or embarrassment. Of course she's heard the rumors. "Everyone else knows too? Kel and Corey and Julia? The real story, I mean?"

She nods.

"So you knew about me all this time and you still . . ."

"Still what?" she says when I let the thought trail off. "Still wanted to be friends with you? Why wouldn't I? You're not a sociopath." Her pale face flushes pink. "Sorry. I didn't mean to sound so crass. My mom's always telling me to stop being crass. It's just—I see how some people treat you around here, like they think you have no business walking the halls like everyone else. As if what happened to you couldn't happen to any one of them. And I've always been the type to root for the underdog, so—" She turns even redder and covers her face with her hands. "Sorry," she repeats. "Not that you're a dog. I'm just going to stop talking now."

I grab my pencil and start doodling on my side of the sheet. "You mean you felt sorry for me."

"No." She drops her hands, looking horrified. "I wanted to be friends with you because I *like* you. To be honest, Ethan's talked about you so much since I met him, I felt like I knew you even before you came back to school."

My pencil halts right in the middle of sketching a five-point star. "Really?"

"Really. And not stuff about what happened with you and his sister either. He talked about *you*. What you were like, you know, before. How amazing he thought you were. And at the end of summer, when he found out you were back in town . . ." She picks up her pencil again and fills in the rest of my star. "He was *freaked*, Dara. Not because he didn't want to see you, but because he wasn't sure if you wanted to see him. He was convinced you thought he hated you."

"I did," I say, swallowing hard. Knowing these things about Ethan makes me feel sad and frustrated, like I missed out on something good I didn't even know I had.

"Well, let me assure you, that boy has never hated you. Even when he couldn't forgive you, he still didn't hate you. I'm glad you guys were able to move past everything and be friends again." She nudges me with her elbow. "Or should I say friends with benefits? I hear Corey walked in on you two after band practice on Saturday. That couch is pretty comfortable, right? Hunter and I get a lot of use out of it too."

I manage to smile thinly in response, even though my brain is stuck on something else she said. *Even when he couldn't forgive you* . . . What does she mean? What exactly has Ethan told his friends that he hasn't told me?

All this time, I assumed he meant it when he said he didn't blame me for Aubrey's death. But hearing this makes me wonder if there's something to my parents' suspicions, after all.

Maybe, buried so deep he doesn't even fully realize it, Ethan is angrier at me than he lets on.

My mother recently instated a rule that we all must do something together, as a family, every Friday evening. Like our mandatory family dinners, these evenings feel forced and unnatural. Tonight, it's a kid-friendly movie in the living room, but I'm having trouble following the plot. I feel restless and distracted, and for the first time since Aubrey died, I'm not even trying to keep still. It's like my body suddenly needs to make up for all those months of inertness.

About halfway through the movie, my phone vibrates with a text from Ethan. You free?

Kind of, I type back.

Free enough to come out? I'm right outside your house.

I want to go to the window and peek through the curtains, but that would arouse suspicion, so I don't. Instead, I text Be right there and stand up. My mother looks at me.

"I'm going out for a couple of hours."

She frowns. "Dara, it's family time."

In order to have family time, you need to feel like a family, I want to reply, but that would probably set my father off again, so I say, "I know, but I forgot I made plans to go for a drive with Ethan. Sorry."

Dad's face twitches, but he doesn't say anything. Tobias doesn't even glance away from the TV, and Mom sighs like I just ruined her life. I take that as permission.

"I won't be late," I promise as I head for the front door. I throw on my coat and leave before anyone has time to change their minds.

I fully expect to see Ethan's car when I get outside, so I'm surprised when it's nowhere on my street. As I'm about to pull out my phone and text him, he steps out from behind the neighbor's tree and scares the hell out of me.

"Damn it, Ethan," I say as he wraps his arms around me, pulling me against his cold body. My heart races, partly from the scare and partly from his proximity. "I thought you meant you were picking me up in your car so we could go for a drive."

"My car's low on gas, so I'm picking you up for a walk instead."

"You walked here from your house?" Aubrey and I used to walk to each other's houses whenever our parents were unavailable to drive us, so I know it takes about fifteen minutes at a brisk pace. "Wasn't it cold?"

Obviously it was, because his skin is like ice. The temperature is actually pretty mild for December, but the wind adds a damp chilliness that settles into your bones.

"I'm nice and warm now," Ethan says, pressing his freezing nose to my cheek.

I squirm and glance behind me. We're a safe distance from my house, but still, we have lots of neighbors. Nosy ones. Gripping the sides of his jacket, I drag him back behind the tree, out of sight.

"Why didn't you come to my door?" I ask him.

He grins and slips his hands into the back pockets of my jeans. "Because I'm scared of your father."

Okay. I'll give him that. My father is sort of terrifying, especially when he's mad.

After warming up for a while behind the tree, we decide to walk to Juniper Park. On the way, we pass several decorated houses, reminding me how close it is to Christmas and New Year's. And Aubrey's birthday.

"Do you still want to be a cop?" Ethan asks as we cross the street.

I shrug. Mrs. Dover brought the topic up again yesterday, when she called me in to discuss why I haven't yet applied to any colleges. I didn't have an answer for her, and I don't have one for Ethan. Things are different now; that naïvely confident fifteen-year-old no longer exists. Police officers risk their lives to protect people, and I can't even work up the nerve to drive a car.

"I haven't decided yet," I answer.

Thankfully, he doesn't push. A few minutes later we arrive at the park, which—due to the late hour and increasingly frigid weather—we have all to ourselves. Hand in hand, we walk along the gravel path that cuts through the grass, pausing when we reach the stone fountain. We sit on the edge, facing the deserted playground area in the distance.

"Remember when you walked across the monkey bars?" Ethan says.

"Of course."

"I thought you were going to fall and break your neck." He lifts a hand and brushes it against my fortunately undamaged neck, making me shiver. "You were so fierce back then. Fierce and fearless. I loved that about you."

I feel a prickle of hurt and look away, not wanting him to see it on my face. Since those traits no longer exist in me, what's left for him to love? Shame and anguish? Not exactly attractive qualities. "I was more reckless than fearless," I tell him, making my tone light to cover up the sting. "Not to mention a show-off."

He grins and hooks an arm around my waist, tugging me toward him. "Yeah, but you were a *cute* show-off. I couldn't even think straight when I was watching you up there, and not just because I was afraid you were going to fall. You had on those little white shorts that showed off your legs and all I could think about was how sexy you looked. And how much I wanted to do this."

He tips my face up and kisses me, extinguishing my hurt and igniting a much different feeling. The kind I'm still not entirely used to experiencing around Ethan. Sometimes, when I think about what we're doing, about how it's *him* I'm kissing and touching and wanting, I feel like I'm breaching some sort of ethical code.

Ethan, however, has no such qualms. His hand slides under my coat, inching toward the hem of my shirt. I can feel the iciness of his fingers even through my clothes, so I yank his hand out and hold it firmly in mine.

"Don't even think about touching me with your ice cube hands," I scold him. "You might be bigger than me now, but I can still take you in a fight. I used to be very good at kicking your ass."

"I know. I thought that was hot too."

"Sure you did."

"No, really." He leans back a bit and sticks his other hand under the back of my coat, where I can't easily block him. When his cold fingers meet my bare skin, I shriek and try to jerk away, but he grips me even tighter and presses his entire palm against my lower back.

"Ethan," I gasp, and before I even realize what I'm doing, I revert to my old playful self for a moment and push him.

Neither of us is prepared for what happens next. The force of my shove knocks him off balance and he slips off the edge of the fountain, landing on his knees on the hard pavement below. He laughs and gets right back up, so I know he's not hurt. But knowing this doesn't stop the wave of panic that hits me when I realize what I did.

Just like the day in the truck with Dad and Tobias when we drove down Fulham Road, my breathing shallows as the memories flood in, pulling me under.

Garbage reeking under the sun.

A small, still foot, nails painted blue.

Crimson blood on the asphalt, spreading, soaking . . .

So much blood.

"Dara. *Dara.* Look at me."

Ethan's voice breaks through, and suddenly I'm back on the fountain again, arms wrapped tightly over my abdomen and fingers curled into fists. I focus on Ethan's face, which is pale and anxious. Seeing him so worried makes *me* worried, and it takes a few seconds to regulate my breathing again.

"I'm okay," he says, taking hold of my wrists and prying my arms away from my body. He lifts my right hand and presses it flat to his chest, right over his heart. "You didn't hurt me. I'm okay."

Tears spill over my lids and I nod, unable to speak. His heart thumps steadily against my palm, rhythmic and alive, but all it does is remind me of how fragile bodies are. How quickly and easily the life inside them can cease and fade away.

"I'm sorry, I can't—" I drop my hand from his chest and stand up, prepared to walk away and leave him there, alone but safe, on the lip of the fountain. But he's in front of me before I can even take one step.

"Please don't be sorry," he says, gripping my shoulders. "You didn't do anything wrong. Honestly, I kind of liked it when you pushed me. You were like the old Dara again for a second. It was nice."

"But I'm *not* the old Dara anymore, Ethan." I take a step back, out of his reach. "I'll never be her again."

He lowers his hands and stuffs them into the pockets of his jacket. "I know that."

"No. I don't think you do." Another tear escapes and I swipe at it angrily. "I'm sorry I can't be fierce and fearless and whatever else you loved about me back then, but that girl is gone. Forever. Don't you get it? I'm different now."

"And you think I'm not?" he says, his mood darkening in

a flash like it did the other day in the hallway at school. "She was your best friend but she was my *family*. Losing her changed me too, you know. I'm not that innocent little kid anymore. I stopped being a kid the day my sister was crushed to death by a fucking truck."

The words hit me like darts, making me flinch. I knew he felt these things, but hearing him say them, feeling the potency of his anger *while* he says them, is a different experience altogether. It also confirms the suspicions I've had ever since my conversation with Noelle in chemistry a few days ago. Ethan is still mad at me. And even if he isn't completely conscious of it, he *does* blame me, at least on some level.

"I'm sorry," I mumble after a few moments of heavy silence. "Do you want me to go?"

He sighs and takes my hand, weaving his cold fingers through mine. "I'm sorry too. Don't leave. Please."

There's not enough light to see his face clearly, but I can hear the vulnerability in his voice, feel it in the way he squeezes my hand. Something inside me melts.

"Walk me home?" I ask softly.

He nods, his tensed shoulders sagging in relief. Still holding hands, we exit the park and start down the sidewalk to home. The colorfully lit houses seem almost garish on the walk back, like someone went and jacked the wattage up to maximum. Or maybe it's because everything feels clearer and more intense after what happened in the park. Even the smallest things seem amplified now.

When we get close to my house, Ethan leads me behind the neighbor's tree again. I tilt my head up, expecting a kiss good night, but he's not even looking at me. He stares at the ground in front of him, lost in thought.

"Ethan?" I touch his arm and he looks up, blinking like I just woke him from a dream.

"Do you think this is a mistake?" he asks out of nowhere. "Us, I mean? Is it becoming too much?"

Too much. Does he mean our relationship? The conflicting mix of guilt and desire that rushes through me each time we kiss? The feeling that we're betraying Aubrey's memory in selfish, dishonorable ways? Everything about this is *too much*.

"I—I don't know," I tell him. It's mostly the truth. I don't know what the hell I'm doing anymore or what I want or how I feel. All I know is I'd be devastated if I lost him forever too.

"Okay," he says, even though it's clearly not the answer he wanted from me. I've never been too much for him. Not even now, when I would be for anyone else. "Can I ask you one more question?"

"Of course."

The wind picks up, rustling what's left of the leaves on the branches above us. Ethan glances up as if gathering courage from the sound and then returns his attention to me. He shifts his weight from one foot to the other, suddenly nervous.

"My parents are going out for New Year's Eve," he says.

"They won't be home until the next day sometime, so I'll have the house to myself for about twenty-four hours. Do you want to come over and celebrate Aubrey's birthday with me?"

I don't know what I was expecting, but it's not this. My first instinct is to decline. I haven't been to the McCraes' house since Aubrey died, and the thought of going there again makes me light-headed with dread. Aubrey's school pictures are probably still on the walls, her room still exactly as she left it. Or maybe not. For all I know, her parents could have scrubbed the house clean of all traces of her. I'm not sure which would be harder, seeing things that remind me of her or not finding anything at all.

But Ethan's waiting for an answer, so again, I give him a noncommittal one.

"I'll think about it."

It's the most concrete promise he's going to get from me right now and he knows it. Without saying anything else, he walks me up to my door and kisses me lightly on the lips before disappearing back into the dark.

twenty-four   **Sophomore Year**

---

class right at the bell and waited for Ethan near his locker.
When I saw him approaching, I gave him an expectant look.
In response, he frowned and shook his head.

"I don't think she's talked to him," he said, stopping in
front of me.

To my horror—and probably Ethan's—my eyes filled with
tears. I'd given Justin plenty of time to do the right thing and
own up to his mistake. I realized now he'd probably never had
any intention of telling her. He'd missed the deadline I'd given
him on purpose, forcing me to do his dirty work for him so he
wouldn't have to. Coward. I couldn't believe I'd ever liked him.

"Are you okay?"

"Yeah, he's just such a . . ." Frustrated, I squeezed my eyes shut, trapping the wetness inside. "Never mind. Do you know where Aubrey is?"

"No, but we have a lunch meeting for orchestra in a few minutes and she said she'd—"

"What's going on?"

Adrenaline flared in my stomach and I turned in the direction of the voice. Aubrey stood about two feet away, watching us. Ethan and I stared back at her, mute.

"Dara, why are you crying?" she pressed when we failed to answer her question. "Are you—did something happen?"

These were the first words she'd spoken to me since Sunday. On a normal day, I would have felt relieved she still cared enough to ask. "Aubrey," I said, and then immediately ran out of words.

"What is it?" Her hands rose to her hair, but it was already in a braid, so they just lingered there for a moment before dropping to her sides again.

I glanced at Ethan, who gave me a tiny nod of encouragement. "Can we go somewhere and talk?" I asked her, stalling again.

"No. I need to know now."

"Aubrey . . ." I trailed off helplessly.

She crossed her arms. "Just tell me, Dara. Does it have anything to do with Justin? You seem to hate him all of a sudden. Obviously something happened and you're both keeping it from me for some reason. Travis told me he heard you two fighting in the hallway yesterday, but I thought he was exaggerating or imagining things. Now I'm not so sure. Just tell me," she repeated, her eyes boring into mine. "Are you and Justin . . . is something going on between you two?"

This was something I'd worried about for the past two nights as I lay in bed wondering what would happen when she found out—that she'd think Justin and I were fooling around behind her back. Still, hearing her actually voice the suspicion out loud sent a tremor down my spine.

"No, Aubrey," I said, taking a step toward her. "Of course not."

She continued to stare at me, waiting, silently begging me to explain. And I didn't have any other choice, because no matter what repercussions might come from this, no matter how impossible it felt to say the words, I owed her the whole truth.

"The other night at Paige's party," I began, keeping my eyes on the scuffed floor, "Justin came up behind me in the garage and he pressed up against me and he . . . he put his hands on me. I stopped him, but he was so drunk it was like he didn't even realize what was going on. That's it, Aubrey. Nothing else happened. I didn't tell you right away, because I wanted to give him a chance to come clean to you first. But he hasn't, so . . . I'm sorry."

I looked up in time to see her face go from expectant to shocked to bright red with anger. At first, I thought the anger was for Justin, since he'd crossed a line no boyfriend should ever cross, but then she opened her mouth.

"I can't believe you," she said, eyes blazing. "You're just saying this because you're jealous. You've been jealous this entire time and you're doing whatever you can to sabotage this for me. What kind of friend does that?"

"That's not it at all." I kept my voice low, hoping she'd take my cue and do the same. People were starting to stare, and no wonder. Tears were rolling down my face and Aubrey looked like she wanted to kill me.

"That's *exactly* it. You've been trying to turn me against him, telling me I can do better and maybe we're not *meant* to be together. And now you're trying to convince me he hit on you? That's *low*, Dara. Justin would never do that to me."

"Yes, he would," Ethan cut in.

"Ethan," Aubrey said, tossing him a quick glance. "Maybe you should go. This doesn't have anything to do with you."

"It does, actually. I was there Saturday night, in the garage. I saw it happen. Dara's not lying."

She looked at him again, and this time her gaze lingered. Ethan was unfailingly honest, especially with her. She knew he was telling the truth, which meant I was telling the truth too.

After a long pause, the anger in her face softened into hurt and she turned and walked away, dodging the small crowd of nosy bystanders who'd paused to listen to our fight. They watched her until she disappeared, then spun their heads back to Ethan and me, hoping for more drama.

"I should probably go talk to her," Ethan said, sounding apologetic. But I understood. Aubrey was his number one, exactly as she should have been.

"Thanks," I told him, blinking back more tears. "For what you said, I mean. And I'm sorry you got involved in this."

He shrugged as if it were no big deal and headed off to find his sister. Now it was just me, standing in the hallway and crying, wondering once again if I'd just screwed things up even worse.

twenty-five

Senior Year

"ARE YOU SURE?" MY MOTHER ASKS ME FOR THE umpteenth time this week. "We don't have to go tonight. We can all stick around here and order Chinese food."

"No," I say, swirling my spoon around in my cereal. "You should go. You'll get charged if you cancel your hotel room now."

Mom sighs into her coffee cup. She's been freaking out for days about leaving me alone on New Year's Eve. Months ago, before they knew I was coming back, she and Dad bought tickets for a concert and reserved a hotel room nearby. They never do things like this anymore, and I know they need the break from work and stress and me.

"True," Mom says with a definitive nod, and I know I've finally convinced her. "It would be a shame to have to pay a cancellation fee. And Tobias is really excited about sleeping over at Brock's house tonight."

Keeping my face smooth so she won't see my relief, I put my empty bowl in the sink and go to my room. There's a text from Ethan waiting for me on my phone.

Have you decided?

I stare at the screen for a moment, my mind reeling. Since the night he asked me to celebrate Aubrey's birthday with him, I've been putting off giving him an answer. It's not just that I'm worried about going to his house for the first time since she died. I know it won't be easy, and being there will trigger more memories and anxiety than I'm probably ready to handle. That part is inevitable. What I *can't* predict is how tonight will impact the new, still-fragile connection I've managed to build with Ethan over the past few months.

But maybe that old fierce-and-fearless part of me still exists somewhere and I can tap into it again, at least for a little while.

I refocus on my phone and tap out a response. I'm in.

When Ethan arrives at seven to pick me up, it's snowing. Not the dry, flurry kind we've had until now, but big, fat flakes that stick and make the roads treacherous.

"Oops, I've never really driven in snow before," Ethan says when his tires skid on the way out of my driveway. He gestures to the plastic-wrapped plate in my hands. "What's that?"

"It's a cake I made earlier." I peer out the windshield at the swirling snowflakes. "I really suck at baking, but . . . Aubrey would've wanted a cake for her birthday."

He smiles. "Only if she could bake it herself. From scratch."

I smile too, remembering how picky she was about store-bought pastry and the kind that came out of a box, like this one. But I think she'd give me credit for trying.

We make it to his house in one piece, and Ethan parks his car in the empty driveway.

"Where are your parents?" I ask as we walk up to the front door. I don't really care where they are, but I need to distract myself somehow.

"Some party at one of their friends' houses." He opens the door and motions me inside. "I'm not exactly sure. They hate me, so we try to avoid speaking to each other as much as possible."

"Oh," I say, feeling my heart start to pound. The inside of the house looks exactly the same, perfectly coordinated and impossibly neat. It even smells the same, like cinnamon and citrusy wood polish.

A surge of dizziness passes over me.

"You okay?" Ethan touches my arm and gives me a sympathetic look. Of course he understands. Getting used to living here without Aubrey must have been much more difficult for him than this brief visit is for me.

I let out a breath and nod. "I think so."

"Come on." He takes the cake out of my hands and leads me toward the kitchen. "I have something that'll help."

The "something" turns out to be an almost-empty bottle of vodka that he digs out from a bottom cupboard. He sets it on the counter beside the cake, finds two shot glasses, and fills them both, shaking the bottle to get the last few drops.

"Cheers," he says, sliding my shot toward me and picking up his own.

I've never liked alcohol—probably a good thing, as I might have drowned myself in it after Aubrey was killed—but I'll do pretty much anything to calm this shaky feeling in my stomach. "Cheers," I echo, then tip the shot in my mouth like I did at Paige's party so long ago. This one is only marginally better. Ethan gulps his at the same time, wincing as it goes down.

"So," I say, leaning against the counter beside him. "Why do you think your parents hate you?"

He tosses the empty bottle in the trash. "Because I rebelled, or whatever. Stepped out of the box they kept me in. They're just pissed I started living for myself instead of for them."

I feel my muscles start to loosen, warmed by the vodka in my belly. The dizziness has passed. "I doubt they hate you. If your parents hate anyone, it's me."

"What makes you say that?"

"They charged me with criminal negligence, Ethan. I'm pretty sure there are some hard feelings."

He gets quiet for a moment, his fingers absently tapping against the counter. "They dropped the charge, though."

"Yeah, and I still don't know why."

An odd expression crosses his face, like embarrassment mingled with pride. He turns away to get a glass of water, suddenly unable to look at me, and that's when it sinks in.

"*You* convinced them to drop it?"

He downs a mouthful of water and then offers the glass to me. I take a small sip, studying him carefully over the rim.

"I told them you'd already been through enough," he says, meeting my eyes. "And if they didn't back off and leave you alone, I'd find some way to fuck up their lives even more."

I almost choke. "What would you have done?"

"Ruin their reputations around town somehow? Get a tattoo? I don't know. I didn't really need to provide details . . . the threat was enough."

All I can do is shake my head, amazed. He'd stood up for me, fought for me, even after I'd taken his sister away. *Right after* I'd taken his sister away. That he was still willing to help me after what I did makes me feel even more undeserving of him.

"Thank you," I tell him, and press my lips against his. It's inadequate, but it's all I've got at the moment.

He kisses me back for a minute, then pulls away and says, "How about we take that cake down to the family room and not come back up until it's gone."

"Sounds good to me."

We gather up forks and napkins and the cake and carry everything downstairs in one trip. The family room hasn't changed much either, aside from new lamps on the end tables. A fire crackles in the wood stove, making the room feel cozy and warm. We dump everything on the coffee table and settle on the couch.

"Do you remember the last time we were down here together?" Ethan asks.

It takes me a minute to summon up the memory. "It was spring. May, I think." About a week before Paige's party and everything that happened with Justin. I remember, because it's one of the last times I was in this house with Aubrey. "We were watching *Harry Potter*."

"Right." Ethan smiles and puts his arm around me. "I was sitting where I am right now and you were stretched out beside me, your head by my leg. I couldn't concentrate on the movie at all. You had on this shirt that was sort of low cut, so I had an awesome view."

Emboldened by the vodka shot, I reach out and swat him. "Ethan."

"Sorry. Most of my memories involve lusting over you." He tugs my legs over until they're draped across his. "Anyway, right after the movie ended you guys left to meet Travis and Paige or something, and my heart was broken."

I remember that part too. Justin was busy that night, so it

was just the four of us for a change. We went to the movies and then to Starbucks for frappuccinos, and Travis spent the whole night joking around with Aubrey.

"Do you think he was in love with her?" I ask before I can stop myself.

"What?"

"Travis. Do you think he was in love with Aubrey?"

He looks at me like he's wondering if it's possible for a person to get drunk from a couple of ounces of liquor. "Why would you think that?"

My mind flashes on the day I found the two of them together in the library, how red Travis's neck got when he saw me. "You've seen the way he acts around me," I say, picking at a loose thread on my leggings. "He hates me. He looks at me like I'm a murderer."

Ethan's jaw twitches. "No. I'm almost positive he wasn't in love with her. They were just really good friends. She was the only one who never made him feel dumb, you know? I think even Paige made him feel like an idiot sometimes. Still does, probably." He runs his fingers over my kneecap, tickling me. "And I'm sure he still has a soft spot for her because of what she did for him."

"What she did for him?" I ask, confused.

His eyes widen. "She never told you about that?"

"About what?"

"She tutored him in math and English for an entire year.

He would've had to go to summer school or repeat tenth grade if it weren't for her."

I gape at him. How did I miss this? What else was going on in Aubrey's life I didn't know about?

"Maybe he asked her not to tell anyone," he adds. "Even you. I probably wouldn't know either if he hadn't come over here a few times to study."

I lean my forehead against his shoulder, feeling a bit rattled. "Wow. I had no idea. All this time I thought he might be the one putting those papers in my locker because he loved her and hated me for—"

"Wait." He pulls back, causing my forehead to drop off his shoulder. "Papers? Plural? There was more than the obituary one?"

"Just one more," I assure him, and I describe the stick-figure sketch of me pushing Aubrey, that big, happy smile on my penciled face.

"And you think Travis is behind it?" His hands, both resting on my leg, clench into tight fists.

"I don't know. Maybe. I think he started some of those rumors about me, at least." I touch his cheek, run my thumb over his tensed jawline. "Forget I said anything. Tonight's about the good memories, okay?"

His features relax and he nods, capturing my hand in his. And for the next two hours, that's what we do—talk about our good memories of Aubrey. The funny things she said and did.

Her amazing talent. Her quirks and pet peeves. How sweet and thoughtful and loyal she could be. How much she loved us both. How much we both loved her.

It's cathartic, exchanging these stories with Ethan. I can talk all I want to Dr. Lemke or Mrs. Dover or my mom, but none of them knew Aubrey like Ethan did. None of them shared a connection with her that was forged through years of laughter and kinship and pain. None of them truly understand how it felt to lose her so early, long before she was ready to go.

"What do you think she'd be doing now?" I ask after we've exhausted every happy memory in our collective brains. It's close to midnight, minutes away from a brand-new year and the day Aubrey would have turned eighteen. We haven't moved from the couch, and the cake still sits in front of us on the table, untouched. We decided to wait until it's officially January first to eat it.

"Probably freaking out about college," Ethan says, sprawling back on the couch.

"Yeah." I feel a pang of sadness. She'd never get to go to college, or get married, or have kids, or sit around with us like this, talking about old times.

"Two minutes," Ethan says, checking the time on his phone.

"Do you have candles for the cake?"

He glances around, then gets up and crosses the room to a

set of shelves in the corner. "I have *a* candle," he says proudly, swiping a squat, red candle off one of the shelves. He brings it and the lighter from the wood stove back to the couch. I unwrap the cake, and he sticks the candle right in the middle, causing the thick, white icing to ooze up the sides. "Time?" he asks as he lights the wick.

I peer at his phone. "Fifteen seconds."

He settles back on the couch again and grabs my hand, and that's what we're doing when midnight and Aubrey's birthday arrives—sitting together and remembering her. I think about last year, how I'd spent the holidays at my aunt and uncle's house because I wasn't ready to come home. Mom and Dad and Tobias flew in for a few days so we could celebrate together, but it didn't feel like a celebration. Not like right now.

"What did you do last New Year's Eve?" I ask after the candle has been blown out and we both have forkfuls of cake.

Ethan hacks off another bite. "Hunter got me drunk."

"Hmm." I lean closer and use my thumb to wipe a smudge of icing off the corner of his mouth. "I guess eating crappy homemade cake is sort of boring in comparison?"

Instead of answering, he kisses me. His mouth is sticky and sweet, and I kiss him back like I can't get enough of it. Soon, we're tangled together on the couch, cake and everything else forgotten.

"Want to go up to my room?" Ethan asks sometime later, after he notices me shivering for the second time. The fire died off a while ago, and the room has been growing increasingly chilly. "I don't mean—we can just talk. Or whatever. It's a lot warmer up there, that's all."

I hesitate for a moment. If we go up there, we'll probably do a lot more than talk. My chest is pressed against his and I can feel his heart pounding. He wants me, and going by the way my own heart races in sync with his, I want him too. I want us to get lost in each other and let everything else fade away. Just for a while, I want us to forget.

"Okay," I reply.

We slowly make our way upstairs. I feel a bit unsteady, like my limbs belong to someone else. I'm grateful when we reach the top floor, because it's much warmer up here and I don't have to climb any more stairs.

"Oh my God," I gasp when we walk into his room. The last time I was in here, it looked almost like a hotel room, tidy and bland and impersonal. Now, the walls are virtually covered in posters, and his floor is littered with clothes and music magazines and guitar picks. For the first time since I've known Ethan, his room looks like it belongs to a teenage boy. "You're really committed to pissing off your parents, aren't you?"

"I live for it." He pushes a balled-up sweatshirt off his desk chair. "You want to sit down?"

I ignore the chair and kiss him instead. He wraps his arms around me and walks me backward toward his bed, which—surprisingly, considering the state of his room in general—is very neatly made. Not for long, though. We pick up where we left off downstairs, only now we have more room to maneuver. Without removing his lips from mine, Ethan rolls us over until I'm on top of him, my knees on either side of his hips and my hair falling forward, shielding our faces.

"I love you," he mumbles against my neck as his hands slide over my rib cage, pushing my shirt up, unhooking my bra. "I love you so much. I always have."

Tears sting my eyes, but I force them back. I don't want to cry. Not now. All I want is to get even closer to him, closer than I've ever been to anyone, and let these feelings take over until there's nothing left but his body against mine.

"We still good?" he asks as our clothes join the jumbled mess on the floor.

"Still good," I say, because even though I haven't loved him for years like he's loved me, I've always been able to trust him. And that hasn't changed.

Ethan lies there and watches me for a while, like he's giving me time to change my mind. When I don't, he reaches beside him to the nightstand and opens the drawer, pulling out a small, square package. The fact that he has an open box of condoms in his room makes me pause for a second.

"You've done this before?" Right now is the worst possible time to broach this subject, but I have to know.

"A couple times. With Lacey." He touches my bare

shoulder, his fingers trembling against my skin. "But it was nothing like this."

As he leans in to kiss me, I realize it doesn't matter. None of it does. Not who he's been with or what he's done or what I've done or if we'll end up destroying each other. For the first time in a long time, I can't see anything but what's right in front of me.

I wake up just before dawn, thirsty and disoriented. Propping myself up on my elbows, I glance over at Ethan, who's stretched out on his stomach beside me. I can barely make him out in the grayness of the room, but I can tell from his even breathing that he's deeply asleep.

Heat floods my cheeks as images of last night push through the sleep-fog in my brain—the vodka shot, the cake, the New Year countdown, and then . . . this bed. That part of the night feels like a surreal blur, and I'd probably think I imagined it if it weren't for the tenderness between my legs, assuring me it really happened.

I feel a twinge of regret. Before, we might have been able to go back to being just friends—or even walk away from each other entirely—if the Aubrey-shaped wedge between us ever became too big to manage. But there's no going back after last night. Now our lives are tangled together even more.

I glance down at my body, naked underneath the covers. Too late for second-guessing now.

Ethan stirs and rolls toward me, his hand grazing my bare hip. "You okay?"

"Yeah," I tell him, even though my eyes are suddenly prickling with tears. Why am I so emotional all of a sudden? "I just . . . I need to use the bathroom. I'll be right back."

"Okay," he mumbles, and seconds later he's breathing evenly again.

Quietly, I get up and feel around on the floor for some clothes. I grab the first thing my hand touches, which turns out to be Ethan's Black Sabbath T-shirt, and pull it over my head as I leave the room.

In the bathroom, I gulp some water from the tap and then splash some on my face, avoiding my red eyes in the mirror. As I reach for a towel, my gaze catches on a yellow tube of lip balm on the counter next to the hand soap. It probably belongs to Mrs. McCrae, but Aubrey used to use the same kind.

A memory flashes through my mind. Aubrey and I, in this room, sitting side-by-side on the edge of the tub. Aubrey crying over Justin, wiping her tears with toilet paper because the Kleenex box is empty. Me with my arm around her, telling her she's worth the hassle. Her in the hallway with Ethan, assuring him that she didn't mean to yell. Both of us forgiving her instantly, knowing that even when she pushed us away, there was nothing either of us could do to make her stay mad at us forever.

I let go of the towel, my body growing cold despite the warm air pumping out of the vent by my feet. Maybe there *is* something I could do to make her that angry. Ethan was a willing participant these past few months, but it's me she'd blame for crossing the line.

Aubrey would hate me for this.

I pause at the threshold of the bathroom, shivering and unsure what to do next. I'd told Ethan I'd be right back. My body aches for his warmth, for a few extra hours of sleep, but instead of turning left toward Ethan's room, I veer right and head for Aubrey's instead.

The door is closed. I push it open slowly, praying the hinges don't squeak. They don't. I slink inside and flip the light switch, squinting as the brightness hits my eyes. Right away, I can see it's not Aubrey's room anymore. Almost everything of hers is gone—laptop, books, makeup, the miniature violin I'd given her for her thirteenth birthday that always sat on her bookshelf. All gone.

I cross the room to her closet and ease open the door. Her clothes are gone too, probably packed up and given to Goodwill. Some other petite size two could be wearing her favorite navy blue sweater right now.

The only thing left of her in here is the bed, still covered in the same light purple comforter she owned since I met her. I lie down on it, running my hand over the familiar velvety fabric and trying to pick up her scent. But that's gone too, faded away with time.

Despite how different the room looks, cleansed of any trace of her, I still feel like she's in here somewhere. Watching me. Judging me for what I've done. Lying here on her bed, I can feel her disgust for me. And I don't blame her. Somewhere along the way, I lost sight of why I came back here—to remember my best friend the way she deserved to be remembered. Instead I got caught up in this crazy romance with Ethan, thinking that if he still wanted me after what I'd done, then maybe it was okay for me to want him too.

But wanting Ethan won't help me. It just gives me one more thing to feel guilty about. Not only did I cause Aubrey to die . . . I had the nerve to fall in love with her little brother a year and a half later.

I had the nerve to feel happy.

"I'm sorry," I whisper to the quiet room. "I'm sorry."

It's just beginning to get light when I slip back into Ethan's room. He's sound asleep again, but now he's on his back, one hand resting on his chest and his head tilted slightly to the side. He looks different while sleeping, young and sweet and vulnerable, like the Ethan I knew before that day in June, when his life was altered forever. Because of me.

Bile rises in my throat. What am I doing here? What have I done?

As quietly as possible, I find my clothes and put them on, every so often checking to make sure I haven't disturbed Ethan. He doesn't even stir as I creep out of his room, and then out of his house. The snow has stopped, leaving behind a thick blanket of white. I walk home in the early morning cold, my head thumping like a heartbeat with each step.

twenty-six   **Sophomore Year**

"GOOD LUCK," MOM SAID WHEN SHE DROPPED ME off at school for my biology exam.

I grabbed my backpack and climbed out of the car. The June sun beat down on the top of my head, already hot at eight thirty. It was going to be a gorgeous day. I breathed in the fresh morning air and felt the headache I'd woken up with that morning begin to subside. "Thanks."

My bio exam, along with several others, was due to take place in the gym. I headed straight there and dropped off my backpack at the front of the room as was exam protocol. The gym was only about one-third full, so it didn't take me long to spot Aubrey.

She sat in the middle of the second row of desks, back straight and eyes trained on the front of the room. I could tell from her stiff posture that she'd spotted me too, but was pretending she hadn't. Looking away, I sat down on the opposite side of the room, my temples throbbing with fresh pain.

We hadn't spoken to each other in over a week, since the day I told her about Justin. I'd considered going up to her a million times, but every time I saw her, I remembered all the hurtful things she'd said to me and changed my mind. I'd already apologized—now it was her turn. Ethan had revealed to me that Aubrey really missed me, and she wanted to work things out but was too embarrassed to make the first move. She was mad at herself for misjudging Justin so completely and mad at me too, for not telling her what he'd done right after it happened.

One good thing to come out of all this—she seemed to be officially done with Justin. I never saw them together, and the way he avoided my eyes whenever we passed in the halls only strengthened my suspicions. Either he'd grown balls and confessed, or Aubrey had finally accepted that the boy she loved wasn't the person she'd thought.

Aubrey was one of the first to finish her exam. I watched as she rose from her seat and carried her booklet to the teacher at the front of the room. Mrs. Gimbal smiled at her like teachers always smile at smart, proficient students, and Aubrey went to dig out her backpack from the colorful pile by the door. Once she was gone, I tried to finish my essay on the various threats to ecosystems, but after a few minutes of crossing out sentences, I gave up and handed in my exam too. I'd done enough.

The first thing I saw when I emerged from the gym was Aubrey, standing by the trophy display case and talking to Ethan. They turned to look at me, two sets of dark brown eyes burning into mine. Ethan seemed uncomfortable, and a hint of sadness flickered across Aubrey's face before it went completely blank.

She turned back to her brother. "You coming?"

"No, I think I'll stick around here for a couple of hours. A few people are getting together in the cafeteria to study for the math exam."

"Okay. See you later, then." She started backing away slowly, as if giving me time to put some distance between us before she followed me.

As I passed them, I saw Ethan glance at me and then nudge Aubrey's arm. "Will you just go talk to her?" he said with an edge of impatience that told me it wasn't the first time he'd said those words.

I paused for a moment with my back to them, waiting to hear her response. But there was nothing but silence, so I kept on walking.

She caught up to me on Dwyer Street, just a few yards from the entrance to the school. When she called my name, I paused and turned around, shading my eyes against the glare of the sun. She was sprinting toward me, her lacy white skirt swishing around her legs and her hair billowing out behind her.

"Hey," she said, sounding more tired than mad. I felt my first glimmer of hope.

"Hi." We fell into step beside each other on the sidewalk. I was already sweating through my shirt from the heat. Or maybe it was nerves.

"Can I talk to you for a minute?"

I bit my lip and stared down at the ground, focusing on the sound our flip-flops made on the pavement. Aubrey's toenails, I noticed, were painted blue to match her top. "Okay."

Her fingers went to work plaiting her hair. "I wanted to tell you I'm sorry," she said. "What happened with Justin . . . I should've believed you right away. None of it was your fault. I know that now, and I'm sorry."

The knot that had taken over my stomach for the past few days began to loosen, and I let out a breath. "I'm sorry too. I should've told you right away instead of waiting around for Justin to do it. I was wrong."

A car zoomed past on the street beside us, music blaring out of its open windows. Aubrey glanced up at it, her stride slowing to match mine. We didn't speak for the next twenty-three steps. I counted.

"Justin's a douchebag."

Surprised, I looked over at her. She was gazing straight

ahead, her pretty face twisted in disgust. It wasn't directed at me, though. Not this time.

"Too bad it took me almost nine months to figure it out," she went on. "I wasted the entire school year on him. Lied to my parents for him. Gave him so many second chances, I lost count. And that's how he repays me? By going after my best friend?" She undid the braid and flicked her hair off her face. "I confronted him about it the day you told me. He tried to deny it at first, but I could tell he was lying. That made it even worse, you know? He didn't even have the decency to come clean. He's a liar *and* a douchebag."

We turned onto the paved walking path and slowed even more, grateful for the shade of the trees. When we passed the yard with the tree house, my thoughts spun back to that cold day in November: Justin and me, our legs dangling into the air, the entire neighborhood stretched out before us.

"Yeah, he's a douchebag," I said, tearing my gaze away from the decaying boards. "But I'm no better, Aubrey. I liked him, you know, more than I should have. He was your boyfriend, and instead of feeling happy for you, I was jealous."

She stopped walking and peered up at me. I slid my gaze to hers, expecting shock or anger or the same disgust she'd expressed toward Justin. But she just looked sad.

"I know that, Dara," she said, and started walking again. Numbly, I followed suit. "I could tell you liked him the very first day, when he came up to us in the cafeteria after you hit

Wyatt Greer with the tray. The way you looked at him . . . I'd never seen you act like that around a guy. I knew you were interested in him, but I let him flirt with me anyway."

"Why?"

She glanced at me. "Because I was interested in him too. For once I wanted someone to look at *me* like I was fun and interesting, like people look at you. Then I realized he liked me and the rest just sort of happened. I assumed you'd be okay with it—you were always telling me I needed to live a little. But that was just me being selfish." We stepped out of the shade and into the dazzling brightness of Fulham Road. "So I'm the one who's 'no better.' Not you."

I was silent for a moment, digesting this. All these months, she knew. She knew, and she never once gave me any clue or called me on it. It amazed me how much we'd held back from each other since Justin entered our lives.

"Then I guess we're both horrible people," I said, my voice almost cheerful. The glimmer of hope from before had turned into something brighter than the sun. "Either way, this year was mostly crap. I hate fighting with you."

"I hate it too." She shifted to the side, dodging an empty tomato sauce can that had escaped from someone's trash. It looked like the crows had visited, ripping through the shiny black bags for the treasures within. "Truce?"

Something loosened in my chest and I smiled. "Truce."

Behind us, the rhythmic sound of feet hitting pavement

echoed through the air. I glanced over my shoulder and saw a woman jogging a few yards away, her ponytail bouncing against her shoulders. The street was so quiet, I could hear strains of the music blasting from her headphones.

"I wouldn't say this year was *mostly* crap," Aubrey said, her step lighter now that the tension between us had dissipated. "I made first chair in orchestra, got my license, and lost my virginity. All in all, not a total loss."

"What about me?" I asked, looking over at her. "What have *I* accomplished this year?"

She pretended to seriously consider my question, but I saw a trace of laughter in her eyes. "Let's see. Hmm . . . you got even taller?"

"Wow. So impressive."

"And," she said with a giggle in her voice, "you managed not to break your neck while doing incredibly dangerous dares, like walking across monkey bars in your bare feet in the dark. Now *that's* talent."

Laughing, I nudged her shoulder with mine. She nudged me back, her tiny body barely making an impact. Realizing this, she used her hands instead, pushing against my upper arm. And like I'd done countless times before—with her and everyone else—I pushed her back.

I pushed her back.

The next few moments seemed to happen in slow motion. In other ways, they flashed by in a blink. One second, Aubrey and I were standing there together on the sidewalk, tussling like little kids, laughing and carefree. The next, her foot was tangled in the remnants of a ripped garbage bag and she was tumbling backward toward the street, eyes widening as she realized she was falling.

She was falling so fast and so unexpected that by the time it actually sunk in—this nightmare in front of me—it was too late. All I could do was watch. Watch her tiny body land in the direct path of a large gray pickup truck that seemed to appear out of nowhere. Watch the truck's right front wheel roll over her chest, pinning her underneath for a moment before continuing to the pavement on the other side of her.

I started screaming.

Everything after that happened in fragments, brief flashes of sound and color and awareness:

A woman dressed in running clothes, her ponytail brushing my neck as she held me close and murmured, "Don't look, honey. Don't look."

A man in a red baseball cap, kneeling with his back to me on the sidewalk, his body quaking with guttural moans that sounded almost primal. "I didn't see her. I didn't even see her," he repeated, over and over, his hands pressed to his head like he was trying to squeeze the images back out.

Aubrey's foot, bare and resting against the curb, and the random, nonsensical thought that popped into my head when I saw it. *What happened to her flip-flop?*

A voice, talking into a cell phone. *Please, please, come quick.*

Blood, so much blood, staining the asphalt, soaking into Aubrey's white skirt, spreading up toward the top half of her body, which I couldn't bear to see.

Sirens, loud and close.

Me, crumpled on the grass in someone's front yard, my eyes never straying from Aubrey no matter how hard people tried to get me to look away.

And then the sound of my screams, fading into heavy, shocked silence when I realized what I'd done.

twenty-seven · Senior Year

ON THE FIRST DAY BACK TO SCHOOL AFTER BREAK, I know before I even open the door that Ethan will be waiting for me at the front entrance. I also know what his face will look like—concerned with a hint of irritation simmering underneath.

I'm right on both counts.

"What the hell, Dara?" he says when I stop in front of him. "I've been trying to get ahold of you all weekend."

I start walking again, willing myself not to cry. He falls into step beside me, and I can feel the frustration radiating off him, a pot of boiling water about to spill over. I can't blame him. I walked out of his house Friday morning without so much as a note, and aside from one brief text letting him know I was alive, we haven't spoken since. I've been avoiding his texts and calls, even though it kills me to shut him out like this.

"I had a headache," I mumble, my eyes on my feet as I climb the stairs.

"For three days?" He reaches the top of the staircase first, then turns to face me. "For three days, you couldn't pick up your phone and answer a text? You had me going crazy, you know. I almost went over to your house, but I thought maybe you got in trouble with your parents and they grounded you or something."

I pause on the second stair from the top, my knuckles white on the railing. It would be so easy to use that as an excuse, to tell him my parents grounded me and took away my phone, but they hadn't. I'd done everything possible to make it seem like I rang in the New Year alone—answered every check-in text they sent, forwarded the landline to my cell in case they called the house, kept the lights on for the nosy neighbors. My parents are blissfully unaware of what happened that night.

I kind of wish I was too.

People stream around us like water channeling around rocks, and I finally look up at Ethan. The desperation in his face makes my heart squeeze. I'm hurting him, and I don't know how to stop. It's like pain surrounds me, infecting everyone who loves me. Everyone I dare to love. My body may seem whole, with intact ribs and a beating heart and breath in my lungs, but I'm just as broken as Aubrey was, lying dead in the road.

"Talk to me, Dara." Ethan moves down a step and places his hand over mine, still wrapped tight around the railing. "Tell me the truth. I think you owe me that much."

He's wrong. I owe him everything. My honesty is just a drop in the bucket of all the things I owe him, all the things I'll never be able to pay back.

"New Year's Eve was the best night of my life," he says, low enough for only me to hear. "Then I woke up and you were gone. You just *left*. No warning, no explanation. Nothing. How am I supposed to take that?"

I slide my hand out from under his and step around him. "I can't do this right now."

"We *have* to do this right now," Ethan says, catching up with me again. "Or I'm going to spend the rest of the day torturing myself over it, and I've already done enough of that over the weekend."

We reach my locker and I bend my head over the combination lock, letting my hair spill forward. "What do you want from me, Ethan?" My voice sounds steady behind my curtain of hair, but my fingers tremble on the lock, betraying me. I will them to keep still, like the rest of me.

"I want you to tell me we're still good. That's it. That's all I need to hear and then I'll leave you alone."

My lock finally pops open, but I don't move my fingers

from it. Because if I do, I'll probably end up touching him. I'll touch him and kiss him and assure him we're still good. That we'll always be good. And I can't. After being in Aubrey's room, after lying on her purple comforter and trying to soak in what was left of her, I find it hard to believe that anything good can come out of something so unspeakably horrible.

"You probably would've been better off hating me," I say.

"What?"

I flick my hair off my face and look at him. "When I came back here. You were probably better off hating me instead of—" My voice breaks and I take a deep breath, steadying myself.

"What? Loving you?" Ethan says. When I don't answer, he stares at me for a moment and then shakes his head. "Right. I think I get it now. You want me to make your life hell as some sort of payback for an accident that happened a year and a half ago. You think people should hate you, and any other possibility freaks you out. Because if people don't hate you, then you might actually have to face the possibility that it wasn't your fault and you aren't a terrible person."

The truth in his words makes my face burn and I bend over my lock again, sliding it from its latch with a shaking hand. When I pull open my locker, a folded sheet of paper falls out and flutters to the floor. My breath hitches in my chest. Already? School has barely been open ten minutes. How is it possible that someone dropped this off so quickly?

Unless it's been there since before Christmas break. I didn't visit my locker at the end of that last day, I remember. I felt sick after lunch, so I went home early. Whoever left this for me probably did it to cast a little pall over my two-week vacation from school. Or to remind me that even when I'm not here, they still have the power to ruin my day.

I make a grab for the paper, but Ethan gets to it before me and opens it up, his eyes scanning whatever waits inside. And it's clearly nothing good, because his body tenses and his eyes go flat and the anger arrives the same way it always does, like a switch going off in his brain, soaking everything in darkness.

"Ethan. Give that to me."

He's not listening. His hurt over me is colliding with his rage over this and the result is downright scary. I reach out to take the paper from him, desperate to remove it from his sight, but he evades me and walks away. His stride is quick and purposeful, like he knows exactly where he's headed and what he's going to do when he gets there. Several other people in the hallway watch him too, apprehension on some faces and drama-hungry excitement on others.

I hurry after him, catching up just as he rounds the corner to another bank of lockers. Travis Rausch stands at one of them, a pen lodged between his teeth as he sifts through some books on the top shelf. I open my mouth to say something, snap Ethan out of it before he does something he'll probably regret, but he's on Travis before I even get the chance.

"You think this is funny?" he snarls, shoving the paper into Travis's chest hard enough to send him reeling back against the locker door. His jaw drops in surprise and the pen tumbles to the floor.

"What—" Travis straightens up and locks eyes with Ethan. "What the fuck is your problem, McCrae?"

Moving closer, I put my hand on Ethan's arm. It's like touching marble. He ignores me and keeps his eyes on Travis, pinning him in place with his glare. I step back out of the way as he pushes the paper into Travis's chest again. This time, Travis is prepared and braces himself.

"Did you put this in her locker?"

The bell rings, punctuating Ethan's question. Travis's gaze shifts to me, then behind me to the hallway, where a small crowd has gathered. No one moves to go to class. All eyes are riveted on Ethan's rage-filled face and on Travis, as he takes the paper and looks at it. His face reddens.

"Dude," he says, shoving it back at Ethan. "Aubrey was my *friend*. Why the hell would I draw something like that?"

Ethan's fists tightens on the note, crumpling it. "Who did it then, if it wasn't you?"

"I don't know. Anyone could've put that in Dara's locker. She's not exactly well liked around here."

"Yeah, you made sure of that, didn't you."

"No idea what you're talking about, man."

Ethan takes a step closer to him, muscles coiled. "I know it was you who started those bullshit rumors. They all trace back to you. What kind of sick asshole does something like that? Dara was your friend too, remember?"

Travis's expression turns stormy and he leans in closer until his face is inches from Ethan's. "*I'm* sick? You're the one who has a fucking hard-on for the girl who killed your sister."

Ethan's hand shoots out, connecting with Travis's face. The sound of bones crunching echoes through the hallway. Somewhere behind me, a girl shrieks.

It feels like forever, but it's probably only a minute or so later when two teachers arrive to break it up. One of them is Mr. Haggerty, my chemistry teacher. He gets ahold of Travis and pulls him away while the other teacher grabs Ethan.

"Both of you," Haggarty wheezes, his fingers wrapped around Travis's bicep. "To the office. Now."

Travis jerks out of his grasp and spits on the floor. With his bloodied nose and fat lip, he definitely got the worst of it. Ethan's face is untouched, but his right hand is scraped and bleeding and already starting to swell. I want to go to him, wrap my arms around him and make sure he's okay, but I can't make myself move. So I stay where I am, frozen by the lockers and trying to ignore the drops of blood everywhere, while he and Travis are ushered down the hall toward the office.

Once they're gone, the small crowd disperses. I'm about to leave too when I remember the piece of paper. It's still on the floor near Travis's locker, half ripped and trampled. I snatch it up and smooth out the wrinkles until the images come into focus. It's another stick figure me, but this time I'm wearing a Santa hat and standing—no, *dancing*—in front of a headstone. Aubrey's headstone, which I've never actually seen in person. That same wide smile is on my face, like I'm delighted to be there, doing what I'm doing.

Beneath the sketch are some letters, big and bold and printed in red:

HAPPY HOLIDAYS, MURDERER!

My fingers stiffen on the paper. For a moment, I consider folding it up so I can place it in the green notebook with the obituary note, but then I notice a tiny spot of red on the upper-left corner. At first I think it's marker, but when I run my fingertip over it, the spot smears. It's blood.

Without even hesitating, I rip the paper into a dozen pieces and toss the scraps in the nearest trash can.

I spend the rest of the day and most of the night trying to contact Ethan, but he doesn't answer any of my texts or calls. Payback, I guess, for doing the same to him all weekend.

It's not until the next morning that I find out what happened to him after the fight. Before class, I search the halls for Noelle or Hunter and find them both at Noelle's locker.

"I talked to him last night," Hunter tells me before I can ask. "Three-day suspension. And he's in major shit with his parents."

I squeeze my eyes shut, not wanting them to see how red and watery they are. Noelle notices anyway and lays a hand on my arm.

"Everything will be okay," she says, even though she has no idea what happened between Ethan and me or why he got into the fight in the first place. She's just one of those people who believe things eventually work out. I used to be.

First period is a wasted effort. I can't stop worrying about Ethan. Seeing that fight yesterday jump-started a new level of protectiveness in me, something much deeper than the little-sibling kind I used to feel for him. I know I won't be able to rest until I make sure he's all right.

On Tuesdays I have a free period right before lunch. Students are supposed to use their frees to study in the library, but seniors can leave school grounds if they sign out in the office first. So I scrawl my name on the sign-out sheet and make the short trek through the biting cold to Ethan's house.

As I expected, neither of his parents' cars is in the driveway. Ethan's Saturn is there though, its windshield crusted with ice. I walk past it to the door, then hesitate before jabbing the doorbell with my numb finger.

He doesn't answer. I wait another minute before ringing the bell again, accompanying it with a knock for good measure. Another minute passes. Just as I'm about to turn into a human icicle, the door swings open and there he is, wearing a T-shirt and shorts and rubbing his eye like he's just woken up.

"What are you doing here?" he asks, his voice thick and scratchy with sleep. So I *did* wake him up. "Shouldn't you be in school?"

"I'm on my free." I cross my arms over my chest and bounce on my toes a few times. "Can I come in? It's freezing."

"Oh," he says, snapping out of his sleepy daze. "Yeah. Sorry."

He opens the door wider and steps aside so I can enter. As I do, I notice the bruising and swelling on his hand. I think about yesterday, how it sounded when he punched Travis, that sickening *crack* of knuckles meeting bone. It's all I've been hearing, and seeing, since it happened.

A burst of anger charges through me, hot and sharp and completely unexpected.

"What were you *thinking?*"

He blinks at my tone. "What?"

Frustrated, I push past him to the living room and sink down on the couch, my coat still zippered to my chin even though it's really warm in here. I can't stop shivering. Ethan follows and sits next to me, keeping plenty of space between us.

"I was *thinking*," he says brusquely, "that ever since you told me Travis was probably the one who spread all those lies about you, I could hardly wait to get my hands on him. I was *thinking* how freaking good it would feel to punch him in the face. It did, by the way. Feel good."

I glance at his battered hand again and wonder when, exactly, he became so consumed with hostility. What was his tipping point? Aubrey's funeral, when he could no longer deny that she was never coming back? The aftermath, feeling the pressure of everyone's stares and hearing the same empty words of comfort over and over? Or did it start the day she died, when he was faced with the kind of news that changes a person forever, destroying something inside them that can never be restored?

"You shouldn't have hit him," I say, my rage fizzling.

"Well, he deserved it. I did some digging over the weekend and talked to a few people. The rumors lead right back to Travis, like I said."

Sighing, I unzip my coat and shrug it off. "But it doesn't matter. The notes, Travis, the things people say about me . . . none of it matters. I told you why I came back here, remember?"

"Right," he mutters. "Because you felt guilty for not thinking about Aubrey every second of the day and you wanted to punish yourself for it."

I clench my teeth and look away. I don't like way he says it, like it's the dumbest reason he's ever heard for anything. Like I'm crazy for believing I'm not worthy of peace.

"Is that what this is, then?"

My eyes swing back toward him. "What?"

"This. Us." He rakes his good hand through his disheveled hair, making it even messier. "Is that why we're together? Because it hurts you to be with me? Am I just another way for you to punish yourself?"

Coldness spreads through my stomach and into my veins. Until he said it, the notion never once crossed my mind. It did hurt to be around him, at first, but as time wore on, he became separate from Aubrey, in a way. Disconnected from the boy I knew when she was still alive. He became just Ethan, the boy who helps dull the edges of my grief. No one understands the void of living without Aubrey better than he does.

"No," I say, holding my hands stiffly in my lap. I'm back to being a statue again, rigid and still. "If anything, you're the opposite. Being with you makes me happy, and in some ways that's even harder—"

"Because you think you don't deserve to feel happy," he finishes for me. He shakes his head. "Either way, I can't win, can I?"

Frustration simmers in my chest again. Unlike him, my anger comes on slowly, gradually, building and rising instead of exploding in a blaze. "You know what? I'm sorry my head is so screwed up. I'm sorry I'm so conflicted about my relationship with you. But God, Ethan . . . did you ever stop and think about how *she'd* feel about all this?"

"Who? Aubrey?"

"*Yes.* Do you ever wonder what she'd think about us if she were here?"

His eyes stray to the wall directly across from us, which is lined with framed pictures. The portrait in the middle, the biggest one, shows a much younger Ethan and Aubrey, posing together with their violins. I forget sometimes how alike they were.

"She'd hate it," I go on when he doesn't reply. "She'd want me to look out for you, not . . ." *Kiss you. Fall in love with you. Lose my virginity to you.*

"I don't *need* you to look out for me. I can take care of myself now. You're not my replacement big sister, okay? You're not—" He suddenly winces and looks down at his hand. Without realizing it, he'd balled it into a fist, aggravating the swollen tissue there. "Anyway," he adds, gritting his teeth through the pain, "it doesn't matter if she'd hate it, because she's not here. She can't hate anymore. She can't think anymore. She can't do *anything* anymore. She's dead, and I'm getting sick of you using your guilt over it as an excuse to drive us apart."

Each word is a brick, dropping from a great height and slamming into me, one by one. If I ever had any doubts about the resentment he holds for me, deep down inside, they're all gone now.

I stand up on shaky legs and turn to face him. "I don't get

it, Ethan. How can you even want me? Has this all been some kind of experiment for you or something? Your way of seeing if it's even possible to forgive me?"

He stands up too, his face drawn in confusion. "What? No. Dara—"

I grab my coat from the couch and walk out of the living room, stopping him from talking. Stopping him from reaching for me and putting his arms around me and making everything okay. Because despite what Noelle believes, things don't always work out in the end.

twenty-eight

Senior Year

LATE SATURDAY MORNING, MY MOTHER WAKES ME up with a firm knock on my bedroom door. "Brock has the stomach flu," she says.

I roll over and look at her, my brain scrambled with sleep. "What?" I croak.

"Brock," she repeats, and I dimly notice that she's wearing dress pants and a blouse. "Tobias's friend from down the street? Tobias was supposed to spend the afternoon at his house, but his mother just called and said Brock woke up with a stomach bug."

I don't know why she's telling me this. "Are you going to work?"

"Yes, Dara. I mentioned yesterday at dinner that I needed

to go to work for a few hours today, remember?"

I don't, but this shouldn't come as a surprise to either of us. For the past few days, I've done nothing besides go to school and sit alone in my room. And whenever Mom makes me emerge from my cave to do necessary things like eat, I do them as quickly and quietly as possible before escaping to my room again. I know it worries her, this sudden backsliding into my old reclusive ways.

"I can't get out of it," Mom goes on, glancing at her watch, "so you're going to have to look after Tobias today."

I freeze under my blankets. Look after Tobias. Just him and me. I used to babysit him all the time before Aubrey died, back when our relationship was easy and affectionate and fun. Since then, I haven't been alone with my brother for longer than a few minutes. My parents never ask me to babysit, and I never offer. The thought of being fully responsible for him makes my palms clammy.

"Where's Dad?" I ask, trying not to sound as panicked as I feel.

"He's got that big job today." Mom gives me an exasperated look. Clearly, Dad's big job was discussed during dinner last night too. I vaguely remember something about heavy snow causing some sort of roof collapse, but I'm fuzzy on the details. "You're okay with it, right?" she says, unsure. "Taking care of your brother for the afternoon?"

"I guess," I tell her, because what else can I say? *I'm the* reason my parents work so much. The least I can do is make it easier for them.

After Mom leaves, I wander out to the kitchen. Tobias is at the table, squirting glue onto cotton balls and then sticking them into an open shoebox.

"What are you doing?" I ask as I open the fridge and take out a carton of orange juice. My voice sounds falsely bright, even to my own ears.

"Making a diorama." He uses his finger to remove some excess glue from the edge of the shoebox. "I have to do an animal habitat for science. I picked a polar bear."

"Oh." This explains the mass of snowy-white cotton balls. "Do you need any help?"

"No."

Something twinges in my chest and I have to force myself to swallow the juice in my mouth. Tobias doesn't even answer when I tell him to stay put for a few minutes while I go take a shower.

We don't speak again until lunchtime, and only because we have to figure out what we want to eat. Tobias decides on grilled cheese and I make one for each of us, piling on the cheese the way I know he likes. We eat at the table amid the diorama mess and awkwardly try to make conversation. I ask him about school, and then he asks me something that almost makes me spit out my sandwich.

"Are you better now?"

I clear my throat and wipe my buttery fingers on a napkin. "What?"

"Mom and Dad keep saying you'll be better soon." He picks up a pair of scissors and starts cutting out a kidney-shaped body of water he's drawn on a sheet of blue construction paper. "Are you better yet?"

I watch him cut for a moment, trying to figure out what I can possibly say to him. "Not yet, Tobes, but hopefully soon."

He glances up at me, surprised, and two things hit me at once. One, I called him by his nickname for the first time in ages. And two, his eyes are on me and not on his hands, where they should be when he's using a pair of sharp kitchen shears instead of the safety scissors he's supposed to be using.

Like everything else horrible, it happens in slow motion, yet quick as a blink. The scissors slip and collide with the index finger of his left hand. Blood immediately spurts out, rolling down his hand, dripping on the table, spattering the cotton balls and construction paper and the leftover crusts of his sandwich.

Tobias drops the scissors and screams.

My throat aches to do the same, scream and scream until someone comes, someone who can deal with this. Someone who can act quickly and confidently instead of sitting here like a statue, too stunned to even move. But no one is coming, and all my brother has right now is me.

"Tobias," I say, but my voice is too weak to carry over his panicked crying. So I say it again, louder, and the force behind it propels me out of my chair and over to his. As I get closer, I can see the skin on his finger, gaping wide like a mouth. The copper tang of blood hits my nostrils and I hold my breath, willing myself not to faint.

"I want Mom," Tobias wails, staring wide-eyed at his sliced finger.

Instinctively, I grab a clean dishtowel from the drawer beside the sink and fold it into a thick rectangle, then wrap it around his finger. He flinches, which makes me flinch, but I keep going, pressing the cloth snugly against the cut.

"Hold that there so I can call Mom," I tell him, snatching my cell off the table. "And keep your hand up high, okay? It'll help with the bleeding."

Mom doesn't pick up, and my call goes to voice mail after a few rings. I hang up and try Dad, but his voice mail kicks in after only one ring, which probably means he's precariously balanced on a high roof somewhere, unable to take calls. I try Mom again, anxious sweat gathering along my hairline as I wait. When she doesn't answer the second time, or the third, I take a deep breath, try to ignore my rising panic, and force myself to think.

Tobias needs stitches. That much I'm sure of. Stitches require a doctor, and seeing a doctor requires a trip to the hospital. But how do we get there? It's too far to walk, and I don't have any cash for a taxi. A cut finger isn't serious enough for an ambulance, even with all this blood. The bus takes too long, and even if I did have my license, I don't have access to a car.

The only option left is asking someone to drive us.

"Dara?"

Ethan's voice sets off a blast of conflicting emotions inside me—relief and confusion laced with sharp pangs of longing. We haven't seen or spoken to each other since I walked out of his house four days ago, interrupting a conversation that begged to be finished. And unlike the first time I walked out on him, on New Year's Day, he hasn't attempted to reach out to me even once. I know he's probably just giving me time to think and figure things out on my own, but his absence still hurts. Missing him is an ache that never subsides, not even now, when my mind is overwhelmed with urgency.

Finding my voice, I tell him about the scissors and Tobias's finger and my inability to get ahold of my parents. He's silent through it all, listening and evaluating.

"What do you need?" he asks when I'm through.

I glance at Tobias. He's still sitting at the table, his wounded hand exactly where I told him to position it, raised above his heart. His scared blue eyes are fastened on me, waiting for me to make this okay. "A drive to the ER," I tell him. "I'm sorry, but you were the first person I thought of."

A long pause follows, and if I weren't so desperate I'd

probably feel like a total idiot. But there's no time right now for awkwardness and leftover tension. Not when my little brother's blood is quickly soaking through his dishtowel.

"Well," Ethan says finally. "I'm grounded, so I'm not supposed to be going anywhere in my car . . ." There's another pause, but this one is much shorter. "Fuck it. I'll be right there."

I spend the entire ride to the hospital watching Tobias, monitoring his color, making sure he's not going to puke or pass out. My mind is so focused on him, I don't even have a chance to dwell on the strange, edgy vibe between Ethan and me. I'll do it later, when my head is clearer and my senses aren't overwhelmed with blood.

"Thanks," I say when Ethan stops in front of the emergency entrance. I push open the back door. "Let's go, Tobias."

Ethan twists around to look at me. "Are you gonna be okay?" he asks, like I'm the one with the gaping flesh wound.

I nod quickly and get out, then reach inside the car to help my brother. His dishtowel is soaked through again, the blue and yellow stripes obscured with bright red. I wonder how much blood an average-sized nine-year-old boy can lose before he collapses. I don't want to find out.

The second we enter the busy ER waiting room, I forget about Ethan and focus on the tasks at hand. First, I get Tobias registered, using the insurance card I keep in a safe section of my wallet. After he's been triaged and we're back in the waiting room, I pull out my phone again. No messages from either of my parents, so I send Mom a text, explaining what happened.

As I'm typing, I dimly notice someone sitting down in the chair next to me. The place is packed, so I assume it's another patient until I catch Ethan's familiar woodsy scent.

"I thought you left," I say, surprised.

He shrugs carelessly, but his shoulders are tense. "Figured I'd keep you company while you wait."

Looking at him, it occurs to me that he probably hasn't been in this hospital since Aubrey died. The ambulance brought her here, even though it was too late, and one of the doctors had to break the news to him and his parents. Being here can't be easy for him.

On my other side, Tobias shifts in his chair and whimpers. The triage nurse redressed his cut with tape and gauze, but even that's not keeping the blood from seeping through. "It hurts," he whispers, his eyes glassy with tears.

"It'll feel better soon," I assure him, even though I have no idea if it will or not. "Remember the time you fell off your bike and scraped up your knees? It only hurt for a little while, right?"

He nods, bottom lip wobbling. "Mom cleaned the scrapes and put stuff on that made them sting."

"But then you felt better, and you were back on your bike a few minutes later. It hurts now, but keep reminding yourself it won't last forever."

He nods again, but I'm not sure he's all the way convinced. My words seemed to have calmed him, though, and he sucks in a breath, steeling himself against the pain.

I look over at Ethan, meeting his eyes for the first time since he sat down. "I'm sure my parents will be here soon," I tell him. "You don't have to stay. I got this."

He holds my gaze. "I know you do."

Tobias's name is called, making me jump. I say good-bye to Ethan and lead my brother over to the waiting nurse, who leads us to an emergency room bed. Tobias settles on the crisp white sheet while I sit next to him in a chair.

"What are they gonna do?" he asks, going pale again.

Before I can answer, a doctor in blue scrubs slips between the privacy curtains. He's absolutely huge, with bushy hair and hands the size of dinner plates. He introduces himself as Dr. Thayer and shakes Tobias's hand. Tobias gapes at him, entranced, while I wonder how a man with fingers the size of sausages is going to put intricate stitches in my brother's skin.

"It's a clean cut," Dr. Thayer says as he examines the wound. "A few stitches and you'll be good as new."

Tobias glances at me, terrified. "Can my sister stay with me?"

"Of course she can." He smiles at me. "Be right back."

Once he's gone, I climb up on the bed beside my brother. "You can squeeze my hand," I say, offering it to him. He takes it, folding his grubby little fingers around mine, and all the distance and wariness that's built up between us over the past few months melts away. I didn't realize how much I miss this, being his big sister. Having him rely on me for comfort instead of circling me cautiously, like he's been doing for so long.

Tobias handles the stitches better than anticipated. For most of it, he's the one comforting *me* as I cringe with each stab to his skin. But Dr. Giant does a good job, and we leave with an even bigger bandage, along with instructions on how to keep it dry and clean. And Tobias is smiling, suddenly thrilled with the whole ordeal.

Back in the waiting room, I'm surprised to see that Ethan still hasn't left. I'm so focused on him, I almost fail to notice my mother.

"Mom!" Tobias lets go of my hand and runs over to where she's standing, in front of the reception desk. "Mom, I cut my finger with the scissors and Dara took me to get it sewn back together. Look. I got three stitches."

He holds up his dressed hand, but Mom's too busy hugging him to give it more than a cursory glance. "Are you okay?" she asks, straightening up and patting his shirt, which is stiff with drying blood. I understand her alarm. He looks like he's been shot.

"It doesn't hurt much anymore," Tobias reassures her.

Mom looks at me, standing next to Ethan and watching them. "My phone died," she says, sounding close to tears. "I didn't get your messages until I plugged it into my charger. I just got here two minutes ago. Ethan told me what happened."

All three of us over look at him, and he stuffs his hands into his pockets, embarrassed. "I should get home," he says, his eyes skimming mine as he backs away.

"Ethan, wait." I follow him and we stop a few feet from the main doors. "Thanks again for everything. I'm sorry if I got you in more trouble with your parents."

He shrugs lightly and gives me a small, quick smile. "You're worth it," he says, and turns and walks away before I have a chance to respond.

As he's leaving, he almost collides with my father, who's on his way in. Dad eyes him warily as they pass each other, and Ethan nods at him once before picking up his pace. I can't blame him. Dad looks extra intimidating, his face red from the cold and his clothes filthy from working. He spots us right away and strides over, his boots leaving wet prints on the floor.

"What the hell happened?" he demands.

It takes me a few seconds to realize he's directing this question to me. I look up at him, my mind suddenly blank.

"He cut his finger and needed a few stitches, Neil," Mom says as Dad's gaze sweeps over Tobias, pausing on each splotch of blood. "Not a big deal."

"Dara saved me, Dad," Tobias says, waving his mummified hand. "Can we go home now? I wanna ride in the truck with you."

Without a word, Dad lays a hand on Tobias's head and points him toward the exit. The four of us separate in the parking lot, my father and brother to the truck, my mother and me to the car. As soon we're settled in our seats, Mom places her finger under my chin and tilts my face toward hers.

"Your brother is fine, Dara. You did everything right. Okay? No one is mad at you."

I think of my father, glaring at me like I purposely sliced my brother's skin myself, and something in me snaps. "Yeah, right. Dad's mad at me. He's been mad at me since I came back from Aunt Lydia's. I know he didn't want me to come home, but how long is he going to hate me for it?"

Mom pulls back a little, color rising in her cheeks. "Dara," she says firmly. "Your father does not hate you. How can you even think that?"

"I heard you guys, months ago. Fighting in the kitchen. I heard Dad say I should've stayed there, graduated at Somerset Prep. He didn't want me to come back."

Her mouth twitches and she fusses with her scarf, adjusting it against the front of her coat. "Yes, he said that," she admits. "But of course he wanted you to come home. He just didn't think you were ready. He thought staying away would be best for you."

I shake my head, unconvinced. She can't deny what I heard with my own ears.

"Listen," Mom says, leaning toward me again. "You have to understand something about your father. He's a fixer. He fixes things for a living, but he can't fix you. He can't make everything better for you, Dara, and that eats him up inside. He loves you and your brother more than anything in the world, and watching you suffer makes him feel frustrated and helpless." She smooths my hair, tucking it behind my ear. "Try cutting him some slack, okay? He was just scared for Tobias. He knows it wasn't your fault, and you shouldn't blame your-self either."

She's not going to let it go until I agree with her, so I force myself to nod. Still, I can't help beating myself up just a little. "I shouldn't have let him use those scissors."

"True." She faces forward and starts the car. "But it still could've happened to anyone. It could've happened to me or his teacher or even your father. Remember when Tobias was a baby and he fell off the couch while I was changing him? I took my eyes off him for *one second* to get the diaper cream, and the next thing I knew he was on the floor, screaming. I thought I gave him brain damage or something. It took me months to forgive myself."

I do remember. He ended up in the ER for that one too.

"Mistakes happen," she continues, turning back to me. "We can hate ourselves for them all we want, but it doesn't help anything. It just ends up hurting us too."

My anger dissolves as fast as it arrived and all of a sudden I'm crying. Mom gathers me into her arms and holds me tight as big, gasping sobs shudder through my body. I'm not sure if I'm crying because of her words or because of my father or because the stress of the day chose this exact moment to catch up with me. Maybe it's none of those things. Maybe it's everything at once. All I know is, it feels good to finally let go.

twenty-nine   Senior Year

TOBIAS BURSTS INTO MY ROOM LATE SUNDAY
morning while I'm still in bed to show me his finger in between
dressing changes. He seems fascinated by its gruesomeness.

"You were really brave, Tobes," I tell him, remembering
how still he sat in the hospital, his eyes staring resolutely ahead
while his fingers stayed locked around mine.

"So were you," he says, flashing his big-toothed grin. He
hasn't smiled at me like that in so long, the sight of it now
makes me want to hug him. Before I can even think about it,
that's exactly what I'm doing. I breathe in his little boy smell
of sweat, kid shampoo, and peanut butter, and something in
me unravels.

"Ahhh," he yelps, wriggling free. "You're crushing my bones."

"You mean these bones?" I tickle his ribs and he runs for the door, giggling.

After Tobias leaves, I take a long, hot shower. By the time I'm dressed, my stomach is growling and there are strange noises coming from downstairs. Banging sounds, like metal clanging against metal.

I shuffle downstairs to the kitchen and almost trip over my father, who's stretched out on his stomach on the floor in front of the dishwasher with a flashlight in his hand. Various tools are scattered on the tile around him.

"What are you doing?" I ask, grabbing a bagel and popping it in the toaster.

"Dishwasher's leaking." He sticks his hands into the opening at the bottom and moves some tubes around. "Looks like the drain hoses are cracked."

"Where are Mom and Tobias?"

He lifts himself into a kneeling position and wipes his hands on his jeans. "Grocery shopping. Your brother wants homemade pizzas for dinner tonight, and he insisted on being in charge of picking out all the toppings."

My bagel pops, and I'm glad for the excuse to turn away. It's the most my father's said to me in weeks and I'm not sure how to react.

"I have to go to Home Depot for new hoses." He gathers

up the tools, his back to me. "Feel like tagging along?"

I concentrate on buttering my breakfast, feeling torn. Clearly, Mom told him what I said in the car yesterday, about him hating me for coming home, and now he's trying to prove me wrong. But then I think about what she told me about him, that he's a fixer who can repair everything except people, and how helpless it makes him feel to watch me suffer. Seeing me broken probably eats at him the same way guilt eats at me, and there's no quick cure for either of us. All we can do is avoid being devoured completely.

"Yeah," I reply, finishing the rest of my bagel. "I do. Just give me a few minutes to get dressed."

Home Depot is a madhouse, but for once in his life, Dad doesn't linger in the aisles, drooling over expensive tools he'll never have any use for. He finds the hoses he needs and pays for them, and we're back at the truck in under ten minutes.

We barely speak on the way home, unless it's to comment on something trivial, like the weather. As we pull into our driveway, I wonder if this is how it'll always be for us now— long silences interspersed with safe conversation. But then my father shuts off the truck and lets out a long, weary sigh, and I brace myself for something bad.

"I didn't mean to snap at you yesterday," he says gruffly. "At the hospital. I was worried, and sometimes when I'm worried it comes across like I'm mad, even when I'm not. And I wasn't. You did a good job yesterday, taking care of your brother like you did. I . . . I'm proud of you. And I'm glad you're here with us, at home. It's where you belong."

He says all this to the side window, face hidden from my view. Slowly, I reach out and touch his hand, which is rough and twice the size of mine. Still facing away, he grasps my fingers and squeezes hard, like he used to when I was little and we went somewhere crowded. Whenever I complained about him holding my hand too tight, he'd say, *Sorry, baby girl, just trying not to lose you.* Hearing it always made me want to stick close.

"Thanks," I say, blinking back tears. Crying would just make us both uncomfortable.

Dad clears his throat and lets go of my hand, reaching in back for the Home Depot bag. We climb out of the truck and walk up to the house together.

"So," he says as he unlocks the door. "You and Ethan. What's going on there?"

My face gets hot. "What do you mean?"

"I'm not going to have to take him down to the basement to show him my rifle collection, am I?"

We step inside the warm house, and I concentrate on my jacket zipper. "No, Dad. We're not— It's not like that with us."

"No?" He raises his eyebrows. "That's not the impression your mother and I got. Seems like you two spend a lot of time together."

I take my jacket off and hang it up. "We do. Well, we did. I'm just not sure it can work."

"And why's that?"

I sigh. My father and I never talk about things like this. But he's clearly trying to connect with me, so I explain. "Because of Aubrey. Because it's too hard. Because his parents hate me. Pick one."

He looks at me for a long moment and then shakes his head. "That's doesn't sound like the Dara I know."

I'm not sure how to respond, so I shrug and head for the kitchen.

"The Dara *I* know," he goes on, following me, "doesn't back down from challenges. She tries things, even when they seem impossible. She tries things just *because* they seem impossible."

I sidestep the dishwasher mess and get a glass from the cupboard, keeping my back to him so he won't see the tears in my eyes. He's describing the old me, the girl who died on that warm June morning. The girl I'm not sure I can ever get back.

"She's one of the bravest people I know."

My fingers tremble on the glass. I set it on the counter, empty, and turn to face my dad. "Was," I say. "Past tense."

"No." He opens the Home Depot bag and takes out the hoses he bought. "Pretty sure I used present tense. Want to help me install these?"

"Dad," I say, ignoring his question. "Remember what happened when you drove down Fulham Road? I still haven't gone back there, or to the graveyard either. I can't even bring myself to look at her headstone." I let out a breath. "I'm not brave."

"I disagree." He crouches next to the dishwasher and starts digging around in his toolbox. "You came home. You went back to school. You faced Ethan and the rest of your friends. You stepped up to take care of your brother yesterday even though you were probably terrified. You think a coward could do all that?"

My brain scrambles for another argument but comes up empty. Maybe because there isn't one. Maybe the old me isn't as dead as I thought.

I kneel next to my father and pick up a wrench, turning it over in my hands. "Okay, so I'm not a coward," I say, humoring him. "In that case, it should be easy for me to go talk to Ethan, right?"

"Easy? No. But definitely possible." He looks at me, a ghost of a smile on his face. "Your mom says he grew up nice. He's always been a good kid."

I get what he's trying to tell me—he and Mom don't mind anymore if I want to be friends with Ethan. More than friends, even. He drove Tobias and me to the hospital and stuck around the entire time, so obviously, his intentions toward me are good. He cares about me, and that's good enough for them.

Can it be enough for me too? I think about what he said in the shed that day, weeks ago, after our second kiss: *I'm done with hiding.* I thought I was done hiding too, until it turned out

I wasn't. Not entirely. When I returned to Hyde Creek last August, I thought I was prepared for what was to come. And I was, for the most part. I knew it wouldn't be easy. I knew things would never be like they were.

But I hadn't been prepared for Ethan. After everything I've taken from him, after all the pain I've caused, he still believes I'm someone worth loving.

Maybe I can be that girl again. The one Ethan still sees. The one my father believes still exists inside me. Someone who's brave and worth loving. Someone who's finally ready to be done with hiding too.

After I help my dad install the new hoses, I bundle myself against the cold and walk over to Hunter's house. With any luck, the band will still be practicing.

They are. As I approach, I can feel the thrum of the bass under my feet. It's familiar now, like a welcome. I wait for a break between songs and pound on the door instead of walking right in, because I haven't been here in a while and it seems less presumptuous to knock first.

Kel answers the door, guitar still strapped to his chest. "Hey, Dara," he says casually, as if I'm just returning from a bathroom break. He motions me inside, and I gratefully step into the warmth. Everyone's here today, band and girlfriends, but as usual, my attention goes directly to Ethan.

He's wearing the same T-shirt he had on the first day I

saw him at school back in September, the Iron Maiden one. I remember how surprised I was to see him in it then. Now I'd be surprised to see him in anything else. I've grown accustomed to the changes in him.

"Hey," he says, surprised.

"Hi," I say back, sitting on the couch next to Noelle, who gives me a quick sideways hug in welcome. On her other side, Julia glances up from her phone and flashes me a smile before dropping her gaze to her phone again. No one acts like it's a big deal, my being here. That's what I like about this place— even I can blend in. Because here, it's all about the music.

"Okay, one more and then we gotta quit for the day," Hunter says from behind the drums. "I have a huge physics test tomorrow I haven't even fucking studied for yet."

Everyone agrees, and they launch into an original, one I've heard many times and often find stuck in my head. As usual, I watch Ethan as he plays. Today he seems distracted, like he's going through the motions more than anything. I wonder if he's been like this the entire practice or just since I arrived.

When the song is over, they take their time packing up, stalling their inevitable departure from the cozy warmth of the shed.

"We're gonna go raid Hunter's kitchen for food," Noelle says, nudging me with her elbow. "Want to come?"

"Um . . ." I look over at Ethan as he secures his guitar inside its case. Noelle follows my gaze, smirking. She probably thinks I'm going to jump him the second they all leave.

She pats my knee and stands up. "See you later."

I nod, my eyes still on Ethan. He glances up at me, and like the day we had our second kiss on this very couch, he quickly catches on that I want to be alone with him. Only this time, there won't be any kissing. At least not until after we settle a few things.

Ethan drags out collecting and packing up his belongings until everyone's gone and it's just the two of us, alone with our unresolved tension.

"I thought you were grounded," I say to fill the silence.

"I am, but my parents have barely been home all weekend so they don't even know I'm out. I don't really care, anyway." He snaps his guitar case closed and joins me on the couch. "How's Tobias?"

"He's fine."

We're both quiet for a few moments, so quiet I can hear the faint hiss of the space heater in the corner. My mind scrambles for something to say, something smart and profound that will magically transform our relationship into something effortless and normal. But there's nothing, because our relationship will never be effortless and normal. Our memories of Aubrey won't ever fade. My part in her death will always be between us, and that's something we both need to accept if we're going to move forward.

"Ethan," I begin. "I came over here because I wanted to talk about—"

"Wait." He touches my arm, stopping me. "Before you say anything else, I need to ask you something."

I shut my mouth and look at him, waiting. He lifts his hand from my arm and shoves it through his hair.

"What was the last conversation you had with her? Right before she . . ." He swallows and shuts his eyes for a second. "What did you guys talk about? You've never told me."

My mind immediately flashes back to that day, and it's like I'm there again, reliving it all. The humid June heat. Our flip-flops, slapping against the pavement. Aubrey's blue-painted toes. *Justin's a douchebag.*

"Justin," I say, my voice cracking. "We talked about Justin and all the chances she gave him. She talked about what she accomplished that year in spite of all the drama we went through. I apologized to her, and she apologized to me. We . . . we made things right again."

He nods like he's known this all along. "She forgave you."

Truce?

Truce.

"Yeah. Of course she did. Aubrey was the most forgiving person in the world."

"She was," he agrees, his gaze steady on mine. "You were her best friend and she would've forgiven you for anything."

Wide, frightened eyes. A lacy white skirt, soaked through with blood.

"Not anything," I say, tearing my eyes from his. They're so much like Aubrey's. Sometimes I can forget, but now, with her presence surrounding us, it hurts me to see her in them.

"Yes," he says firmly. "Anything, Dara. Even that."

My gaze flicks back to his face. He can't actually believe what he's saying. Aubrey was compassionate, sure, but she wasn't a saint. "How can you possibly know this?"

"Because I knew *her*. Because that's the way she was. What happened to her was a terrible accident. She never would've held you responsible."

"But you do, right?"

His dark eyes glitter and I brace myself for the inevitable explosion of anger. But all he does is shake his head. "I don't know where you're getting the idea that I blame you. I told you I didn't and I meant it."

Just like in the car with Mom yesterday, something in me breaks, long-supressed thoughts boiling to the surface. "Noelle said something once, about how even when you couldn't forgive me, you never hated me," I say, the words spurting out of me. "And you get so angry sometimes. You were never like that before Aubrey was killed. So what the hell am I *supposed* to think?"

"Aubrey dying isn't what I couldn't forgive you for," he fires back at me. "Don't you get it?"

"No. No, I *don't* get it. What else did I do to hurt you so badly?"

He springs off the couch and walks to the other end of the room, his hands clasped at the back of his head. Stunned, I keep my eyes on his rigid back, watching it rise and fall with each breath as I wait for him to speak.

"You *left*, Dara," he says hoarsely, keeping his back to me. "You left me and I had no one. My sister was gone, and then the second most important person in my life was gone too. And you didn't say a word about it to me."

"But . . ." My mind drifts back to that time, all those dark, endless days of grief. "You didn't even look at me during the funeral, you didn't talk to me after . . ."

"I didn't talk to anyone. I couldn't. Losing Aubrey decimated me. I didn't eat. I didn't sleep. I pushed everyone away." He lowers his arms and presses his palms to the wall in front of him. "Then I started hanging around with Hunter and playing guitar and working on the farm and I finally started to feel a bit like myself again. But by that time, you'd already left. I figured you wanted to be done with everything back here, including me."

A different kind of guilt overtakes me. He's right. After Aubrey died, it was all I could do not to follow her. Even breathing felt like too much effort. I needed to get away from the constant reminders, the whispers and pitying looks. But I never once considered how my absence would affect Ethan.

I never once considered he might need me here, so he didn't have to mourn alone.

He lost Aubrey, and then he lost me too.

Ethan turns around and comes back to the couch, reclaiming his seat beside me. His eyes are red, but he's calmer now. Back in control.

"Noelle was right," he says, reaching for my hand. He laces our fingers together, and his touch warms me straight through. "I hated that you left, but I've never hated *you*. It's impossible for me to hate you, Dara. I've loved you since I was ten years old."

I lean forward and bury my forehead in the space between his shoulder and neck. "I'm so sorry for leaving you. I seem to have a habit of taking off without warning, don't I?"

"Maybe a little one."

I pull back. This time, when our eyes meet, I see only him. "For the longest time, my first instinct when something feels good was to resist it. Pull away. You're something good, Ethan, and I don't know if I'm ever going to feel like I deserve you."

"Is that why you freaked and ran off after we . . ."

"I ran because I was scared. You're Ethan. Aubrey's little brother. One of my best friends. How I felt about you terrified me. It still does." I touch his cheek, run my fingers along the defined bones, the coarse, bristly skin on his jaw. "But in spite of the way I acted afterward, I don't regret a second of that night. I'm glad it happened."

"Good." His arm circles my waist and he leans in closer, his lips grazing mine. "Because I want it to happen again."

I let myself melt into him. Right now, in this moment, I'm not the cold, motionless statue I became. Right now, I've never felt more alive.

thirty

Three Months Later

IT'S THE FIRST WARM SATURDAY OF SPRING WHEN Ethan pulls up in front of my house, music blaring out of the speakers of his Saturn and the windows rolled down as far as they can go. When I see him, I exhale and rise from my spot on the steps, where I've been waiting for the past five minutes, soaking up the sun.

"Ready?" he asks once I'm settled in the passenger seat.

"I hope so."

He switches off the stereo, either because he thinks loud, heavy music is inappropriate right now or because he's worried that *I* do, and pulls away from my house. We drive across town in silence, but it's a reflective quiet, not an uncomfortable one.

Neither of us wants to disrupt it with words.

Too soon, Ethan parks the car and reaches behind us to the back, where the flowers lie across the seat. Twelve purple tulips, secured in place with a simple white ribbon. Aubrey loved tulips, and purple was her favorite color. Ethan hands them over to me. They smell fresh and faintly sweet, like spring.

We get out of the car, and Ethan comes around to my side, taking my hand. "We don't have to do this today."

"I want to," I say, peering across the parking lot to the wide expanse of grass in the distance, the tidy rows of marble and granite, bearing names of the dead. I don't know if it's the sunshine or Ethan's solid presence beside me or the new medication my doctor put me on that makes life seem more manageable, but I feel surprisingly calm here.

Ethan leans in to kiss me, wedging the flowers between our chests. "Then let's go."

We head toward the graveyard with Ethan slightly in front of me, leading the way. I haven't been here since the burial, almost two years ago, but Ethan—as I recently learned—visits about once a month. He doesn't always bring flowers but when he does, they're never in a vase like most cemetery flowers. He'd rather place them directly on the earth, as close to her as possible.

"Here it is."

We stop in front of a simple, black granite headstone with a swirling floral design along the edges. She's buried near a tree, which she'd like, and close to the road, which she wouldn't. I stare at her name—*Aubrey Elizabeth McCrae*—and think about the last sketch I found in my locker: me, wearing a Santa hat and smiling, dancing on Aubrey's grave. The same sketch I shredded to ribbons and tossed in the trash. I'd considered doing the same to the paper I'd stored in my green notebook, but I ended up giving it to Mrs. Dover instead.

It happened about a month ago, when she called me into her office to talk about my future after graduation, which was creeping up fast.

"No pressure," she said, handing me a small stack of what looked like brochures. Then I looked closer and realized they *were* brochures—for police academies. One had a picture of a uniformed woman on the cover who looked a little like the cop I'd seen in that movie with Travis and Paige, so long ago. "Just think about it."

I put them in my backpack and promised her I would.

She let it go at that and went on to ask me the usual questions about how things were going. Instead of answering, I dug the photocopied obituary out of my backpack and gave it to her. At first, I felt silly for complaining about a few nasty notes when the things I did to earn them were so much worse. But now I can acknowledge the difference: I never meant to hurt anyone, but whoever left those notes clearly meant to hurt me.

"Someone keeps putting things like this in my locker," I

told Mrs. Dover. "I don't know who they are, but I want them to stop."

When she saw what was on the sheet, her pretty face turned stony. "If you ever find out who's doing it," she said, "please let me know."

I promised her I would, even though I knew the culprit would probably remain a mystery. He or she is a coward, hiding behind their anonymity like a troll on the internet.

The good news is, there hasn't been any passive-aggressive locker mail since. And if I ever do get more, I won't hang on to them. My green notebook is being used to store something else now—the police academy brochures. Maybe someday soon, I'll take them home with me.

"Dara," Ethan says, jolting me back to the present. "You okay?"

I nod and pass him the flowers. "You do it."

He crouches down and rests the tulips against the grave, right under the etched words *Forever in our hearts*. Before he straightens up again, he eases one flower from the bunch and closes his fingers around the stem. I don't ask him why. Maybe he keeps one every time.

"Do you . . . feel her here?" I ask him.

"Not really. I feel her more at home. Especially when I'm alone in my room, playing guitar. I'm not sure why."

I press my hand to the top of the stone, feeling vaguely relieved. I don't feel her here either. Like Ethan, I mostly sense her presence around the house—his and mine. It's where most of my memories with her took place.

Back in the car, Ethan puts the single purple tulip on the dash and pulls back onto the street. I assume he's taking me home, so I'm confused when he goes in the opposite direction.

"Ethan, where are we—?"

He makes another turn and it suddenly hits me what he's doing. Where he's taking us. And my entire body freezes.

The last time I was here, back in September when my father took this way by accident, it was raining and I was so upset I barely even registered my surroundings. But today, it's sunny and clear, and Fulham Road looks as peaceful and picturesque as ever. Exactly like it did the day Aubrey was killed.

The calmness I felt at the graveyard has abandoned me completely. My pulse quickens and my breathing shallows, a precursor to the flashbacks that always follow close behind. Suddenly, I feel Ethan's hand on my shoulder, and I realize the car has stopped moving and we're parked on the side of the road, mere feet from where Aubrey's life was crushed out of her.

"You can do this." Ethan's face is inches from mine, all I can see. "You can. I'm right here with you. I love you."

I focus on him, on the words he just said. Inhale. Exhale.

"I come here too, you know," he says. "Every month, after leaving the cemetery, I come here. I feel like I owe her that, to stand in the last place she was alive. It's hard, but I do it.

And if I can do it, so can you."

My heart is still racing, and the memories are still looming, but I keep my eyes anchored to Ethan's and breathe through it. This time, I'll try not to let them consume me. This time, I'll try digging deep, past the thick, murky layers of guilt and hate and pain, to the fierce-and-fearless me who possibly still exists down there somewhere, waiting to be freed.

For Ethan, but mostly for myself, I'll try.

"Okay," I tell him.

He drops a kiss on my forehead and gets out of the car, grabbing the lone tulip as he goes. I take one more deep breath and get out too, nausea swirling in my stomach. But I breathe through that too and join Ethan on the sidewalk. We walk for a minute, passing neat houses and winter-worn lawns, until he comes to a stop near a spindly tree poking out of the strip of grass between the sidewalk and curb.

"No," I say, tugging him forward several steps. "Right here."

We stand together on the sidewalk for a while, looking out at the road. The occasional car passes, but no one seems to notice us. To them, and to the rest of the street, it's just another ordinary day.

"You do it," Ethan says, holding out the tulip.

I take it and step closer the curb, my shoes sinking into the new spring grass, and look down at the clean, unblemished pavement. These are the things I see now:

Rows of shortbread cookies, cooling on the counter.

A violin bow, cutting through the air.

A pair of dark brown eyes, watching me with love.

I lift the tulip to my nose, inhaling its subtle fragrance until it's all I can smell. Then I hold it over the empty road, open up my fingers, and let go.

acknowledgments

THANK YOU TO MY EDITOR, CATHERINE WALLACE, for loving *These Things I've Done*. Your spot-on editorial notes pushed me to dig deeper into the heart of the story and figure out exactly what I was trying to achieve. The final product is a thousand times better because of you. Another huge thank-you to the rest of the HarperTeen team, for turning my little manuscript into a gorgeous book that people can hold in their hands.

A million thanks to the remarkable Eric Smith, both for taking me on and for being the best agent an author could ever dream of having in her corner. Your enthusiasm for this book (all books, really) knows no bounds. Your kindness, humor, and infinite supply of happy tears helped sustain me through all those long, agonizing waits. To everyone at P.S. Literary, thanks for always having my back. And of course, big group hugs to #TeamRocks. Your support makes the stress-inducing world of publishing a lot easier to navigate.

These Things I've Done literally would not exist without Cara Bertrand and her fateful email about a book idea. Cara, no words can adequately express my gratitude. You always believed I could write Dara's story and do it justice, even when I had my doubts. We haven't even met in person (yet), but you've made an impact in so many ways. This book isn't just mine—it's ours.

Thank you to Shannon Steele, my forever first reader and definitely my number one fan (Annie Wilkes has nothing on you). Your friendship, encouragement, and unflagging belief in me is always appreciated. And thanks to Tanja Sullivan, my talented critique partner, for taking the time to read my books and offer such thorough and thoughtful feedback.

One of the best parts of being a YA author is the YA community. Thanks to Nicole at YA Interrobang for the last-minute cover reveal, and to all the other bloggers who talked about and looked forward to *These Things I've Done*. You're all amazing.

Thank you to my friends, real-life and online, for keeping me connected to the big and exciting world beyond my desk. I'm so fortunate to have such a wonderful support system. As always, thank you to my family, extended family, and in-law family. Your pride in my accomplishments grows stronger with each book, and it means everything to me.

Thank you to my beautiful and supportive children. If there's one thing I hope I taught you guys, it's that impossible dreams are possible if you put in the work and never quit.

And thank you to Jason, my best friend and my heart. I couldn't do this without you. Parts of this book brought me right back to when I was a band girlfriend, sitting around with the other band girlfriends as we waited for Dark Waters to finish their set. Over two decades have passed since then, and you don't play guitar much anymore, but I'm still as big a fan of yours as you are of mine.

rebecca phillips lives in beautiful
Nova Scotia, Canada, with her husband, two teenagers, and
one spoiled-rotten cat. She's also the author of the Just You
series, *Out of Nowhere*, *Faking Perfect*, and *Any Other Girl*.
Visit Rebecca on her website, www.rebeccawritesya.com,
and on Twitter @RebeccaWritesYA.